IGNITED BY HIM

THE MERGE SERIES, BOOK 4

KYLIE KENT

Ebook ISBN 13: 978-0-6452572-1-2

Paperback ISBN 13: 978-0-6452572-2-9

Cover illustration by
RJ CREATIVES GRAPHIC SERVICES

Editing services provided by
Kat Pagan – https://www.facebook.com/PaganProofreading

This book contains scenes of sexual acts, profanity, and violence. If any of these are triggers for you, you should consider skipping this read.

This is a work of fiction. Names, characters, businesses, places, events and incidents are either the products of the author's imagination or used in a fictitious manner. Any resemblance to actual persons, living or dead, or actual events is purely coincidental.

This book is dedicated to the very lovely Bree Porter. Bree, you have been an inspiration to me throughout my journey so far as an author. I know I'm the much older one, but when I grow up, I want to be you! Your mafia romances are unlike anything I've ever had the pleasure of reading. I have devoured every single word you've written, and I hope I have done justice with Breanna's character, based on your badassery and brave soul. Thank you for letting me use your name for this story!!

BLURB

Ash

She's the unattainable, untouchable. The one I've both loved and lusted after from the sidelines.

For years, I've kept myself distracted with work, turning my family's company into an empire.

And, more importantly, I've kept my distance. It's best for everyone.

But when she walks into my club and tries to cheat me out of money, all bets are off.

One way or another, she's going to pay back what she's stolen.

Although, it won't be in the form of cash.

Breanna

I love winning, even if I have to cheat to get to the finish line.

I knew better than to come to this club to play.

I knew he'd more than likely find out I was here.

What I didn't expect was to see him up-close. I've hardly seen him over the last few years.

I wanted him to notice me. To see that I wasn't a little girl anymore.

And that was my mistake, because he did more than notice.

There is no going back now.

That flame we've both been dousing in denial has just been ignited.

Can I really play with fire without getting burned? Or will everything around me turn to *ash*?

PROLOGUE

Ash

S ix years earlier

I DON'T KNOW when it happened, when I stopped looking at her like a little kid who was just always around. Another younger child for me to protect, like I did with all my cousins. When she was born, Aunt Ella took me to meet her while Emily was still in the hospital.

I was only six, but I vividly remember being drawn

in by her big blue eyes. I couldn't stop looking at her. When I reached out to touch her, Josh pulled her away. I hated him then. I wanted to hold her, but I was told I couldn't.

I remember thinking it was a stupid rule. I was allowed to hold Lily and Hope when they were born. It didn't matter though. Because on the drive home from the hospital, Aunt Ella told me that one day baby Breanna would be big enough to play with me and the twins.

I never thought much more of it. By the time I was ten, she was only four, and she'd follow me around everywhere whenever our families got together. Which was often. By the time I was fifteen, she was nine, and she'd stopped following me around by then. She was always with Lily and Hope, or Dominic (Aunt Ella's son), our mutual cousin. I was glad. At that age, I had better things to do than entertain the little kids, or so I thought anyway.

It wasn't until she was sixteen that I started to wish she was still following me around everywhere. It's like she went from being an annoying little kid to the most beautiful creature I had ever seen. The only problem was... *she was fucking sixteen.* There wasn't a damn thing I could do about those feelings she was stirring in me.

Because now that I'm twenty-fucking-two, I have no business lusting over a damn teenager. She's not just jailbait, she's fucking pig-food-bait. I know all about how her father likes to feed bodies to his pigs, or at least he did before Breanna came into the world. I've heard the whispers. I also know he wouldn't hesitate to make me the pigs' next meal if I touched his little princess.

Not to mention, Breanna's mum (Emily) is bloody crazy. She'd be just as likely to bleed me dry if I so much as looked at her daughter wrong. I wonder how two of the craziest people I know made someone as remarkable as Breanna.

Emily's been watching me like a damn hawk all night. Have you ever had to sit across from the one you want, but can't have? All the while, surrounded by your family and friends, and having to act like everything is fucking hunky-dory. It's a fucking nightmare. I need to find a way to rid myself of these thoughts.

I can't be thinking about a sixteen-year-old like this. It's not fucking normal. I have no intention of ever acting on these thoughts, but just having them is making me feel like a predator. I should not be in the same room as this girl, let alone sitting across from her.

It doesn't help that she's wearing a scrap of black fabric she's passing off as a dress. She's purposely reaching over or bending forward, giving me a full and clear view of her cleavage, which for sixteen is already fucking well-developed.

Turning away from her, I tune into my cousin Lily and listen to her drone on about the university party she went to on the weekend. Lily's just started university, although hearing about her going to parties sounds more like her twin sister's idea of fun. Lily's always been more the *stay home and read a book* kind of kid.

Out of the corner of my eye, I watch Breanna get up and walk over to another table. Where the hell is she going? She hugs and sits down next to some teenage douchebag. I'm about to jump out of my seat and drag her ass back to our table, when Lily grabs hold of my arm. She winks at me, then calls out over everyone's chatter.

"Hey, Josh, who's the guy Breanna's getting all cosy with over there?"

I've never seen the man move so fucking fast. He's out of his seat and storming towards his daughter. Two minutes later, Breanna is sitting back at the table. *Right across from me.* I want to know who the fuck the kid is. Is it her boyfriend? For the life of me, I can't figure out if it'd be better if she *did* have a boy at her side. Maybe these thoughts I'm having would be easier to ignore if she belonged to someone else. Or maybe I'd fucking kill him...

Breanna crosses her arms over her chest, and my eyes immediately fall to her cleavage. Fuck me, I'm going straight to fucking hell. It's a shame my Uncle Bray couldn't convince the twins to join the nunnery. I really could have used the family connection to wash me of the sins I want to commit with the girl who is way too young for me.

"Problem?" She smirks at me.

"Yes, there is. A huge one," I admit, while attempting

to adjust myself in my pants without drawing attention to it.

I need a distraction. I need to get these thoughts of Breanna out of my fucking head. Work, that's my escape. It's nearing nine p.m. I now have an excuse to leave this dinner.

"Mum, I gotta go to the club. Thanks for organising all of this. It's been… *eventful*." Standing, I walk around the table and kiss my mum goodbye.

"Ash, you know you can take a night off. It's your birthday." My mum tries to reason with me.

"I could, or I could go to work and do what I'm good at. Making money." I smile; it's really fucking hard to say no to my mum.

"Zac, tell him he should stay." Mum turns to Dad for backup. Great, there is nothing my dad won't do for Mum. If she says jump, he'd be the one reaching for the stars.

"Ash, your mother wants you to stay. You should stay a while longer. The club will still be there in another hour." Dad uses his *don't fuck with me* voice. Great, I guess I'm staying.

"Fine, I'll stay for a bit. Shove over, squirt." I pick up my little sister, moving her along to the empty spot to the left, and take the seat between her and my mum. Ava's just turned twelve, but I swear she thinks she's twenty already. Is that…? "What the hell? Who the fuck let you wear makeup?" I yell, probably louder than I needed to.

"Ash, I'm twelve. I can wear makeup if I want to."

She puts her hand on her hips. I turn to Dad. Surely, he is not okay with this.

"Are you really letting her out of the house like that?" I question my parents.

"It's a little bit of lip gloss and blush. It's not a big deal, Ash." My mum rolls her eyes.

"Not a big deal? It may just be a bit of lip gloss today, but what about tomorrow? The next thing you know, it will be miniskirts and boyfriends!"

"Ew, Ash. No, I don't like boys. They're gross," Ava says.

"Don't worry, Ash. Any boy who comes near Ava will have to go through me first," my little brother Axel chimes in, holding his fists up.

"Thanks, Axe. I'm glad someone around here cares enough to save our sister's virtue," I grumble.

"Okay, we are not having this conversation. Ava knows she's not allowed to date until she's thirty. *At least*," Dad grunts.

"Axe, have you been taking lessons with Uncle Bray? Dad's gone soft, so it's up to us to keep Ava away from boys." I laugh and dodge the slap my dad was about to give the back of my head.

"Yep, sure have. I'll be able to take you soon, Ash." Axe chuckles. The kid is nine. I always said my parents got bored when I started school, so that's why they had Ava and Axel. I'm about to finish my business degree at uni, and Ava's just starting high school. Part of me wishes I was at school with her—that way, I'd be able to make sure no jerks were hanging around.

"You do know Ava looks just like Lyssa, right, Zac?" Aunt Reilly asks.

"Yeah, thank God," Dad jokes.

"So, you remember how hot you thought she was twenty-three years ago? How you couldn't keep your hands off her? Imagine how many guys are going to be all over little Ava here when she's older." Aunt Reilly and Mum laugh. I, however, do not.

"Reilly, when I need your opinion, I'll ask for it. And FYI, my wife is still fucking hot as hell, and I still can't keep my hands off her." Dad follows up by kissing my mum like no one's watching.

"On that note, I'm out. Thanks, everyone. Catch you around." I bend down and kiss Ava on her forehead. "Stay away from boys," I whisper to her, before I walk around the table and hug the women, and shake the hands of the men. It's the one excuse I can use to touch *her*.

I make sure I save Breanna's hug for last, probably lingering longer than I need to. And squeezing tighter than necessary. I bury my head in her hair and inhale the scent of raspberries. Then I close my eyes, trying to embed this moment in my memory. This is the last time I'll touch her. I need to keep myself the fuck away.

CHAPTER 1

Ash

"Mr. Williamson, we're preparing to land. We should be touching down in approximately twenty minutes. Can I get you anything?" The blonde hostess, who's been trying to gain my attention all night, bats her eyelashes and waits expectantly.

I'm not sure what it is she's fucking expecting. That I take her into the galley and fuck her senseless? Sure, everyone in this first-class cabin might be asleep, and if she weren't a blonde, I might have taken her up on the unspoken offer. But I don't fuck blondes. *Haven't touched a blonde for over six years.*

"No, thank you." I lean my head back and close my eyes. Hopefully, she'll get the message and leave me the fuck alone.

Every time I see a mass of blonde hair, I see *her*. Breanna McKinley, the one girl who's always on my fucking mind. The one I have been avoiding. At all costs. For the past six years, I've buried myself in work.

I've expanded my family's nightclub in Sydney, branching out and opening The Merge in every capital city around the country. It's been great for the business, but it also gets me out of Sydney as much as fucking possible, giving me excuses to miss as many family gatherings as I can get away with. The few I have been forced to attend have been pure torture—the cruel reality of being near her and not being able to touch her.

She never makes it any easier. I swear she lives to taunt me with the little dresses she wears. And the whiff of fucking raspberries I get whenever she walks past torments me with the unattainable. No matter how much I want her, I can't have her. She's my cousin's cousin. She's practically family. And you don't shit where you eat.

There was a time I thought differently, so sure that once she turned eighteen, I'd claim her. *To hell with the consequences and all that.* I was certain, when she was old enough, I'd finally be able to make her mine. She's twenty-two now, and I'm still waiting for the right time. It just never seems to come.

Maybe I should have asked for a whiskey. Rubbing my eyes, I try to get her image out of my head. Fuck, I'm tired. This isn't the first time I've caught the redeye from the other side of the country. It won't be the last either. You'd think, with the amount of flying I've done, I'd be used to it. I'd be able to sleep on planes. But I can't seem to ever put my mind at rest. Not when I'm in the air.

I pull out my phone and open my emails as the plane descends into Sydney. I briefly check the sender and subject line of each, not bothering to open a single one until I see a message from Chase, my best mate, who moonlights as my second in command. He's the one person on my payroll who I trust ninety-nine percent.

Trust is a fickle thing; you can never trust someone one hundred percent. And if you do, you're a bloody idiot. People are assholes, greedy fucking assholes, who always want something from you. I blame my mother for my trust issues. She was betrayed by her best friend, and all over jealousy and money. She warned us: *it's those closest who can hurt you the most.* I don't think she's ever gotten over that incident.

The only people my mum said we should trust with absolute certainty are her and my dad. The loyalty those two have for each other is unlike anything I've ever seen. *Or experienced.* The lengths my dad will go to for my mother are immeasurable.

Don't get me wrong, I trust my parents to always have my back no matter what. You couldn't ask for a better, more stable, caring set of parents than the ones I've got. They both love unconditionally, openly, and really would do anything for me and my siblings.

But do they know all the ins and outs of my dealings: business and personal? *Absolutely fucking not.* I may trust and love my family, but I'm also not a fucking idiot. Then there's the disapproving look my mother can give. One I don't like receiving, and I'd find myself on the other end of, if she knew just how I was able to expand the family company so quickly.

Am I a mummy's boy? Fucking oath, I am. Am I ashamed to admit it? Not a fucking chance. My mum is the one person I know who will always be my cheerleader in life. She's the kindest, most generous and authentic person I've ever fucking met. There is nothing I wouldn't do for her.

Opening the email from Chase, I read the message:

ATT: Bossman,

Do me a favour. Check your fucking text messages! Now!!

FROM YOUR TOO-YOUNG-TO-DIE BEST FRIEND,

Chase

I cough to conceal my laughter. He's a fucking idiot. Who sends an email to someone just to tell them to check their messages? Closing my emails, I open my texts. Sure enough, there's five unread messages from Chase.

The wheels of the plane touchdown, and my hand clamps around my phone, my knuckles turning white. The image on my screen can't be right. She can't be in my club… No! Not just in my club, *in my fucking poker room*.

I've known for a while now that she and her friend play high-stakes games. *Play* being used lightly here, considering what they do is fucking cheat. I thought she was smarter than to step foot in my club though. She should know better than to steal from me.

Fucking Breanna McKinley, the untouchable princess. The heir to the McKinley dynasty. She's about to learn just how touchable and breakable she fucking is. Nobody gets away with stealing from me. Not even her. *Especially not her.*

I send Chase a message back.

Me: Keep her there. Do not let her fucking leave. I'll be there in thirty minutes.

Chase: Why me? Can't someone else do it?

Me: Don't let her leave.

Chase: You're going to get me killed. You know who her father is. I know you do.

I choose to ignore his last message. If I respond, I'm only encouraging his paranoia. If he thinks Josh is the one he has to worry about, he's clearly underestimating me. With that thought, I type out a reply.

Me: No one touches her, Chase. If even a hair on

that pretty little head of hers is out of place, Joshua McKinley will be the least of your concerns.

His response comes immediately.

Chase: I'm quitting. For health reasons. Being employed by you is clearly a danger to my wellbeing.

I was planning on heading home and sleeping, not going into the fucking club tonight. But thoughts of Breanna, at my mercy, have given me a second wind. I feel more awake than I've been in a long time.

Baggage seems to take forever. The longer I'm waiting, the more agitated I'm getting... knowing she's in my fucking club. I'm tempted to just leave my suitcase here and process it through lost baggage.

After fifteen minutes, I finally grab my bag and jump in a rideshare. The thirty-minute trip to the club allows my mind to wander... to all the places it shouldn't. Not when those places consist of bending Breanna over my desk and spanking her pert little ass. I can't exactly treat her the way I would any other thief. No, I have to be more creative with whatever punishment I dish out. I groan and adjust my cock, as images of Breanna McKinley hit me like a fucking freight train.

CHAPTER 2

Bree

"Come on, Benny. Stop dawdling. They won't let us in if we're even a minute late." I tug at the arm of my best friend (and partner in crime).

"Beebee, I'm not so sure this is a good idea. I mean, this is *his* club. We should just sit this one out. Let's go get wasted at some trashy dive bar instead. You can do that thing where you pretend to break up with me, and leave me heartbroken, so someone else can come along and try to fix me."

"Benny, I'm sorry to say this, because I love you and

all. But there is no fixing you." I laugh as I continue to drag him along the sidewalk, straight past the queue of people lining up to get inside. I don't *ever* wait in lines —one of the many perks of being Breanna McKinley, I guess.

I'm the heir to the McKinley dynasty (or so everyone says). A dynasty I'm not entirely sure I want to take over. Luckily for me, my dad is a little bit of a control freak. He's also young, healthy, and no matter how many times someone or something has tried to take him down, he always comes out on top. I don't think there is anything my dad can't do.

The main benefit of being Joshua McKinley's daughter is the fear it incites in others. I've never told a single soul, not even my best friend. But when I tell people my name, that moment recognition flashes across their face, mixed with uncertainty and fear, I fucking love it.

It's not normal. To like watching how anxiety dilates the pupils. I know it's not directed at me, but rather my dad's reputation for being a little... *unhinged.* But I relish it all the same. I look over to Ben, and wonder what he'd think of me if he knew just how much I liked that level of hesitation at the mere mention of my name. I suspect my dad knows about my... *proclivities*, but he's never questioned it.

There is only one person who's called me out on it. Ash fucking Williamson. No one's ever watched me, observed my every move, like he has. He's calculated.

His words are always well thought out. He could probably manipulate his way into anything he wanted.

It would be creepy as hell—the way he watches me —if that same gaze didn't send a thousand bolts of electricity thrumming through my body, igniting every nerve ending along its way. It's rare though... having to endure his scrutiny. He doesn't show up to many of the family events anymore, and when he does, he never stays long.

That's whose club we're going to tonight. I've known about Ash's other business ventures (the ones he holds in the underground of his clubs) for a while now. I also know that if he were in town tonight, I would have absolutely no chance of getting a seat at one of the tables. Luckily, I have it on good authority (that authority being Hope, his cousin and the local gossip of the family) that he's currently in Perth.

I couldn't *not* jump at the opportunity to take advantage of his absence. I straighten my spine and saunter up as if I own the place, as we approach the bouncers at the door.

"The line's all the way back there," one of the over-steroided gym junkies says.

"I think you forgot to ask me my name." I smile sweetly at him.

"I don't give a shit what your name is. The end of the line is back there." He turns away, dismissing me. He either doesn't watch the news, or pick up a paper, or he's just plain stupid.

"Let me introduce myself." I hold out my hand, as if I'm willing to shake his. "Breanna McKinley."

I smile as I see that familiar glint of recognition in his eyes. He extends his hand, and I drop mine. "Now, should I call Ash, and let him know you're not letting his friends into his club? Or maybe I'll just reach out to Uncle Zac or Uncle Bray directly?" I don't ever refer to Zac or Bray as my uncles, but this idiot needs to know just how close our two families are. My Uncle Dean is married to Ash's Aunt Ella. We share a mutual cousin— that kind of close—which is also why my crush on the guy is never going to lead to anything, no matter how bloody hot and bothered he makes me with just one look. I can't even imagine if I did manage to get his hands on me.

Shaking the thoughts of Ash out of my head, I walk through the now-open door, propped ajar by the humiliated bouncer. "I'm so sorry, Miss McKinley. Head on up to VIP. I'll make sure there's a table ready for you."

"That won't be necessary," I say, looking around. I've been here a few times with Hope and Lily, Ash's cousins. But every time, he's also been here, watching from a safe distance. I usually choose other clubs to go to. Ben and I love finding new dive bars to occupy our evenings—something my dad would probably have a coronary about if he knew.

I lead Ben through the crowd of people to the back of the club. I may have extorted the code for the lift from Hope. We've partied together way too much for us to not have shit on each other. Shit we'd both rather stay hidden...

Please, God, let the code she gave me work. Waiting for the doors on the lift to shut, I punch in the series of numbers and immediately feel the carriage descend downwards. Yes! When the doors open, we are greeted by more security.

"Good evening. Miss Breanna McKinley and Mr. Ben Scott. I believe we have seats at tonight's game." Again, I revel in the expressions that cross both grown men's faces.

"Ah, sure, this way, Miss McKinley." When we reach a big metal door, the man points to a bowl on a hall table just outside. "Your phone stays here."

"Sure, but if it's not there when I come out, I won't be very happy. You see, my father gave me this as a birthday gift last month. It'd be a shame if I had to tell him someone stole it. *In this club.*" I smile, pulling out my phone and powering it down.

"Ah, maybe... you should just keep it turned off and in your bag. Don't let anyone see it. They get a little weird about having technology present." He nods his head towards the door.

I lean up on my tiptoes and kiss his cheek. "Thanks a bunch. I won't forget you made this concession for me." I may go a little overboard on the batting of the eyelashes, but the noticeable swallow in his throat, his Adam's apple bobbing, and his sizable puppy-dog eyes tell me he's hooked on the Bree charm.

I should feel bad using my womanly wiles on the

helpless guy, but it's not my fault men are stupid, simple creatures who only think with their dicks. If this idiot had an ounce of brain cells, he'd be on the phone with Ash by now, letting him know I was here. There's no way I would have made it this far if he were around.

The moment I step through the door, four sets of leery old man eyes go straight to my cleavage. *Suckers.* I smirk at Ben. These geezers don't know what's about to hit them. I wore this dress for a reason. Its black shimmery material clings to every one of my curves. The top hangs down low on my breasts, and I forwent a bra. I want these idiots to be distracted by a set of nipples. The dress stops just below the curve of my ass, and my black Louboutin stilettos snake around my lower legs.

I was blessed with my mother's looks. Does it make me conceited to admit it? To know that I'm beautiful? Probably. Do I care? Absolutely not. Do I use my looks to my advantage? You bet your sweet ass I do. *Unapologetically.*

I pull out a chair and take a seat. Ben strategically positions himself on the opposite side of the table. We need to be able to see each other head-on, in order to pull this off without the others catching on. We've perfected the art of making sure the odds are always in our favour.

The fact that these old men, who can't get it up without a blue pill, also can't stop staring at me is starting to piss me off.

"Gentlemen, are we going to play poker? Or just stand here all night, admiring what God and my mumma gave me?" I ask, while motioning my hands up and down my torso.

"Well, I'm sure I can manage to do both, sugar." Mr. Edgar ogles me, taking the seat next to mine. He's in his fifties, on wife number six, and very close to gambling away what little remains of his family's fortune.

I smile sweetly at him. "Well, you can always try, right?"

Ugh, sometimes it's a wonder how I manage not to throw up while leading these men on, letting them think they have a chance to touch me.

Everyone else takes a seat, and the dealer calls the entering. The small and big blind bets are placed—the minimum set at ten thousand. I try not to laugh. *Ten grand? That's it?* I thought we were playing for real money here.

After a few rounds, my pile of chips is growing larger. Ben's is purposely getting smaller. This is our tactic: He flops and folds, losing his money quickly, while I play for the win. Until he gets a set he knows no one will beat. That's when I get reckless and go all in, forcing the rest of the table to fold. It works every time. I lose, of course, and Ben acts like it's his lucky payday.

We've been sitting here for an hour. Mr. Edgar has been trying to lay on the flirt the whole time. It's really starting to grate my nerves, and I can feel my mask of indifference slipping further and further with each touch or comment he makes.

Honestly, I'm mostly pissed he's ruining the high I usually feel as I rip off these old, greedy assholes. Ben and I don't play because we need the money, and the money we win we always donate to charity. We're kind of like the Robin Hoods of Sydney... is my way of thinking anyway. No, we do it for the thrill of not getting caught. Well, *I* do it for the thrill of not getting caught. Ben's my ride or die; he'll follow along with any stupid plan or idea I have, and I'd do the same in turn.

"Maybe I can rub some of your luck onto me," Old Man Edgar says. I'm momentarily confused by his statement... that is, until I feel his cold, wrinkly fingers crawling their way up my bare thigh.

"You have exactly three seconds to remove your hand," I warn him with a sweet smile. Ben rises to his feet; he knows that tone way too well.

"Breanna." His warning is too late.

"Three," I say at the same time I grab those fingers, twist, and bend until I hear the breaking sound. My wannabe suitor screams out a few colourful, derogatory words at me while he slaps me across the face with his other hand. *That* is his biggest mistake.

I reach under my dress, retrieving the tiny blade I have strapped to my inner thigh. Flicking the pocket knife open, I don't waste any time as I slam his hand—the same one that just slapped me—onto the table and stab the sharpened edge right through the middle.

"I did ask you nicely, Mr. Edgar. Gentleman, it's

been a pleasure, but I think I'll call it a night." I smile at the stunned faces of the other three players, who are all smart enough to keep their mouths shut. Turning to leave, I stop dead in my tracks.

"Fuck." That must have been what Ben was trying to warn me about. Fucking Chase, otherwise known as Ash's best friend. Great, there is no way Ash doesn't already know I'm here now.

CHAPTER 3

By the time I make it to the club, I'm fuming. What kind of stunt is Breanna trying to pull by coming to play here? To cheat at my table? I hand my suitcase off to one of the bouncers as I walk through the back entrance. I'm on a mission to my office, where I know Chase has my little prisoner held.

The lift takes exactly fifty-eight seconds to reach the third floor. It then takes twenty-three steps to walk down the hallway to the door. The closer I get, the louder the voices are. Or should I say the louder *her* voice is? No one else is yelling.

A smile forms on my lips, as I picture her tearing up my office and cursing out Chase for refusing to let her leave. I imagine she's threatened him with all kinds of bodily harm by now. A strange sense of calm overcomes me as I place my palm on the handle. She's behind this door. It's been five months since I've laid eyes on her, yet I could give you a very detailed description of every inch. Every curve.

From the blonde curls that run down the length of her back, to those piercing blue eyes. A button, slightly turned-up nose. Lips so plump and thick I can't help but think how fucking great they'd feel wrapped around my cock. Full D-cup breasts, that small waist, and what would have to be the most perfect fucking ass I've ever seen. Then there's those legs: long, toned, tanned.

Fuck, this is not helping. Her image is only making me fucking hard. The moment I open the door, the room goes silent. I take two steps over the threshold before any ounce of calm I had flies out the fucking window. I walk straight up to her, grab her chin in my hand and turn her face, inspecting the big red mark currently residing on her left cheek.

"Who the fuck hit you?" I yell, letting her go. She takes a step back and shakes her head.

"I'm fine. Don't worry about it." She smiles.

"I didn't ask how you were. I asked. Who. The.

Fuck. Hit. You!" She doesn't answer. Instead, she clamps her mouth shut.

"Someone better start fucking talking, before I assume it was one of you two fuckwits." I point at Chase, and then turn to that fucking idiot who's always following Breanna around like a lost puppy.

The idiot cracks first. "It was the old man. *Edgar*. He was sitting next to her and got a little handsy."

"A little?" I raise my eyebrows, before gesturing to Breanna. "Stay here. Do not leave this fucking office." Then I direct my anger at Chase. I told him not to let anything happen to her. "Chase, a word."

"Shit, Ash, stop. It's not his fault. He wasn't even in the room when I broke the old guy's fingers." Breanna jumps in front of me, a palm on my chest to halt my steps.

Looking down at her hand, I wonder if she can feel the erratic beating of my heart. She shouldn't be touching me. I can handle being in the same room as her. I can't be held responsible for whatever actions I make if she starts touching me. Then her words seep through my rage-infused fog.

"What do you mean you broke his fingers? Why'd you break the old man's fingers?" I ask curiously.

"That's not important," she says. Looking behind me, she glares at Ben. I'm guessing to tell him to keep his mouth shut.

Without taking my eyes off her, I ask, "Ben, why'd she break his fingers? And think twice before you try to lie to me."

"Ah, well, I'm not sure. I was on the other side of the table, so I didn't really see too much," he stammers out.

"Ben, why did Breanna break someone's fingers?" I ask again. "Unless of course, you'd prefer I call Josh down, and we can watch the security footage together to see exactly what happened for ourselves?"

Breanna's eyes go wide. I'm guessing she doesn't want her dad involved. "Don't be stupid, Ash. You want the whole fucking city burnt down?"

"He felt her up," Ben says from behind me.

"Jesus, Ben, shut up. You are not helping."

"He felt you up? Where?" I ask her.

"It doesn't matter, Ash. It's not like he's the first guy to ever try to cop a feel, and he won't be the last."

Leaning in, I whisper in her ear. "I want names, Breanna, every single fucking one. And you can bet your sweet little ass that he'll be the last one to ever lay a hand on you again."

I walk around her and out the door, with Chase following close behind. As soon as we're in the hallway, I land a right hook to his jaw.

"Fuck, what the fuck did I do?" he grunts.

"I told you not to let anything happen to her. Where is the fucking old man with a death wish?"

"I'm gonna let you have that one shot, because I know how much that girl screws with your head. I left Edgar downstairs. He was screaming about lawsuits, while trying to remove the blade your girl put through the middle of his hand." Chase smirks.

"She stabbed him?" I don't know why that surprises me.

"Yes, and she did it with a fucking smile on her face. I'm telling you, Ash, that girl is not right in the head."

"She is everything right, and unless you want a matching shiner on the other side, I would refrain from ever saying that again," I grumble.

Chase stands there and laughs.

"I want you to take Breanna to my apartment. Keep her there until I get home." Opening the door to the office, I step back inside, while Chase is cursing under his breath behind my back.

"Bree, Chase is going to escort you to my place. I want you to wait for me there. I won't be long."

"No, I don't think so. I'm going home." She tries to walk around me. Grabbing her waist, I lean in, inhaling that fucking scent of raspberries.

"You can't go home with a handprint across your cheek, Breanna. What do you think your folks will do?"

We all know about her mum's past before she ended up with Josh. It's not pretty, and I'm certain that Emily seeing her daughter with a mark on her face, a mark that was left there by a man, is not going to end well. For anyone.

People think it's Josh they should fear, but really, Emily's the scariest McKinley there is. She's a silent assassin, that woman.

"Okay, but I'm only going to your place because I'm tired. And I'm taking Benny with me." She tries to untangle herself from my arms.

"Breanna, that's really not a smart idea. He can go home, or sleep in a dumpster for all I care."

She opens her mouth to argue, but she must see something on my face, because she closes it without saying anything. I kiss her forehead, and my lips linger longer than necessary. The tingle that courses through me, when I make contact with her skin, has me wanting to trail my mouth all over every fucking inch of her.

"Good girl," I whisper into her hair before leaving the room. The way her body leans into mine, the little shiver that runs through her, and how her cheeks turn red tell me I'm not alone in this attraction.

***

"Did you really think you could get away with touching her? That there wouldn't be consequences for your actions?" I ask as I land another blow to his ribs.

"I didn't know, Ash. I'm sorry. I-I didn't know." He spits blood on my floor.

I've been laying into him for thirty minutes. His right eye is swollen shut, and blood drips down the side of his face. But I'm not done. I've got so much pent-up anger. The thought of this fucker's hands on her skin sends a rage through me like I've never felt before.

I hear the door open and close, but I don't bother to turn around to see who's entered. Right now, the only thing I care about is showing this old man what happens when people think they can touch what's mine.

"You didn't know? Please, everyone knows who the fuck she is. What you didn't know is that she's mine. You touched something that belongs to me. And that is the last mistake you'll ever make."

His eyes go wide as he stares over my shoulder. Turning my head, I see Josh leaning against the wall, dressed in a black suit, his ankles crossed and his hands in his pockets. His lip tips up at the corner like he finds something amusing.

"Carry on, Ash. I'd love to hear all about how you've come to the conclusion that my daughter belongs to you." He smirks with an odd calmness.

Fuck, this is not what I need to be dealing with right now. As I've mentioned before, I'm not an idiot. I've grown up around Josh. I know exactly what he's capable of. But I'm also too far gone to back down. I shake my hand out, because my knuckles fucking hurt like hell right now.

"Josh, I'd love to chat, but I'm kinda busy right now." I know I'm not going to be able to blow him off, but it's worth a shot.

"I can see that. Care to explain why you let something happen to Breanna under your roof?" He still hasn't moved from his spot against the wall.

"I didn't *let* something happen to her. I'm too tired for this shit. I took a fucking redeye from Perth. I landed forty minutes ago to find out Breanna and her dipshit friend thought it'd be a good idea to sneak into my game room."

Josh smiles. "She's really good at getting into places she's not meant to be."

"Yeah, not sure that's something we should be encouraging."

"Probably not." Josh shrugs his shoulders. "So," he says as he takes very measured, very precise steps towards the old man, "I heard you thought you could put your grubby little hands on my daughter?" Josh picks up the blade that was pulled out of the old man's hand.

"No, I didn't mean to. It won't happen again." He pisses himself—literally pisses—staining the front of his pants.

"You're right. It won't happen again." Josh picks up the blade and slices right down the side of the man's neck, severing his carotid artery. Blood spurts everywhere, making a fucking mess I'm going to have to have cleaned.

"Great, thanks, man. I wanted to redecorate the place. With blood," I smart.

"You're welcome. Now, where's my daughter, Ash?"

"I had Chase drive her home." I don't mention that the home was not in fact her own.

"Is she okay?" he asks.

"She has a red handprint across her left cheek. Other than that, she seemed like her usual self."

I see his jaw tick as he looks down at the body on the floor. "I'll be stopping by tomorrow to see her. I'm trusting you... to not let anything else happen to her,

Ash. I'm sure I don't need to tell you what the ramifications will be if you fail."

"Wait, seriously? That's it? No threats of cutting off my fingers if I touch her? Nothing about being fed to the pigs?" I'm not going to lie. I'm in shock. What fucking *Twilight Zone* have I entered here?

"The threat is always there; I don't need to verbalize it. She can't see her mother with a mark on her face. I also know you're probably the only other person on this earth she trusts. So, like I said, I'll be by tomorrow to see her."

"Sure, no worries. That friend of hers, Ben, what do you know about him?"

"I know he's her best friend, and she's not going to let go of that for anyone." The fucker laughs as he walks towards the door, before offering his parting words. "A cleaning crew is on the way. Don't touch anything."

***

During the drive back to my apartment, I hear Josh's words replay over and over in my head. *"...you're probably the only other person on this earth she trusts."* What the fuck is that supposed to mean? I feel like I'm walking into a damn trap. There is no fucking way Josh is okay with Breanna being at my place. And how the fuck did he know she was there?

The apartment is quiet as I step off the lift and into the foyer. Walking through, I find Breanna, Chase, and Dominic (the cousin we both share) out on the balcony.

"Dominic, what the fuck are you doing here this late?" All three heads turn to look at me.

"Thank fuck you're here. I'm out." Chase wastes no time leaving.

"Uncle Josh called me. Told me I had to come sleep over with Bree. What's going on? She won't tell me anything." Dominic, who's only just turned nineteen, sprawls out on a lounger, drinking my fucking whiskey. I should have known Josh would never knowingly leave her alone in my apartment. With me.

"*She* has a name, asshole. Use it. And you're replacing that bottle of whiskey. I'm tired. I'm going to shower and jump into bed. Breanna, you can have a guest room. And don't even think about leaving this apartment. Dom, I don't give a shit where you sleep, as long as it's not with me." I turn to walk back inside.

"What if *I* want to sleep with you?" Breanna's sweet, sugary voice says.

"You can sleep with me anytime, sweetheart." I dodge the glass Dom throws at my head.

"That's my fucking cousin, asshat," he growls.

"Yeah, but she isn't mine."

CHAPTER 4

Bree

"*You* *can sleep with me anytime, sweetheart.*" Ash's words are like a broken bloody record in my head. Was he serious? Was he just trying to get a rise out of Dom? I've been tossing and turning for three hours. I can't sleep. I'm horny. I'm confused. And I'm bloody pissed off I didn't get to collect my chips from the table before I was marched up to the boss's office. That boss being Ash.

Was his offer to sleep in his bed, to sleep *with him*, genuine? And if it was, what the hell am I going to do about it? Argh, I usually have so much confidence. I know what I want, and I always get it. But with Ash, it's like every ounce of low self-esteem, of self-doubt, I've ever had comes crashing down around me.

There are very few people whose opinions about me matter. My parents. Sometimes Ben. And always Ash. His opinion of me is the one I stress over the most. I used to go out of my way to get him to notice me. But I stopped trying to impress him when I was around nineteen. I already knew he was impressed by the way he looked at me. However, his lack of action told me he was never going to do anything about it.

But now his words are haunting me like a damn poltergeist. What does he mean? I throw the heavy blankets off. I'm wearing a tank top and my underwear. I found a singlet in the closet. I'm assuming it belongs to Ava. This is the room she uses whenever she sleeps over here.

I decide to get up and grab a glass of water. I'm obviously not going to get any sleep tonight. But when I open the door, the kitchen is not where I find myself. Instead, I'm tiptoeing down the hallway and end up at Ash's room. It's dark, the only illumination coming from the moonlight shining through the sheer windows.

I stare at the outline of his body on the bed. It would be too easy to climb in and snuggle up to him. I'm debating what to do when he speaks, scaring me half to death.

"Are you just going to stand there and watch me

sleep like a creeper, or are you getting in?" he says, holding up the blanket by way of offering.

Do I get in? Jesus, what the hell do I do? If I get in, there's no turning back from that. If I walk away, am I going to wonder 'what if' for the rest of my life? Fuck it, I inch towards the bed and climb in. Lying on my side, I face him, and he watches me like I'm a scared animal. His hand slowly comes up and strokes through my hair.

"Why are you still awake?"

"Couldn't sleep."

"Because of what happened tonight?" he asks. Damn it, why does it feel so good to have his fingers stroking through my hair.

"No, I'm not sure." I can't really admit that I can't sleep, because all I can think about is his offer. His body. His hands. Fucking hell, I'm going insane.

And now that I'm in his bed, and surrounded by him, his woodsy scent envelops me like a security blanket. I didn't even realize how tired I was. I can feel my body relax as he continues to stroke my hair.

"Ash?"

"Mm?"

"What's going to happen if I fall asleep?" Will I wake up and realize this was all just a dream? Will I open my eyes and find that I am no longer in his bed? Will I be alone?

"While you sleep, I'll hold you all night. When you wake up, the first thing you're going to see is me. And the first thing you're going to feel is my arm wrapped around you—well, that… and the raging boner I'm likely to have."

"Who knew you were such a romantic?" I laugh. The first part of his answer was probably the sweetest thing I've ever heard, while the last part made my girl bits tingle.

"Ash, I want to feel that… all of it… and so much more," I confess, holding my breath.

"You will. I promise. Go to sleep, Bree. I have a feeling we're getting some early-morning visitors." He kisses me on the forehead. Why couldn't it have been on my lips?

I'm in his bed, in my underwear, and he wants to go to sleep. Huh, maybe I'm seeing things that aren't there.

"Stop overthinking it. If I kissed you right, I wouldn't be able to stop. And I don't think you want Dominic hearing you scream out my name when I make you come."

The moan slips out before I can stop it. His silent chuckle vibrates through me. "Goodnight." I kiss his chest, his bare chest. My lips burn from the heat of his skin.

I close my eyes, my hand resting against his heart, the rhythmic beat under my hand relaxing my mind and body. Then reality sinks in, giving me that "oh shit" moment. I'm in bed with a half-naked Ash Williamson.

"Why does this feel like a dream?" I whisper, not intending for him to hear. '

His arms squeeze me tighter. "Because it is." He lays another kiss on the top of my head.

***

"Mmm, that's good," I mumble as consciousness slowly seeps in. I hear a grunt, a male grunt. That noise makes my eyes shoot open, and I'm suddenly aware of my surroundings, especially the broad shoulders and head currently buried between my legs.

Ash's eyes meet mine as he lazily drags his tongue right up the centre of my clit. What the hell? I look around. I'm in Ash's room. And then last night comes back like a movie playing out in my head: Ben and I going to The Merge. The old man's hand. The hole I stabbed through the middle of it. Me creeping into Ash's room.

"Oh, God." His tongue swirls around my hard bud, while his finger teases at the entrance of my pussy.

"I think the words you're looking for are: *Oh, Ash. Yes, don't stop.*" He pops his head up. He's talking... Why is he talking? He can't be licking if he's talking.

I glare down at him. "What the hell? Keep going," I growl.

"Oh, I plan to, but you need to be fucking quiet. I'm starving, and this is a feast I've been dreaming about for six fucking years. I'm going to be down here for a while, Bree."

Just as his tongue makes contact with my clit again, the unmistak able shrill of Hope's voice rings out through the apartment.

"Uncle Josh, oh my gosh! I've missed you so much! How've you been? Tell me everything," Hope yells.

"Fuck, shit." Ash falls to the floor—in my panic to throw him off me.

"Bree, calm down."

"Calm down? Seriously, my dad's out there and you're in here, doing *that* to me. Calm down!" I ramble. I'm on my feet, looking around the room, when it dawns on me. I don't actually have any clothes here. My dress from last night is in the guest room.

"Babe, it's okay. Go through there and jump in the shower. I'll go out and stall. I'll leave some clothes on the bed for you." Ash's voice is calm, reassuring. Before he leaves, I grab his wrist.

"Ash, wait… I just wanted to say, in case you don't survive the morning, that you were extremely good at that. You know, for the few minutes you were doing it anyway."

Ash leans in and kisses me. "Don't worry, babe, the best is yet to come. The best being *you*." He smirks before walking me through to the bathroom.

I have the quickest shower I've ever had, leaving my hair wet. I dress in the way-too-big sweats and shirt Ash left on his bed for me and walk out to face the music.

"Daddy, what a surprise. What brings you into the city so early on a weekend?" I try for sweet as I approach.

He inspects me, grabbing my face in his hands and turning it both ways, before he pulls me against his chest. His arms hold me a little tighter than usual.

Leaning into my ear, he whispers, "I fucking love you, Breanna."

"I fucking love you, Daddy," I whisper back. Ever since I can remember, my dad has whispered those exact words to me. When I was little, and used to say them back to him out loud, my mum would go on and on about swearing. I quickly learnt to whisper instead.

"Are you okay?" he asks.

"I'd be better if I had coffee," I groan. It's early. I've probably only had about three hours of sleep.

"Want me to take you out for breakfast before we head back?" I guess he wants to escort me home. I evade his question and look around the room. Where is everyone else?

"Where's Dom?" I ask, pulling out of Dad's arms.

"He just left with Hope a few minutes ago. Hope mentioned how you both stayed up, eating junk food and binging on Netflix until around four?"

"Huh, did she now?" I turn away. Not only am I a crappy liar, but I also hate lying to my parents. That being said, I'm not stupid, so I'm hardly going to tell Dad I spent the night in Ash's bed.

"So, what'd you watch?" he asks.

"When?"

"Last night with Hope?"

Crap, this is a trick question. She obviously said something. I'm saved from answering when Ash walks into the living room with a steaming mug of coffee.

"Oh, thank you, Jesus. I could marry you right now." I take the mug out of his hands.

Ash's smile lights up his face. "Well, that could be arranged."

"No, it fucking couldn't. Breanna, we're meeting your mother for brunch. Let's go," my dad growls. Yes, *growls.*

"Shoot, I wish I could, Daddy, but I can't. I promised Benny I'd be his plus-one to his gran's charity event today. And I have to go home. I still don't know what dress I'm wearing. And I need to get my hair done. Do you know how long it takes to do something with *this?*" I gesture to my damp head. I'm rambling, mostly because I want to distract my dad from the murderous glare he's throwing Ash's way.

"Fine, I'll give you a ride home before I meet your mum."

"Ah, sure, let me just grab my things."

After collecting my discarded dress, my shoes, and my bag from the guest room, I walk back out to the living room. I pause, looking between Ash and my dad. You could cut the tension with a knife. Which reminds me...

"Ash, I'd say it was a pleasure, but it really wasn't." I hand him the now-empty mug. "Also, I think I lost my little blade at the club last night. If it gets found, can I have it back?"

"You mean this one?" My dad reaches into his jacket and pulls out my pocketknife. The exact one I left embedded in the middle of Old Man Edgar's hand. Crap on a breadstick, this is so not good.

"Yeah, where'd you find it?" I reach out to grab it.

"We'll discuss it in the car. You got everything?"

"Yep, let's go." I may be twenty-two, but damn, I hate the thought of the "we'll discuss it in private" conversation that's about to happen.

***

It takes all of two minutes of sitting in my dad's car before he starts his interrogation.

"Really, Breanna, Ash fucking Williamson? There are literally six million people in Sydney, and you choose him?"

"What's wrong with Ash? And I haven't *chosen* anyone."

"I can't get rid of him. Your mum would be extremely upset if I were to hurt him. *That's* what's wrong with him."

"Just for the record, *I'd* be extremely upset if you were to hurt him." I glare at him.

"Noted. But really, Bree, have you even tried to date girls?"

I laugh. I'm not sure it would matter who I dated. My dad would never approve, girl or boy. "Sorry, not into girls, Dad."

"So, do you care to explain how that pocketknife I gave you for your birthday last year ended up through someone's hand? And what the hell were you doing playing poker in the Williamsons' club?"

"Well, the old man deserved it. He tried to put his hand up my skirt. Then, when I broke his fingers, he slapped me. So, I showed him a better use for his hand."

"Good, but what you should have done was cut the fucking thing off."

"Sure, I'll try that next time." I smile. "You know, normal parents would be telling me you shouldn't be stabbing people at all."

"Normal is overrated and boring, Breanna. You're too exceptional to be normal anyway." It's a phrase I've heard many times before, and it's one of my dad's favourite things to tell me and my mother.

We fall into an easy quiet for the rest of the drive. Before I get out of the car, Dad stops me. "I'm really not okay with you growing up yet, Bree."

"I'm already twenty-two, Dad. It's a bit late for that."

"It doesn't make it any easier." My dad has always struggled with his emotions. He is cold and closed off to anyone who isn't me or Mum. I know people say he has psychotic tendencies, and maybe he does. But it doesn't matter because he's my dad.

"No matter how old I am, even after I get married and have babies of my own, I will always be your little girl. *That,* you can count on." I lean over and kiss his cheek.

"Those Williamsons have a habit of running off and eloping. Don't do that. Don't take those memories away from your mother," he says.

"Dad, trust me, I'm not planning on getting married anytime soon. To anyone. And whomever *I* do choose will be the perfect person. I know how I should be treated. And I know what love looks like. Because *you* taught me. I won't settle for anything less than what you and Mum have."

"As much as I want your mum to have the grand-kids she's always dreamed of, I'm too young to be that old yet."

"Mmm, I don't know, Dad. I think the grey hairs coming through on the sides kind of suit you," I tease.

"Get out. You're now my least favourite daughter," he grumbles.

"Yeah, but I'm your only daughter, so that means I'm also still your fav. Bye, Dad. Thanks for the lift."

"You'll always be my favourite girl, Bree. Love you."

"Love you too." I wave as I rush inside. Shit, I really do need to start getting ready for this charity thing. It's a lunch event. Who holds a charity lunch? Dinners work so much better.

CHAPTER 5

Ash

She walked out, just like that. What the fuck?! I wanted to stay in bed with her all day. Of course, her father would fucking cockblock with his impeccable timing. I head into my bedroom to retrieve my phone. After all, I've got a charity event I need to crash.

I glance at the bed, and the image of her spread out on her back is clear as day. I can still taste her on my tongue. I haven't even had a coffee yet, because I enjoy the way it lingers there.

I dial Chase. The phone sounds like it's about to ring out when he answers.

"Ash, I love you, man, but you better be fucking dying… to be calling me this fucking early."

"Good morning to you too, sunshine. Get up. Put on a suit. We've got plans." I smile. If she thinks she's going to slip away from me that easily, she doesn't know what's about to hit her. The fact she's going to an event on the arm of another man fucking irritates the shit out of me.

Ben's not gay; I've seen him with plenty of girls over the years. And any man who's not gay can't *not* be attracted to Bree. She's not just a ten; she's a fucking infinity. And I'm about to show her whose arm she belongs on.

Why didn't she ask me to go to this event with her? Great, now I sound like a fucking pussy.

"Ash? Earth to Ash. Are you even listening?" Chase's voice screams through the phone.

"What?"

"Where the fuck are we going? What's so important you're dragging my sorry ass out of bed? A warm, comfortable bed. A bed that currently has not two, but four breasts in it, I might add."

"Breanna is. Now, put your whoring ways on hold for a day. I'll be by to pick you up in two hours."

"Two hours? Great, that gives me time to…" I hang up the phone. I don't need to hear the rest of his conversation to know what he was going to say.

46

Now, to let Breanna know I intend to make my claim on her pretty little ass, I dial the florist.

"Central Bay Florists, how may I help you?"

"Yeah, I need a bunch of tulips delivered within the hour. Six dozen, purple and pink. Can you do it?"

"Ah, it'll be a stretch, but sure. What would you like written on the card?"

"Make it out to: *Breanna, The dream is about to become a reality. Ash.*" Where the fuck is this sappy shit coming from? I have no idea, but I'm going with it.

***

An hour later, I'm heading down to my car when I get a text from Breanna.

Bree: Really, Ash? Six dozen?

Her message is followed by a photo. Six dozen tulips, in a variety of vases, sitting on her kitchen counter.

Bree: I'm donating them to the old people's home. It'll cheer them up. Don't buy me flowers, Ash!

I laugh, only Bree would be annoyed at getting flowers. I've never actually bought another girl flowers before, but here I thought that was something women liked. As I'm contemplating her reply, another photo text comes in. This one's of a cheque—a cheque I know all too well. Thirty thousand dollars made out to Breanna McKinley, from Club M.

Fuck me, I forward the image to Chase with a message for him to find out who the fuck sent it to her. Whoever the fuck it is, they're fucking fired. I don't care how fucking much I love her; nobody steals from me.

Me: Breanna, do not cash that cheque. Rip it up! You won't like what happens to people who cheat in my club.

Bree: And you don't want to know what happens to people who threaten me, Ash!

Fucking hell. This woman is driving me insane. Maybe I need to go back to pretending she doesn't fucking affect me. That would have been possible... if she hadn't spent hours in my arms. In my bed. And if I didn't already know what she tastes like.

I don't bother responding. I know my lack of a reaction will piss her off more. And a pissed-off Breanna is a fucking sexy Breanna.

***

"Tell me again why we're at this event for orphaned cats? Is that even a thing?" Chase laughs from the passenger seat.

"Because Breanna is going to be there. That's why." I don't give him anything else.

"Well, if your girl is going to be there, then what the hell do you need me for?"

I look over to him. "We weren't exactly invited. Our names are not going to be on the guest list."

"So, we're crashing a charity event... *for orphaned cats*. Great, my life is now complete."

"Shut up. Did you find out who sent Bree that cheque?"

"Yep." He smiles.

"So… who was it?"

"Me." He laughs.

"You? What the fuck did you do that for? She didn't win that money, Chase. She's a fucking little cheat." My fists close around the steering wheel. It's not even about the money; it's the principle.

"Yeah, I know, but I thought it would entertain me to see how you handled your little cheat."

"Well, you thought wrong, because you won't be seeing shit. You're fired."

"Okay, great. Can I get out of the car now?" The asshole knows I'm not firing him.

"No."

Driving up to the valet, I hand over the keys and approach the door. I plaster on my biggest smile, and make a mental note to apologise to my mum later. She's my ticket to get into this event; my mum is a well-known philanthropist. If there's a cause, you can guarantee my mum will donate or support it in any way she can.

I'm not sure if she's ever donated to the orphaned cats' charity, but she does do a hell of a lot for orphanages and foster care kids. My mum didn't have the same privileged upbringing my dad did. She grew up in the system after her mum died when she was young.

"Hello, name, please?" the door attendant, who's clinging tightly to a clipboard, asks. My eyes flick to the name tag hanging around her neck.

"Good afternoon, Katie. My name's not on the list. You see, my dear mother—you might know her: Alyssa

Williamson—she asked that I come here today. She couldn't be here herself, but the cats are very dear to her heart."

"Oh, you're Mrs. Williamson's son? Of course, let me just shuffle some things around, and I'll get you and your friend seated at a table." She flips a few pages over on her clipboard.

Peering over, I can see a map layout with a list of names next to each table.

"That one, please. I don't know anyone here. This isn't my usual scene, so I'd be much more comfortable if you could sit me next to Miss McKinley there." I point to Breanna's name.

"Oh, of course, Mr. Williamson. If there's anything I can do to make you more comfortable, let me know." She blushes, looking everywhere but at me.

"Thanks, Katie, you're a real gem." I smirk and walk through the door, with Chase coughing behind me to cover his laugh.

"Okay, Romeo, what's the plan?"

"The plan is: I don't leave here today without Breanna—and that dipshit friend of hers—knowing exactly who she belongs to." I smile when I see my girl already sitting at the table.

However, that smile is wiped from my face when I see the arm wrapped around her shoulder. By the time I actually make it to their table, I'm fuming and ready to chop the bloody appendage off.

Leaning down between their heads, so they both can hear, I say, "You have two seconds to remove that arm from my girl before I rip it out of your goddamn socket, Benny." Turning towards a shocked (and now pissed-off) Breanna, I kiss her cheek. "Breanna, lovely to see you, as always."

While Ben's face pales and his arm makes a speedy retreat from around Bree, her lips tighten, her shoulders straighten, and she grips the butter knife that's on the table in front of her.

"What the hell are you doing here, Ash?" she whispers harshly.

I take a seat in the chair beside her, as Chase takes the one next to me and watches with a fucking smile on his face like this is the best entertainment he's had all week.

"Well, you see… when my girlfriend says she's going to a charity event with another man, you bet your sweet little ass I'm going to attend that same event."

She looks at me like I've lost my mind, which is hilarious, considering she was raised by two of the craziest people I know.

"First off, I'm not your girlfriend. You don't get to just do a one-eighty on me overnight, and decide that I have something you want all of a sudden. Second, threaten my friend again, and I'll have my dad hold you down while I cut your damn tongue out. A task he will gladly do when I tell him just where that tongue was this morning."

There is no doubt in my mind that she'd follow through with that threat.

"Wait, where was his tongue this morning,

Breanna? *This,* I need to hear." Chase's laughter dies off when I kick his shin under the table. Or more likely, when he sees the death glare Breanna gives him.

"Really, Beebee? You had *the* Ash Williamson go down on you, and you didn't tell me?" Ben whispers, but not quietly enough.

"Why the fuck would she need to tell you that?"

"Because, Ash, I've had to endure countless hours of listening to her ramble on about all the fantasies she's had of you, since we were sixteen. And that one came up... *often,*" Ben says smugly.

Well, maybe this friend of hers isn't so bad after all. I could work with this information.

"Shut the hell up, Ben. Unless you want me to tell him your thoughts on his cousins," Breanna hisses.

"Nope, we're good. Sorry, Beebee."

"What about my cousins?" I ask, confused.

"Well, if it's about Lily and Hope, I'm with you all the way, man. The whole twin thing... Not to mention, two hot fucking fiery redheads. Now, *that's* a fantasy worth jerk—"

"Finish that sentence, Chase. I dare you." *Fucking hell.* I'm not overly concerned when it comes to who my cousins date. That is, as long as they're not friends of mine, and I don't have to see that shit. I won't sit here and let anyone disrespect them though, friend or not.

"Now, Bree, your fantasies are ones I very much want to hear more about." I place my arm around her.

"Well, you might die waiting, Ash. Because I can

assure you those fantasies I had, as a naive sixteen-year-old girl, are long gone."

I lean into her ear, kissing the spot behind it. I feel her slight tremor. She can pretend she's over her teenage crush on me. But we both know, whatever this is between us, it is so much more than a crush. "You're a shitty liar, Bree. How exactly do you manage to cheat your way through those poker games? Which reminds me… I want my cheque back."

She turns her head, and for a second, I think she's going to kiss me. However, she doesn't—much to my disappointment. "I've already cashed it, donated it even. So, there is no way you're getting it back."

She smiles. I don't smile in return. She fucking cashed my cheque—the cheque she wasn't meant to have. "You stole from me, Breanna. What kind of relationship are we going to have, when it started with theft?" I ask her.

"Easy, a nonexistent one. We don't have a relationship, Ash. I don't know what's wrong with your mind right now, but I'm sure you're just sleep-deprived or something. Excuse me, I'm going to the ladies' room." She stands, leaving me there—sitting like a damn chump—as I stare after her.

And it's only now I notice what she's wearing. *Fuck me.* A white dress that hugs every one of her curves. It's tight and ends just above her knees, with a high neckline. It's proper, yet so indecent I have no choice but to follow her.

CHAPTER 6

Bree

What the hell is happening? I feel like my brain is in some kind of fog. I can't think straight. Why now, of all times, is this when Ash decides he's interested in me? It's two weeks before Christmas; we have to spend three whole days together with our family. It was hard enough hiding my damn teenage crush from everyone. How am I meant to do it now, when I know what it feels like to be held in his arms? To be in his bed?

Oh, God... I'm going to need an excuse, a reason

why I can't make it for Christmas. I laugh at the idea. My parents are nuts when it comes to creating memories; there is no celebration they don't go big on. There's no way I'm getting out of Christmas.

I am sitting in a cubicle, panicking about Christmas and this crazy urge I have to jump Ash's bones whenever I see him—which, by the way, now that I know he wants to do exactly that, the need for him has intensified tenfold. It also pisses me the hell off. Who the fuck does he think he is? That he can just waltz in here and claim me like I'm some prized pig at an auction?

Asshat. The more I think about it, the angrier I get. I should walk out and kiss the first man I see, and show him just how much he doesn't own me. Nobody bloody owns me. If I give myself to someone, it's because I choose to, not because I *belong* to them.

Maybe I'll just go kiss Benny right in front of him. See how he likes that? Argh, my blood is boiling at just the thought of someone thinking they have that kind of power over me.

I open the stall, determined to head out there and give Ash Williamson a show he won't soon forget. However, I stop in my tracks when I'm met with the hazel eyes of the man in question. He's leaning against the sink, his hands in his pockets. A cocky smirk graces his face, with those full lips I just want to slam against mine. No, angry! I'm staying angry.

"What are you doing in here, Ash?"

"Following you, apparently."

"Well, you shouldn't be. In fact, you probably don't

want to be anywhere with me right now. I'm likely to go into a blind rage and cut your head off. And just what *head* I'm referencing has yet to be determined," I tell him, my arms across my chest as I stare him down.

"You're worth the risk. And, Bree, believe me when I say that I want to be everywhere with you." He doesn't move a muscle, yet I feel like my body is being pulled into his orbit.

"Stop. We can't do this, Ash. The reason we've both been skirting around this for years is because it's wrong. We're practically family."

"We *are* family, Breanna, but we're not blood, which means nothing about this is wrong. I've wanted you since you were way too young for me to be wanting you. This…" Ash points between the two of us. "…is happening. You can fight it. You can deny it. But it's happening."

"No, I can't do this." I shake my head.

"You know, last night, when you climbed into my bed, and again this morning, when you were so close to coming on my tongue, you weren't thinking this was a bad idea."

My thighs squeeze together at the memory of just how good he was with that tongue. "*Please*, I woke up with your head between my legs. It could have been anyone's tongue, and I still would have reacted the same."

When I was issuing the response, it seemed appropriate. However, judging by the intense expression on Ash's face, it most definitely was not the right thing to say to him. He pulls his hands out of his pockets and takes two steps, until he's inches away from me. I have to tilt my head up to look into his eyes.

I don't back down. I'm a fucking McKinley; we don't lose. But when his tongue swipes out and licks his bottom lip, I can't stop myself from repeating the same motion. He smirks down at me, and those damn hazel eyes glisten.

"If I were to kiss you right here, right now, Breanna, are you trying to tell me it would be no different from any other kiss you've ever had?"

I know it would be different, but I'm way too stubborn to admit that to him. "That's exactly what I'm saying, Ash. I've outgrown you."

"Care to test the theory?" He doesn't give me time to answer him. In one swoop, his lips are on mine as his arms go around my waist, effortlessly lifting me off my feet before spinning me around and pinning my back against the wall.

His tongue slides along the seam of my closed lips, and my traitorous body opens right up for him. Like a blooming fucking tulip, my lips part. One of his hands comes up, twisting around my hair and tilting my head back further. His tongue dances with mine, as if they've been in sync forever. This isn't a sloppy, teeth-grating together, trying to get our footing kind of first kiss.

This first kiss is everything I've always dreamed it would be and so much more. My skin feels like it's covered in tiny embers, my whole body lighting up in flames. My core is burning with a need so hot I find myself pressing tighter against him. If it weren't for this damn dress, I'd already have my legs wrapped around his waist.

He pulls back with the biggest grin on his face I've ever seen. "You have no fucking idea how long I've wanted to do that," he says while stroking his fingers through my hair.

"You and me both," I admit before remembering I'm not meant to be enjoying this. "Damn it, Ash. Why? Why now? How am I supposed to sit across the table from you at Christmas lunch this year, and not think about jumping your bones?"

"Babe, you've been looking at me like I was something on the dessert menu for years. The only difference this year is that you can actually take a bite."

"Ah, no, I have not."

"Sure, well, maybe it was just me then? Trying not to stare so your parents didn't go apeshit."

"Oh my God, our parents... What do you think they're going to say to this? Wait, there is no this." I shake my head and try to move back, but I'm trapped between the wall... and *him*.

"This is happening, Bree. But first, I want my thirty grand back." He straightens his spine.

"Fine, I'll write you a cheque," I grumble in defeat.

"I don't want your money. That's not how we are squaring off."

My eyes go wide. He cannot be serious right now. Before I know what I'm doing, I'm reaching for the little knife that's tucked snuggly along the inside of my thigh. I push the blade right up against his crotch. His eyes go wide in shock, but not fear.

"I'm not a fucking whore, Ash. My body is not for sale. I'll write you a damn cheque." I smile sweetly at him.

"Of course you're not a whore. Jesus Christ, Breanna, put the damn blade away. We both know you're not going to cut off the part of me you want the most." His lip tilts up at the side, showcasing a little dimple. A dimple I want to lick. Fucking hell, he's right.

"Trust me, babe, I don't ever pay for sex. And I'm not paying for you. You're going to come work for me. My secretary just quit. I could use the help."

Is he serious? "Do I look like I need a job, Ash? Or that I'd work for you if I did?"

"Come on, it'll be fun. You can work off that thirty grand, and we can spend every day together. What else do you have to do for the holidays?"

"Oh, I don't know? Take Daddy's jet to the Bahamas? There are literally a million other things I could think of."

"We both know the spoilt princess thing isn't you. You'd probably end up in your dad's office, working for him. I'm sure the bonuses you'll get from me will be much more…" he trails off with a wicked smirk before adding, "…pleasurable. You can start tonight. Meet me at the club at ten." He pulls my knife out of my hand. I'm still processing what he's proposing and what he's doing. By the time my brain registers everything, he has his hand up my dress, slicing through the sides of my lace panties.

"Ash, what the hell?" He returns the blade, and I feel the lace slip down my legs before he tucks the shredded material in his pocket.

"Come on, if I leave Chase alone too long in a civilized setting, he tends to get himself in trouble."

Ash takes my hand and leads me through the crowded room. "Ash, they were La Perla. I hope you plan on reimbursing me for those. Better yet, take it off the thirty grand. Those panties you just cut up cost me three hundred dollars."

When we get back to the table, Chase is busy chatting up the socialite next to him and Benny isn't in his seat. Ash pulls my chair out and tucks me in. Then he leans down and whispers, "Who the hell pays three hundred dollars for underwear, Breanna? That's insane. Man, I'm going to be saving you so much money, because you won't be needing panties when I'm around."

***

The lunch was uneventful, thank God. My nerves are frayed, sitting here next to Ash. I keep pinching myself, because surely this isn't real. As much as I want to tell him where to go, and where he can shove his sudden interest in me, my vagina is saying: *Yes, please! Come in. We're open.*

Traitorous bitch.

Benny returned to the table with red lipstick smeared on his mouth. Ash has been making polite conversation with him the whole time. Chase has been tuning in and out of the exchange, while chatting up the bimbo sitting next to him. I call her that because, well, she is. I should know. I went to school with her. How I got stuck sitting at the same table with her, I have no idea. I don't remember her name, but I remember *her,* and the number of times I walked into the bathrooms only to see her pleasuring a different member of the footy team.

I should probably warn Chase that he'd best get a tetanus shot first. But there's a time and place for everything, and I'm not about to make a scene at a charity event and have my family's name spread all over the papers.

When the waiter places a small plate in front of me with a slice of chocolate mud cake, topped with whipped cream and berries, my mouth waters. "Mmm, now, this is a dessert worth waiting for." I close my eyes and moan around my first mouthful.

When I feel a hand slinking up the inside of my thigh, my eyes slide open. Unlike last night, I don't reach down and break these fingers. No, my legs— having a mind of their own—spread wider and grant better access. All the while, I glare at the owner of the hand.

Ash leans over and licks my lips. It would have looked like he pecked me, but his tongue ran along my bottom lip. "It tastes much better on you," he murmurs, as his finger finds its way to my core.

The moment he slides through the lips of my pussy,

he smiles. He's just discovered how damn wet I am. He slowly circles around my clit a few times before he pushes into my entrance, pumps twice, and pulls back out. He repeats this slow, torturous pattern over and over. I'm trying my hardest to sit still. To not start riding his palm like it's my new favourite saddle.

"I want you to come all over my hand, Bree. I want to lick my fingers clean and have the taste of you on my tongue all afternoon." Ash's gravelly voice in my ear tips me over the edge.

My legs clench his hand. My whole body tenses, my eyes close tight, and my hands clamp down around the base of my chair. I let out every curse, and prayer, in my head only. My mouth parts in a silent scream as I do exactly what he told me to do. I come all over his hand.

When I open my eyes, Benny is staring at me with a knowing grin. He's smart enough to not say anything right now, but I know I'm going to hear all about it when we're in private. I look at Ash, who is licking his fingers unashamedly, and the sight has me wanting to drag him back into the bathroom and do very unspeakable things with him.

CHAPTER 7

Ash

"So, I just heard you fired your secretary? What'd she do?" Chase plops himself down in the chair opposite my desk.

"Nothing. I needed the position vacant," I reply while staring at the monitor. I've been trying to run through these finance reports for the last hour. Every time I think I'm focused, I look at the clock and mentally count down the minutes until she'll be here.

"Why? If you think I'm going to be fetching your

coffees or picking up your dry cleaning, you thought wrong."

"When have I ever asked you to fetch anything, Chase?"

"Don't change the subject. Why'd you fire her? You know she can sue you for unfair dismissal? You can't seriously be that stupid."

"She won't; we came to a mutual agreement."

"You paid her off? How much? And you still haven't answered my question. Why?"

"Breanna's coming to work with me for a bit." This time, I look at him and smile like a fool.

"Why the hell would she do that? Did she forget she's got her own little empire waiting for her?"

"She owes me thirty grand, thanks to you. So, I'm making her work it off."

"As your secretary?"

"Yes, as my secretary."

"Well, this is a disaster waiting to happen. Did she actually agree to this madness? I know you're a six-pack short of a carton sometimes, but I expected more from her." Chase shakes his head at me.

I don't care what he says. This is probably one of my best plans yet. I should have offered Breanna an internship or something years ago. I know she's planning on taking over McKinley Industries, eventually. She's just graduated with her undergrad degree and is enrolled to start her MBA next year.

My mum and aunts talk (a lot) and it seems to be a hot topic of conversation. Whenever I'm around them, their discussions always veer towards Breanna. For a while, I used to make excuses to visit my mum when I knew Aunt Ella was going to be there. Aunt Ella and Breanna spend a lot of time together. I stopped hanging around as much when the subject matter became who Breanna was dating.

"She'll be here," I reply with a confidence I don't exactly feel. I fucking hope she'll be here.

"Sure, mate, whatever you need to tell yourself." Chase stands and starts picking up random items around my office. I watch him for a few minutes, but when he comes over and plucks my letter opener from my desk and confiscates every pen, my curiosity gets the better of me.

"What the fuck are you doing?"

"I'm getting rid of any and all sharp objects, which could be used to stab you. Just in case she does turn up." He shrugs like his actions are completely rational.

"What the fuck for?"

"Because she might look like an angelic little thing, but I watched her jab a knife through an old man's hand. With a fucking smile on her face, Ash. She's lethal, and it's best not to underestimate her."

I laugh so fucking hard. Chase, a six-foot-two, bulky guy, who spends more time in the gym than anyone else I know, is scared of Breanna McKinley.

"You're scared of Bree? Really, Chase?"

"She's literally the devil's spawn, Ash. You'd be wise to be afraid of her. Speaking of Satan himself, why the hell hasn't he come to claim your soul yet? Surely word's gotten back to him by now about what you had for dessert at lunch."

I lick my lips. Damn it, I can't taste her anymore. I need to rectify that as soon as she gets here. I should always be able to taste her on my lips. I should find a way to get her taste made into a fucking lip balm. I'd buy it in bulk.

"Emily happens to like me, which means Josh is not going to do anything lethal to me." At least I hope that's enough of a reason for Josh not to feed me to his fucking pigs.

"Right, well, just know if the devil does come for you, I'll write you the best fucking eulogy you've ever heard. Fuck, maybe I should just write it now, so you can hear how great it's going to be." The fucker is actually serious.

I don't get to respond before my door flies open and Breanna walks in. I look at the clock on the wall; she's ten minutes early. I guess she's just as keen on being here as I am on having her.

Rising to my feet, I round my desk and approach her. She's standing in the middle of my office with a smile on her face. "Hi," she says as she undoes her coat.

"Hi, yourself." Leaning in, I kiss her lips. She hesitates momentarily before kissing me back.

"Oh, Chase? Hope and Lily are in VIP tonight. Thought you'd want to know." She winks at him.

"No, fuck no. Stay the fuck away from them. You only get yourselves into trouble whenever you drink together."

"Well, yeah, because unlike you, your cousins know how to let their hair down. Well, Hope does anyway. Lily, we're working on." Chase makes a quick exit from the room.

"Fucking hell, I don't have time to clean up their mess tonight," I grumble, turning around and walking back over to my desk. Leaning against it, I watch as Breanna takes her coat off and throws it on the couch. I think my brain misfires or something, because it takes me a few seconds to register what the fuck she's wearing.

She is oblivious to my internal turmoil as she types something out on her phone. She's wearing a light pink, sparkly scrap of material. I'm pretty sure she's trying to pass it off as a dress—*it's not fucking working*. That is not a fucking dress. The fabric is so thin I can see her nipples poking through.

Fucking hell, my mind might not be onboard with this dress, but my fucking cock is. He's come to life like he's never seen a pair of tits before. She looks up from her phone as I silently stalk towards her. The moment I'm in front of her, I pick her up and throw her down onto the couch.

"What the hell, Ash?" she squeals as I cover my body with hers, and my mouth goes to her throat, nibbling its way up to her ear.

"Did you expect a different reaction, when you decided to wear this pathetic excuse for a dress tonight, Bree?"

I bite down on her neck—that's going to leave a

mark for sure. Her body arches into mine, little moans parting her lips. Her hands slide through my hair as she tugs at my scalp. Fuck me.

"You know, you arrived just in time."

"For what?" she asks, her voice hoarse.

"I was just thinking how I couldn't taste you on my lips anymore. I need to be able to taste you, Bree. I was hooked after one lick. I'm now an addict. And I have no desire for recovery. Ever."

"Mmm, well, maybe I could offer you a lifetime supply," she says.

"Yeah? You want to be my dealer for life, Breanna?"

"We'll see."

I start kissing my way down her body, while sliding the thin straps from her shoulders.

"Ash, wait. Stop." Breanna's panicked voice halts me in my tracks.

"What's wrong?"

"Apart from the fact that someone who is meant to be like a cousin… is about to go down on me?"

"*Like* a cousin. Not a cousin, Breanna." I smirk at her, while silently thanking the gods that she is not, in fact, blood-related.

"If we do this, we need to keep it on the DL for a while. Just between us. Let's get to know each other, and make sure it's the real thing, before we tell our family."

"Breanna, I've known you since you were born. There's not a lot that I don't know about you, babe."

"I'm serious, Ash, and there's plenty. I have a lot of

bad habits that will drive you nuts. Promise me you'll keep it under wraps?"

I sit up, ready to head into a negotiation I'm not prepared to lose. "Okay, but I'm going to need a time-line here. I can't walk around and pretend you're not mine, Bree. It's going to drive me insane if I don't have an end date. A date when I can send a skywriter all over Sydney, telling everyone that Breanna McKinley is mine."

The smile that lights up her face is breathtaking. I pull my phone out of my pocket and snap a picture of her.

"Okay, let's get through the holiday season and reevaluate after Christmas."

"Three weeks? I can do that. But we are exclusive, Breanna."

"Ash, if you so much as look at another girl while we're together, I will destroy her, right before I cut your balls off and feed them to the pigs. My mum says they really like eating the balls of assholes, and I've always wanted to test out the theory." She smiles.

Fuck, maybe Chase is right. She is the fucking devil's spawn. But I don't care. I fucking love it. "Trust me, babe, there is no one on this earth who even remotely holds a candle to you. I've looked for the last six years, trying to get you out of my head. It didn't work."

"Huh, I wonder what Daddy would think if he knew you were lusting over his sixteen-year-old daughter."

"There are a lot of things we don't need to share with our parents, Bree. That's one of them."

"Oh, yeah? What else?" She laughs.

"How much you're about to come all over my fucking tongue. How, when you're quivering from an earth-shattering orgasm, I'm going to slam my cock so far inside your pussy it will lay claim to every inch of you." I kiss down to her hips, lifting the scraps of material over her waist. She's fucking bare; she's not wearing panties. Fucking hell.

"Breanna, where the fuck are your panties?" I growl as my tongue dives in, and my eyes roll back in my head. I really am an addict already. I need to remember to add to our negotiation: she's going to give me my fix at least twice a day.

"Last time I wore panties, you cut them up. I wasn't taking a chance with any more of my nice things, since you have the tendency of destroying them."

I lift my head to look her in the eye. "That's funny, considering the nicest thing you own is about to be fucking destroyed by me in the best possible way." I laugh.

"What's that?"

"This fucking sweet-as-fuck pussy of yours, Bree. It's now mine. I'll share it with you, I guess. But make no mistake, it's mine."

I go back to my task, licking from her asshole all the way up to her clit. Slowly. Over and over again. I can't get enough, and as much as I want to go quicker and make her come, I also don't want this to end. Inserting one finger into her wet cunt, I pump it in and out. Deliberately. Then I add another, hooking them up and rubbing on that spot that's driving her crazy.

My mouth clamps down over her clit. Sucking. Nibbling. My tongue twirling around. It only takes two minutes before I feel her walls pulse around my fingers. Her legs tighten against my head, holding me in place. The best part, though, is the way my name sounds on her lips as she screams out in pleasure. Hearing it just about makes me come in my pants, like a damn teenager.

I trail my way back up her body, fusing my lips with hers. This is where she was always meant to be. Under me. Mine.

CHAPTER 8

Bree

*A*sh's tongue twirls around mine, licking at my mouth with the same precision and skill he just exacted on my other lips. He's freaking good with that tongue. *Like really good.*

"I need you, Ash," I moan, pulling my mouth away from his.

"You have me, Bree. You've always had me."

I roll my eyes. He's nothing if not a charmer. I've seen him at his finest—how he worms his way out of all sorts of trouble with his mum and aunts. I take matters into my own hands. I don't need an invitation anymore, because the body he has under this suit is mine. I feel like I've dreamt about this moment for so long it's almost too good to be true.

Pushing him off me, I climb on top of him, until he has no other choice but to lie down on the couch. My fingers go straight to his belt buckle. "You have no idea how long I've wanted this."

"Oh, I think I might."

Once I get his belt undone, I go for his button and fly. The moment I release his pants, I see I'm not the only one who's gone commando tonight. I raise my eyebrows as I grip his cock in my hands.

"I didn't want to take the chance of you cutting up my Calvin Kleins." He answers my unspoken question.

"That sure is presumptuous of you, Mr. Williamson." I stroke up and down his shaft. I can't take my eyes off it. It's not like I haven't seen a dick before. I'm certainly no innocent virgin here, but damn… I never thought I'd be looking at one, thinking it was the most beautiful thing I've ever seen.

My thumb swipes along the seam, collecting the leaking precum. And I have the sudden urge to have this work of masculine art in my mouth, but therein lies my dilemma. I want it in another place too, and I honestly don't know which I'm more desperate for. I lean down and run my tongue from base to top, wrapping it around the tip and getting my first real taste.

It's heady, and I want more. But I need him buried inside me. Right now. *I'm aching for it.* I bury my hands beneath him and dig through his pockets. I know Ash. He's always prepared for anything. There's no way he doesn't have a condom on him. He watches me as I retrieve his wallet and open it. However, my search is momentarily paused by the image staring back at me.

Why does he carry my photo with him? He cups his hands over mine. "Don't overthink it, Bree. I like to look at beautiful things. You just happen to be the most beautiful thing I've ever seen."

Like I said, he's a charmer. I continue my search and almost squeal when I find that little foil packet. I rip it open with my teeth and roll the condom down the length of him with ease.

"I'm both turned the fuck on and pissed off that you know how to do that so well," Ash groans as I pump his cock a few more times.

I position myself on top of him. "Channel those feelings, love. Angry sex is good sex." I sink down on him, much more slowly than I'd like. But he's fucking huge, and I need to get used to his size. The burn eases away once I'm bottomed out. I roll my hips slightly, getting my body accustomed to accepting him. Because I guarantee this is not going to be the last time I have him inside me.

Ash's hands go to my hips, and in one effortless move, he flips us around, asserting dominance. "You want angry sex, Bree? You want me to fuck you so hard you'll be limping for the next couple of days?" he asks as he drives into me.

"Yes, fuck yes. I want that, Ash. Don't hold back."

He tips his head towards the ceiling and breathes in deeply, almost like he's trying to summon control. I don't want him in control of himself. I want him to lose it and fuck me like his bloody life depends on it.

His head tilts back down, and he makes eye contact with me as the right side of his lips curl slightly. "When you have to sit with an icepack on your vagina, remember you asked for this."

Then he lifts one of my legs, resting my ankle on his shoulder. His body leans over mine, bending my lower half back towards my head. He's just opened me right up. He starts to pump in and out. His fingertips dig in hard as he grabs at my hips, holding me in place as he picks up speed. *And force.*

I'm nothing more than a screaming, wet mess. He hits something deep inside me—a place I didn't know was even there—and it's igniting every spark within me. The world could burn down around us right now, and I couldn't care less. I'd gladly let myself go up in flames before I stopped doing this right now.

I'm so close to coming again. It's a little embarrassing... how quickly this man can make me fall over that ledge. Oh, but what a bloody beautiful fall it is. And I don't want to just fall right now. I want to leap over, headfirst.

"I want to feel your cunt choking my cock, Breanna. I need you to come for me," Ash grunts. And as if my body has been trained to follow his commands, I do just that. I come. Stars. Blackness. The whole fucking lot. I feel Ash thickening, and his movements become rigid as he follows me off the cliff.

His body covers mine, our heartbeats racing, one against the other, as they battle for first place. In both speed and intensity. Mine's winning, even though he's the one who just put in all the work. I run my fingers through his hair. It's soft. I always thought he'd be a hidden diva. I bet he uses fancier shampoo than I do.

"Ash?"

"Yeah, babe?" His head is resting on my chest.

"We're going to be doing that again, right?" I ask, half joking and half trying to reassure myself that this isn't a one-time thing.

"Night and day, Bree. You just try and keep me out of you." He brings his lips to mine, and again I find myself not caring about anything other than keeping him here. That is, until there's a knock at the door, accompanied by a voice behind it.

"Ash, why's your door locked? Oh, God, please tell me you don't have one of your special little friends in there."

"Ah, just a sec, Aunt El. I was getting changed."

My eyes go wide. Fuck! Day one, and we're already getting caught with our pants down.

"Go into the bathroom. I'll get rid of her."

"Ash, she can't find out. If Aunt Ella finds out, the whole damn family's going to know within the hour." In panic, I get up and tiptoe into the bathroom, locking the door behind me. I sit against it so I can hear their conversation.

"Aunty El, what a surprise. I wasn't expecting you. You look beautiful by the way. Is that a new dress?"

I roll my eyes. As always, he is laying it on thick.

"Clearly, you weren't expecting me. It smells like sex in here, Ash. This is a place of business, not whatever it is you were doing. Spare me the details." She raises her palm preemptively. "I don't need to know."

"Ah, sure… Is there a reason for this drop-in?"

"Can't I just be missing my favourite nephew?"

"Well, when my competition is Axel, I'm a shoo-in for that one. But sure. Want a drink? Just out of curiosity, though, who is your fav? Out of *all* of your nieces and nephews? It's me, right?"

"Mmm, nope. I don't have a favourite. Speaking of nieces, I heard a rumour that you were at lunch with Bree today."

More like… he *had* me for lunch. I bite down on my lip, trying not to laugh at my own joke.

"I went to a charity lunch. Bree was there," Ash says coolly.

"Since when do you go to charity lunches, Ash?"

"Since now. Why? Want me to take you as my plus-one next time?"

"God, no. I've been to enough of those things with your mum to last me a lifetime." There's a silent pause, and then Aunt Ella speaks again. "Huh."

"'*Huh*, what?"

"This coat. Bree has one just like it. I bought it for her last month."

"She probably left it here last night."

"Why was she here last night?"

"She snuck into my… club. She was drunk with that idiot friend of hers. Chase gave her a ride home."

"Oh, I just saw Chase. He was getting mighty close to Hope on the dance floor."

"I'm gonna kill him." Ash's voice rises. Shit! Please, don't leave me in here. I hear his footsteps get louder and then stop. Is he right outside the door?

"Aunt Ella, now is really not a good time. Maybe we can do brunch tomorrow? I've got a lot of work to get through tonight."

"Okay, but let's keep Chase alive. He's far too pretty to bury. I can't do brunch, but I'll call next time. Oh, and, Ash? Get better at lying. You're both playing with fire."

I don't release my breath until I hear her heels click, and then a door shut. I can't bring myself to come out of the bathroom. She knows. Shit, my Aunt Ella knows. Ash's Aunt Ella. Bloody hell.

Ella is married to my dad's brother. She's also the sister of Ash's dad. That's how our family trees merged into a family vine. Talk about messed up… I feel like I'm on an episode of *Jerry Springer*. Ash taps on the door.

"Bree, open up."

I stand, straightening my shoulders. *Never show anyone fear. You're a McKinley.* My little mantra plays through my head. With a smile on my face, I twist the knob and yank the door back.

"Seriously, Ash, she's right. You do suck at lying.

What happened to the little sweet-talking charmer who could get out of any kind of trouble when you were young?"

"I'm pretty sure you were thanking me for my... *charm*... not so long ago." He turns the shower faucet on, testing the water.

"Get undressed. We're getting in," he demands. I fold my arms over my chest.

"Maybe I don't want to shower with you."

"Suit yourself." He unbuttons his shirt, and the moment it hits the floor, all arguments leave my mind.

"You know what? A shower sounds like a great idea right now." I pull my dress over my head and walk past him, while he finishes disrobing. I am so not missing out on seeing that body naked... with water droplets running down those rock-hard abs.

CHAPTER 9

"ou're serious?" she screams.

"Deadly. You stole from me, Breanna. No one fucking steals from me." I'm not sure what she's having a hard time understanding, considering we've already discussed this. I took her appearance tonight as unspoken agreement.

"Ash, just let me pay you back. I can't work for you all summer. I have plans." Bree paces up and down the office. She stops at the bar, pouring herself a glass of whiskey and downing it in one go, before she continues her rant. "Ash, really, I can't work for you. What will I tell my parents? They're going to wonder why I'm choosing to work here, instead of McKinley Industries."

"Are you done?" I ask, raising an eyebrow.

"Not even close," she huffs as she plops herself down into one of the chairs across from me.

"You know, you working for me is the best idea I've ever fucking had. Think about it. You don't want people to know about us yet, which by the way, I am prepared to tell the world as soon as you give me the green light." I walk around the desk and squat down in front of her, holding her hands in mine. "This way, we get to spend every night with each other without anyone suspecting anything other than we're working together."

She stands and pulls her hands free. "As you are well aware, I don't really like being told what to do. I'd be a bloody horrible secretary. I can't even make coffee."

"I don't need you to make me coffee, Bree," I argue.

"Well, what is it you need me to do, exactly?"

"I need you to help me get ready for the expansion in Perth. We're three months away from opening. I may have fired my secretary, and I don't trust anyone else to be that close to this project. So, what do you say? Will you help me, Bree?"

Damn it, I wish I could read her mind… see what she's thinking right now. I don't need her help to build this club. I've single-handedly opened the hottest nightclubs around the whole country. I might have been born into the one in Sydney, but it was me who built the rest of them.

There's a tiny part of me that wants to make her work off the fucking money she stole from me. Or should I say cheated from me? But mostly, it's about being able to hang out with her every night. To have repeat performances of what we just did on the couch. So, no, I don't *need* her help, but I sure as fuck want it.

Bree smiles. It's a fake smile—one she uses often. "I thought your secretary quit?" She doesn't pause to wait for my confirmation. She remembers exactly what I said at the charity event. "But maybe you're right. This could be a great thing. Then again, maybe it could be the worst. What if, after spending that much time together, alone, we end up hating each other? I don't want to hate you, Ash. I don't have many people I like as it is." She clamps her lips shut. She didn't want to share that little tidbit of information with me. She should know that I don't care what she has to say. I'll never look at her as anything other than fucking perfect.

Her whole life she's grown up with people scrutinizing her, to see if she inherited any of her dad's anti-social traits. She did, but she's also learnt how to hide them well. It's a little unsettling just how fucking great she is at faking her feelings. But I know, with me, they're not fake. She doesn't have to pretend.

"Babe, we're not going to hate each other. It's impossible for me to hate you. And, well, I'll make sure to remind you every day just how super lovable I am." I wrap my arms around her and hold on tight. Leaning down into her ear, I whisper, "I'm really glad I'm one of the people you like, Bree. You don't have to pretend with me."

I feel her whole body stiffen. She's not ready to have that conversation, to lose the mask she holds so firmly in place. I'll be here waiting... whenever that day comes.

Pulling out of my arms, she changes the subject. "So, what's my first task as your extremely hot secretary slash secret lover?"

Secret lover? Is she fucking joking? She's not my secret fucking lover. I walk over to my desk and retrieve the stack of building reports I received today. "*Steaming-fucking-hot* secretary slash secret *girlfriend*," I correct. "Tonight, I need you to look over these building reports, and highlight anything you think is important or that I should know about."

"Ah, is that something your old secretary would have done? Shouldn't I just be answering phones, making appointments, that sort of thing?" Fuck, I didn't even think about who was going to be organising my schedule. My secretary didn't just answer the phone; she also got really good at screening the many calls I'd receive from women. Fuck, I cannot let Bree answer those. That won't end too well for anyone. I'm going to have to hire a virtual assistant or something, someone to work in the background.

"Well, you can do all that while you look over these

reports. And, no, my old secretary wasn't qualified to look over reports."

"What makes me qualified?" she asks, smirking.

I answer her honestly. "One, I trust you completely —well, with anything other than poker. Two, you're one of the most intelligent people I know. Three, your opinion matters to me, Bree."

She thinks on my words for a moment before agreeing. "Okay, I'll look over them. Is there a game tonight?"

I shake my head. *No, there's not a fucking game tonight, because your psychotic father sliced a man up in my fucking game room.* Those words don't leave my mouth though. "No, downstairs is being… redecorated. There won't be any more games for a couple of weeks. But for you, there won't be another *ever.*"

"Why can't I play at the club? If I'm going to be working here, I won't have time to play anywhere else." She stomps her foot. I try my hardest not to laugh at her dramatics.

"Bree, you don't play. What you and your little friend do is *cheat.* I'm not having you cheat my club out of more fucking money. And you won't be doing it in any other club either. Do you realize how dangerous some of the men in those games are? If they caught onto you and Ben, do you even know what they'd do?"

"Please, I can handle myself, Ash. They're not going to touch me."

"I'm aware of just how well you can handle yourself,

Breanna. I had an old man with one hand broken and the other with a big gaping hole in it last night."

"Exactly, I took care of his wandering hands."

"What about Ben? He's supposed to be your best friend. Can he take care of himself? What if someone went after him to get at you, because you cheated them?"

"They wouldn't. I'd hunt them down."

"I'm sure you would. But I can't have my girlfriend going around to other people's clubs and cheating them out of money. Do you know how that would look for me?"

"Probably not great. But nobody knows I'm your girlfriend yet. We can table this discussion for when people do know. Until then, Benny and I will keep doing what we do best. *Win*." She smiles like that's the end of our conversation.

"You're done with the underground card games, Bree. I'm not backing down on this. Maybe I should give Emily a call. Does she know about this little hobby of yours?"

"Go ahead. I'll give Alyssa a call and tell her all about what your not-so-legal business ventures are." Fuck, she's got me there.

We remain at a standstill, until we both crack up laughing. "Did we seriously just threaten each other with our mums?" I question.

"We did. Jesus, Ash, you should have seen your face. Don't worry, babe. I'd never actually tell your mum. It'd break her heart. Zac, though, I'd love to see how he'd react if he knew." She smirks.

"He knows. There's not much that happens in this club my dad doesn't know about, which reminds me... How'd *your dad* know you were here, and what happened to you last night?"

"I called him when Chase was driving me to your place."

She called her dad? Of course, she fucking did. "Why would you tell him about Old Man Edgar? Did you want to turn my card room into a bloodbath?"

"I can't lie to my dad, Ash. He'd know. I didn't know he'd show up here. I told him I handled it."

"You knew. You just didn't care. There's a difference."

"Maybe." She shrugs her shoulders.

"All right, I do have a shitload of work I need to get through, before I can take you home and ravish you all night. You can work at my desk. I'll grab my laptop and work from the couch. You'll find highlighters and sticky notes in the top-right drawer." I hand her the stack of building reports.

"Great. First day, and I'm already in the boss's seat. Watch out, Ash. After a week, I might just own this place." Bree twirls around in my desk chair, laughing.

The scary thing is she's probably not wrong. This one woman has the power to bring me to my knees. She'd do it with that fucking smile on her face too. Maybe Chase is right to be afraid of her. I laugh at the memory of him collecting all the sharp objects from the room. The idiot left them sitting on the corner of my desk.

"Hey, Bree, do me a favour? Pop your head down-stairs and give Chase a friendly reminder to keep his paws off Hope for me." I smile. The fucker won't take my warnings, but I bet he'll take Breanna's.

"Ah, why me? Why can't you do it? You know Hope likes him, don't you?"

What the actual fuck? No, there is no way my little cousin has the hots for my best friend.

"No, she doesn't. Hope is sweet and innocent." Even as I say the words, I know I'm describing the other twin; Lily is the sweeter of the two. Hope's always been the wild child. "Also, Chase is scared as shit of you. Chances are he'll listen to your warnings."

"Okay, but if Hope finds out I did this, I'm blaming you." She goes to walk past me. I pull her back by the arm, twisting her hair around one hand and tilting her head upwards. I kiss her with all the fire and passion I've built up. I've fantasized, a lot, about being able to do just this. Grab this girl and give her a kiss that will erase all others from her mind.

As I'm standing here, drowning in everything that is her, I'm mentally cursing myself out for taking so fucking long to do this. I should have claimed her the minute she turned eighteen. Why the fuck did I wait? Why now? Maybe I need to stop questioning and just be grateful that I can finally do this.

By the time I pull away from her mouth, her lips are red and swollen. All I can see are those plump lips wrapping around my cock. Fuck, and now I'm ready for round three. I don't know if I'll ever get enough of this girl. She's a fucking walking aphrodisiac.

"I'm really fucking glad we're doing this. *Finally*," I murmur, my lips mere centimetres away from hers.

"Mmm, you and me both. Be right back, babe. Get some of that work done, so we can get out of here."

I watch her walk out the door. I go and sit back down on the couch and open my laptop. Surprisingly, I manage to focus enough on the spreadsheet in front of me, only thinking of Breanna every other fucking minute. I look up to the clock on the wall. I haven't been keeping track of time, but she's been gone for a while now. My stomach feels uneasy, like I'm having withdrawals. Or is my gut trying to tell me something is wrong? Fuck, why has she been down there for so long?

Putting my laptop aside, I head to the VIP floor, where Hope and Lily hang out. None of them are in their usual booth. The one that's always reserved for family. I look around. Spotting Dan, one of my bouncers, I stalk over to him.

"Boss, busy night."

"Yeah, it is. Have you seen my cousins? Chase?" I ask.

"Last I saw, they were all heading downstairs." He points to the staircase that leads to the bottom floor. The busiest fucking floor. It'll be like finding a needle in a haystack. I walk down anyway, folding the sleeves of my shirt up as I make my way through the crowd to the main bar.

"Hey, Ash, how're things?" One of the bar girls leans over the counter, giving me an eyeful of her cleavage as she smiles and bats her eyes.

"Yeah, Ash, how're things?" *This* comes from the blonde bombshell beside me, with the sugary-sweet voice that easily veils the underlying threat.

"Better, now that I found you. What are you doing down here?" I reach out to pull her body to me, when she gives her head a subtle shake. Fuck me, how does she expect me to keep my hands off her? These next few weeks are going to be fucking harder than I thought.

CHAPTER 10

Bree

y blood is boiling; my skin is itching with the need to maim and torture. My victim? The woman currently leaning over the bar, batting her eyelashes and flashing her tits at my boyfriend. I want nothing more than to drag Ash up on this bar and have my dirty little way with him. Claim him publicly for all of these bitches to see that this man, this beautiful creature they're all lusting over, is taken. By *me*.

I need to calm down. It was my decision to keep

this thing between us a secret. For now. And for good reason. I don't want to hear the opinions of our families. My dad knows, which is probably why Aunt Ella came by tonight. He would have told her; they are close like that. Usually, that would mean the whole family would know by now. Hope and Lily haven't said a word to me yet. If they knew, I'd be sure to hear their opinions on me taking up with their beloved cousin.

They look at Ash like he walks on water. He's certainly a god between the sheets, not that we've been between any just yet. Only the couch, and the shower. Mmm, that shower is one I'll be making use of again. Huh, thoughts of a naked Ash distracted me from the damage I was envisioning inflicting on one of his staff members.

"Can I get you anything, Ash?" The little wench reaches out and puts her hand on his arm. And just like that, the bloodlust is back.

I squeeze myself in front of Ash, forcing him to take a step back, which also removes her hand from his arm. Leaning over the bar, I wiggle my finger at her to bring her face closer to me. I smile sweetly, like I'm about to share a secret with a bestie. The fool leans into me. As soon as her head is close enough, I wrap my fingers in her hair.

"Fuck, Breanna, calm down." I hear Ash cursing from behind me; his hands go to my waist like he wants to pull me back. I have a good grip on this bitch's hair though.

"If I see your filthy fucking hands on my boyfriend

again, I'm going to chop them off at the wrist, before I shove them down your throat and watch you choke. One popped ocular vein after the other." I release her, straighten my back, and smile. I feel Ash's body relax behind me; however, his hands don't leave my hips. It's somewhat grounding, having him against me.

The rage that's burning inside me dims slightly with his touch. I can still feel my heart racing; the need to maim this bitch is strong. It's the look of fear in her eyes that I revel in though. Her face visibly pales. Her eyes glass over, like she's about to burst into tears. Good, you should be fucking scared. I tilt my head and watch her; she's staring at me, opening and closing her mouth like a fish out of water. She wants to say something. And I'd *love* to hear what it is. I know she won't though. They very rarely do.

When her eyes glance up and over my shoulder, I know she's looking to Ash for help. I should have smashed her face on the bar. She's pretty... if you like dirty skanks who wear too much makeup. Maybe a broken nose would be an improvement. A makeshift nose job, free of charge. I'm generous like that.

"Go and serve at the other end of the bar. Swap places with someone else. *Anyone else.*" Ash raises his voice over the club music.

The girl doesn't waste any time scurrying away. Damn, I was kind of hoping she'd try to stand up to me, and give me a reason to slam my fist into that pretty little face of hers. Ash spins me around. My back is now firmly against the bar, my front pressed up to his chest. When I tilt my head to look at him, I realize the mistake I just made. I let my mask slip right in front of him. He's going to know exactly how unstable my mind really is.

As I stare at him, I can see the questions in his eyes, but there's also something else: understanding, concern, lust. Lots of lust. That's confirmed when he presses his hard cock into my stomach.

"Bree, as hot as you are when you go all green-eyed monster, I don't have time for the harassment lawsuits from my employees. You have nothing to worry about. You have no reason to be jealous or concerned." He nips at my ear.

My body responds to his, like we have always melded together. All of my senses ignite with his touch, his voice, his smell. It's overwhelming; he is overwhelming. He makes me forget myself. Right now, anyone could see us in this predicament, and I couldn't care less, as long as I can keep his hands and his mouth on me.

Just as I'm pulling his lips closer to mine, all hell breaks loose. Before I can register what's happening, Ash is picking me up and dumping me on the other side of the bar.

"Get down, and stay there. Do not come out from behind this bar," he yells over the chaos.

I nod my head to ease the worry evident on his face. It's cute that he thinks he needs to protect me. I watch him enter the chaos without a second thought. I have no idea what started this, but punches are being thrown in every direction. Bodies are on top of bodies. I see masses of red hair, belonging to Hope and Lily, in amongst the crowd. Shit, I know they can both handle their own, but I can't just sit behind this bar and watch my friends fight without me.

Besides, what would be the fun in that? I flick my heels off and climb back over the counter. The moment I do, I step on a piece of broken glass. "Fuck." Lifting my foot, I pull the small shard out and continue to push my way into the crowd. By the time I reach the girls, some ass has Lily held up against the wall by her throat. *I don't think so.* I pick up a wooden chair and smash it over his head with every ounce of strength I have.

He lets Lily go and turns around to face me. His hands reach out in my direction, but before he can grab me, his face is hitting the ground. I don't know how, but Lily just put him on his ass.

The music stops, the lights come on, and I look up to see we're surrounded by cops. People are being dragged off in handcuffs. Not just people. *Ash.* Ash is being dragged off. A couple of officers approach us. They look at me, then each other, and shake their heads. Hope and Lily are cursing out the officer detaining Ash.

It's when one of them goes to block Hope's path that she reaches up and slaps him across the face. Lily then steps in front of Hope and somehow gets the officer on his ass. As a result, the twins are dragged out in handcuffs, screaming the place down like banshees.

"What the fuck are you doing? Why are you arresting them?" I demand.

"Miss McKinley, it's best if you head home," one of the officers says.

"It's best if you tell me why the hell you're arresting my friends?" What the fuck? All three Williamsons are being dragged off. And I'm fucking certain if my last name weren't McKinley, I'd be sitting in one of those cop cars right next to them. It's insane. I need to get them out of there.

Chase comes up beside me. Why isn't he being dragged off in handcuffs with Ash?

"Breanna, come on. We can meet them down at the station. It'll be quicker if we just go and bail them out."

"Bail them out for what? Self-defence? This is ridiculous. You can't arrest them," I yell at the retreating cops.

"We can, and we are. If you want to help your friends, I suggest you get them a lawyer or prepare to post bail."

I smile, reading the man's name. "Officer Kennedy, I can assure you there won't be any need for bail. Come on, Chase. I'm calling my dad on the way to the station." I smirk when I see the officer pale a little. He doesn't back down though. He drags Lily out the front doors.

***

"Can't this car go any faster? You drive like my fucking grandma, Chase." I'm fidgeting. I can't sit still. I need to get to Ash. My only thought is getting Ash and the twins out of whatever trouble they've landed in.

"I think you should reconsider calling your dad, Breanna. We can just bail them out ourselves. No one has to know."

I laugh at Chase's naiveté. "Oh, honey, if you think my dad doesn't already know, you're clearly more beautiful than you are smart."

"You think I'm beautiful?" His lips turn into a huge grin.

"You're not ugly." I shrug.

I pull my phone out and dial my dad. He picks up on the first ring—he's obviously been waiting for this call.

"Breanna, what happened?" he asks.

"Well, hello to you too, Daddy. I'm fine, by the way. Thanks for asking." My sweet voice usually works to get me out of trouble. I don't think it's going to this time, though.

"I know you're fine. If I thought for a second you weren't, I wouldn't wait for you to call me. What happened?"

I huff, "I don't know, one minute we were standing in the club. The next, everyone was fighting. I don't know if I saw Ash beating the crap out of someone or not. Then some guy had Lily held up against the wall, so I went to help her. Ash and the twins got arrested. I'm on my way to central."

"Someone had Lily against the wall? Who?" he growls. My dad is fiercely protective of our family, extended or otherwise.

"I don't know who. Last I saw, the dude was face down on the ground."

"Okay, I'll meet you at the station. Do not go in without me, Breanna."

"Okay." I don't bother arguing with him. I know he'll fix this.

After I hang up the phone, Chase breathes out a lungful of hot air. "You know, your dad is probably going to want to leave Ash rotting in that cell."

"He'll definitely want to, but he won't," I say with confidence. "With the risk of sounding like a spoilt brat, there is nothing my dad would not do for me."

"You're right. You do sound like a spoilt brat." Chase laughs.

By the time we pull up to the parking lot at the station, my dad is already there waiting. He's not alone though. Both Bray and Zac are standing beside him. None of them look overly impressed right now.

"Hi." I hug and kiss my dad. He pulls me back, giving me a once-over. Seeming satisfied that I'm in one piece, he lets go.

"You okay, Bree?" Zac asks.

"I'm good. Can we go get Ash out of there now?"

All three men look at me with their brows raised. A thousand questions pass through their eyes.

"I'd prefer he stay there," my dad grumbles.

I don't bother to wait for them. I head into the station and speak to the front-desk officer.

"I'm here to get Ash Williamson and the Williamson twins out. What do I need to do?"

The officer looks behind me and straightens. Peering over my shoulder, I roll my eyes at the three men walking towards us with grim expressions on their faces.

"I expect that all three will be released immediately. I've got my lawyers on the way. Their arrest was unwarranted. I think you and I both know that," Zac speaks to the clerk.

"With all due respect, Mr. Williamson, your son had to be pulled off another man. And that other man is currently undergoing surgery with life-threatening injuries to his head."

I smile. *That's my boyfriend, boys and girls.* "I don't know what the other guy did, but there was obviously a good reason," I defend Ash.

"Where the fuck are my daughters?" Bray's gravelly voice booms out through the whole station. He was calm as a damn cucumber. I was wondering how long it would take him to crack.

At that moment, the twins get brought out. "You're free to go."

"Girls? You okay?" They both nod but don't say anything.

Bray takes Lily's face in his hands and tips her head backwards. "I'm going to fucking kill the motherfucker who did this to you."

"I'm okay, Dad. I already sorted him out." Lily wraps her arms around Bray.

"My son. Where is he?" Zac asks the clerk again.

"He's being held until bail is set, which won't be until tomorrow."

"Like hell, he is. You can't hold him. He's innocent." I'm fuming.

"He almost beat a man to death in public view. He's far from innocent," the clerk scoffs at me. I squint my eyes at her; my dad takes hold of my hand and squeezes it.

"Bree, sweetheart, we can come back in the morning. Come on," he tries.

"I'm not leaving him here. He didn't do anything wrong."

The doors to the station open and two men in suits walk in, approaching Zac. They must be the lawyers he was talking about. There're a few hushed whispers before Zac looks at me.

"Breanna, it's best if you let your father take you home. There isn't anything you can do here tonight," he says to me.

"But I…"

"Come on, Bree. I think it's time for a sleepover. You're coming with us. Chase, be a darl and give us a lift home, will you?" Hope takes my hand and walks out of the station. Zac and the lawyers stay behind, while everyone else follows us to the car park.

"Bree, Zac got my sorry ass out of those cells when I was young more times than I can remember. He's good at getting people out of trouble. Don't worry. Ash will be out by morning," Bray whispers as he hugs me goodbye.

Great, does the whole fucking family know about Ash and me already? I search his eyes, looking for the disapproval I'm sure to find there. But there's none. I don't see anything other than compassion.

Once we're in the car, I ask Chase to take me to Ash's place. I want to sleep in his bed. I want to be there if he gets out some time during the night. Both of the twins give me questioning looks, but neither says a thing.

CHAPTER 11

"Tell me again, Mr. Williamson. Why did you attack Mr. Sanders?" the cop, who's been questioning me for the last hour, asks for the hundredth time. I don't bother answering. I'm not stupid. When it's evident I'm not going to respond, he continues anyway. "It's okay, we have a statement from Miss Williamson. Along with at least two hundred other eyewitnesses, who were in your club tonight."

He's trying to goad me. I saw them take Lily and

Hope away in cuffs right behind me, screaming and cursing out anyone and everyone. The thought of the hell those two would have given in the car ride over here makes me smile.

"You find something amusing, Mr. Williamson?"

I don't answer, just stare at him blankly. The door opens and two of our company's solicitors walk in. "Do not say another word, Ash. Detective, this line of questioning is over. You're harassing and baiting my client."

The detective's face reddens. "The interview is over when I say it's over," he yells.

"Actually, it's over now. He's been bailed out." Another officer walks into the room.

I smirk at the asshole who's been trying to break me. "Better luck next time, mate," I say as I stand and straighten my shirt. It's fucking covered in that prick's blood. I can't wait to get home and burn the fucking thing.

"Are we done here?" I ask my solicitors.

"Yes, go home and get cleaned up. We'll speak tomorrow."

I get escorted to the waiting room, only to be greeted by the disapproving look of my father. Of course, one of the twins called him.

"Who ratted me out? Hope or Lily?" I ask as we walk out of the station together.

"Neither... Josh called me. Right after Breanna called him." My dad raises his eyebrows at me, a million unasked questions written all over his face.

"Get in," he demands as we approach his car.

"It's not like I have much of a choice." Honestly, I was expecting Chase to be here waiting for me, not my dad.

When the car is cruising through the quiet city streets, I lean back against the headrest.

"Are you hurt anywhere? Do you need a doctor?"

"No, I'm good," I say with my eyes closed.

"Good," my dad responds, right as he reaches across the car and slaps me up the side of my head. "Don't ever have me fucking worry like this again, Ash. Do you know what it's like to get called in the middle of the night to find out your son has been arrested? Fucking hell, I'm getting too old for this shit."

"Sorry, you didn't have to come."

"Yes, I did. That's something you won't understand until you have kids. What the fuck happened tonight?"

"Some ass wasn't taking no for an answer from Lily. She was on the dance floor with Hope and Chase. By the time I got to them, Chase already had the cunt on the ground. I just took over for him."

"Fucking hell. I can't even be mad about that. Do we know who the asshole is?"

"The detective mentioned his name's Sanders. Apparently, he's in surgery at the general."

I shake my hand out. My knuckles are swollen, the skin broken. I've had worse though.

"Have you seen the twins? How are they?" I ask.

"They're fine. Chase took them home." My dad

looks over at me before adding, "Breanna went with them."

"Breanna was here?" Fuck, that is not what I fucking wanted. I don't want her hanging around a bloody cop shop waiting for me.

"You sound like you're surprised."

"I *am* surprised." I try to act as nonchalant as I can.

"What's happening between you and Breanna? There have been a lot of rumours circling today."

"Of course, there're fucking rumours. Nothing's happening. She's helping me out at the club, until I find a replacement for my secretary who just quit." The lie burns on my tongue. It's not like I've never told a white lie to my parents. I just don't like doing it.

"I heard you *fired* your secretary." My dad laughs.

"Fired? Quit? Same thing, really."

Thank fuck. We're pulling up to my apartment building. I need to get away from this conversation.

"Thanks for the ride, and for bailing me out."

"I'll always bail you out, Ash. Expect a visit from your mother as soon as the sun is up."

"Argh, you told her?" I grumble. I can handle my dad's disappointment, but my mum's? That's just fucking torture.

"When I get calls in the middle of the night and have to leave, she tends to ask questions. Also, I'd rather her find out from me than from someone else."

"Thanks." I step out of the car.

"Ash?" My dad calls out just before I shut the door.

"Yeah?"

"If this thing with you and Breanna isn't the real deal, end it now."

I don't answer him. I shut the door and walk into the foyer. I'm waiting for the lift when Josh fucking appears next to me. That creepy fucker came out of nowhere, giving me a damn heart attack. *That*, and it's Joshua McKinley, the one man you don't want sneaking up on you in the middle of the night.

"Josh, two visits in one day. My popularity must be increasing." I know being a smartass is probably not helping my case. But sleep-deprivation combined with the physical aftermath following the fight—the sudden increase then drop in adrenaline—are negating my better sense.

"I was wondering how long your dad would leave you in that cell. He lasted longer than I gave him credit for. I've been waiting here for two fucking hours."

"And why *is it* you've been waiting here in the first place?"

"Breanna's up in your apartment."

Fuck, she came back here. My need to get upstairs just doubled with the thought of her waiting for me. Has she eaten dinner? I should order some food in. I pull out my phone and open the Uber Eats app, ignoring Josh's presence.

After I've ordered a heap of Chinese food, I pocket my cell and look back up at Josh.

"Hungry?" he asks.

"Not particularly."

"You always order that much food when you're not hungry?"

"Nope, but I'm pretty sure Bree hasn't eaten yet." I shrug like it's a perfectly normal, acceptable thing for me to be buying his daughter dinner.

Josh stares at me blankly for a while, as if he's trying to see into my soul. After a few minutes of this *weird as fuck* stare-off, neither of us backing down, Josh finally speaks up again.

"It'd be easier if I could fucking hate you, Ash. Do something stupid so I have a goddamn reason to get rid of you."

"What?" He's making no sense.

"Whatever's happening with you and my daughter, I don't like it. But I'll accept it, as long as she's happy."

"You know I'd never do anything to hurt her."

"You didn't see her when you were locked up. She won't admit it, but *that* hurt her."

"Fuck. That wasn't exactly planned. I just... when that fucking asshole had his hands all over Lily, I saw red. I wasn't thinking."

"You did the right thing. I would have killed him then and there. They can't press charges when they can't talk, Ash."

With those parting words, he shakes his head and walks away.

Stopping at the door, he turns and says, "Tell Breanna to call her mother tomorrow."

"Sure."

Entering the apartment, I'm greeted with silence.

Thank fuck, finally some quiet. I walk through in search of Bree. I know she's here somewhere. She's left her shoes in the foyer, her coat thrown on the floor in the living room, and the contents of her purse I found tipped out over the kitchen counter.

I find her in my bedroom. In my bed. And my heart fucking swells. She's sleeping, tucked under the covers. She looks fucking peaceful. I leave her and head into the shower. I need to get this fucker's blood off me before I join her.

The hot water cascades down my back. As much as I'd like to stay in here, and wash the stench of tonight's bullshit away, I make quick work of rinsing and drying. Returning to the bedroom, I turn everything off. I pick Bree's phone up from the bed and sit it on top of the charging mat on the bedside table.

I climb in behind her and pull her body to mine. She rolls over, snuggling her head against my chest. "Ash?" she asks.

Who the fuck else does she think is climbing into bed with her? "Yeah, babe, it's me."

"Don't do that again. I don't like feeling helpless."

I kiss the top of her head. "You being here is helping more than you know."

"Mmm, what did you get charged with? How bad is it?"

"Don't worry about it. The charges won't stick." I change the subject. "Your dad was waiting in the lobby when I came in. He wants you to call your mother in the morning."

"My dad was here? And you're still breathing? Miracles do happen. How'd he know I was here? I told him I was going back to Lily's."

"Probably because he's not an idiot. I know you wanted to keep us a dirty little secret for a while, but I think the cat's out of the bag, babe."

"Let's just pretend it's not. Deniability until death, Ash. I don't want anyone else involved in us. Not yet." She kisses my chest, right where my heart is. There's no fucking chance in hell I can say no to her. When she looks up at me, batting those eyelashes with a smirk that would bring down the devil himself, I know I'm going to agree with anything she wants. "Besides, I kind of like the idea of being your dirty little secret. Someone you do very dirty things to."

Yep, anything she wants. "Oh, yeah?" I roll one of her nipples through my fingers, twisting and pulling. The thin cotton of the shirt she's wearing is not doing anything to protect her from my assault. Her back arches, pressing her tits into me. "You want to be my little plaything, Bree?"

"Yes." Her reply comes out in a staggered breath.

"You should be careful what you wish for, little girl," I growl as I roll her onto her back. Straddling her waist, I tug her shirt up and over her head. Her chest rises and falls with her heavy breathing. "This body is fucking perfection. These tits are fucking mine." My hands massage her breasts, squeezing and pulling them together. "I'm going to fuck these tits of yours, Bree. Come all over your chest. Then I'll write my name in the mess before scooping up every last drop and feeding it to you." I look at her face to gauge her reaction. I don't want to scare her away. The moans she lets out, and the way I feel her thighs clench together underneath me, give me all the encouragement I need to keep going. To keep pushing her to her limits.

"Is that what you want, Bree? To be my dirty little girl? For me to do whatever I want with your body? To fuck it, wherever and however I want?"

"Yes," she says with confidence.

One of my hands travels along her torso, circling her belly button. Moving down her body, I discard the little black lace panties she has on. I have no idea where they even came from; she wasn't wearing any panties when we were at the club.

"Tell me, Bree, are you going to be a good girl? Or a bad girl?"

"Both." She smirks.

"When I put my fingers inside this pretty little pussy of yours, is it going to be wet? Are you creaming for me already, Bree?"

Her head tips back, and her hips arch off the bed, like she's offering herself to me on a silver fucking platter. Except, for Breanna McKinley, that platter would need to be platinum and covered in diamonds. Regardless, I'm not one to turn down a gift. I put two fingers in her. She's wet; she's more than ready.

"You're fucking drenched, Bree." I can feel the walls of her pussy clench and pulse around my hand. Her grip is fucking tight. My fingers work her harder. Faster.

"You are going to come for me, Bree. You're going to come on my fingers. And when you do, I'm going to turn you over and spank that ass of yours, before fucking you like the bad girl you are."

She screams my name as her whole body goes rigid. Her head falls back; her mouth hangs open. It's the most beautiful thing I've ever seen. I don't give her time to recover before I remove my fingers and flip her over. I lift her hips and place two pillows under them.

My fingers trail up and down her asshole. She stiffens and looks over her shoulder at me. "I'm going to enjoy fucking this little asshole of yours, Bree. Not tonight, but soon."

"Ash, I'm not... I mean, I haven't..." Her words trail off.

"Babe, I'm never going to do anything to hurt you. I'm only going to make you feel good." As I say the words, I bring my palm down and slap her right cheek. The sting goes through my already-busted hand, and vibrates up my arm.

"Oww, what the fuck?" Bree goes to move away from me, before she stops. "Oh. Wait... do that again."

I love how explorative she is. "You and I are going to have a lot of fucking fun... *fucking*, Bree." I bring my palm down on her other cheek.

This time she embraces the sting. "Do you know why you're getting spanked? Why you were a bad girl tonight?"

"No, and I don't really care." She smiles.

I bring my palm down and slap her right side again. "It's because you didn't stay behind the bar where I told you to."

"I had to help Lily," she argues. I saw her throw a chair over a guy's head. Through the chaos, I didn't know why she'd done it.

"I don't want to talk about my cousin, when all I can think about is burying myself balls-deep inside you and fucking the disobedience out."

"You're welcome to try," she says.

And try I fucking do. Lining my cock up with her entrance, I immerse myself in her with one thrust. I still the moment I do. I didn't get a condom. I've never been with anyone without a condom before. I had one break last year. Thank fuck the woman was on birth control and nothing came of it. I can literally feel fucking everything inside of my girl right now. I don't even know if Bree's on birth control—that's something I should know.

I fucking love the idea of having babies with her. Just not yet. I'm fucking twenty-eight. I'm nowhere near ready to be a father.

I lean over and open the bedside drawer, retrieving a condom. "Are you on birth control, Bree?" I ask her as I rip the foil packet open with my teeth.

"Yes," she replies as she moves backwards and forwards on my dick.

I pull all the way out, hating what I have to do, but it's a necessary evil. As soon as I'm sheathed, I slam back into her. Holding her hair around one hand, her hip in the other, I fuck her, just like her whimpers are begging me to do. Right before she's about to come, I insert one finger in her puckered little hole. And she screams her way through her orgasm, her pussy clamping down on my cock and milking me for everything I have.

CHAPTER 12

Bree

Consciousness seeps in slowly, and my muscles ache as I roll over. I'm not ready to wake up from this dream yet. I smile, remembering the events of last night, and the reason I'm so damn sore this morning.

As much as I want to stay here in bed, my bladder has other ideas. Groaning, I get up and head for the bathroom. The reflection looking back at me in the mirror is hideous. I run my fingers through my hair, doing my best to tame my locks. After washing up, I trudge out, in search of Ash.

The moment I open the bedroom door, the smell of bacon hits me. Mmm, I didn't realize how hungry I was until right now. I head for the kitchen, only stopping when I hear the voices of Ash and his mother. Shit, I do not need Alyssa to see me here right now. I should turn around, go back to the bedroom, and hide out until she's gone.

That's what I *should* do, but I can't make my feet move. Instead, I stay as still as I can in the hallway, hidden out of view, while eavesdropping on their conversation.

"Mum, I'm fine. Really, if I wasn't I'd probably tell you." Ash sounds exasperated, like it's not the first time this morning he's had to tell her as much.

"Ash Grant Williamson, you are not fine. You're not sleeping. You're getting into bar fights in your own damn club. And you got arrested. Now, tell me why you're not sleeping first."

"I'm sleeping enough. I'm busy. I'm in the middle of a new build, located on the other side of the country, which means I'm flying to Perth and back every other week."

"Isn't that what you hired Chase for? To do stuff for you? Take some of the load off?" Alyssa asks.

I was curious as to what Chase's job was within the club. He's always around, but I have no idea what the guy actually does. I wonder if Ash is working too much? Am I taking up too much of his time? It's only been two days, yet I know I've already disrupted his work schedule a lot.

"Well, you're taking the week off over Christmas, right? We're all going to the McKinley beach house."

"Yeah, I'll be there. I've rented a place just up the road from them already." That's news to me. That will make it much easier to have repeat performances of last night over the Christmas week.

"Okay? Why'd you rent a place? You'll be there all by yourself?" I really should go back to the bedroom. I don't know how long Alyssa is going to be here. "Unless you're bringing a special friend to Christmas this year? You know, Axel brought a girl home the other day. When are you going to bring someone home, settle down, and give me those grandbabies I need?"

My heart pounds in my chest as I wait for Ash's answer. "Soon, but you can wait for grandbabies. I'm not near ready for that."

"Soon, huh? Do I know her?"

"Stop digging, Mum. I can't tell you yet, and I don't really want to have to lie to you."

"Okay, well, I have to get going. I'm taking Ava to do some last-minute Christmas shopping." I rush back to the bedroom and hide behind the door. As soon as I hear the elevator ding, I make my way to the kitchen.

"Something smells really good." I smile at Ash, who is leaning against the bench with a coffee cup in his hand. He smirks as he brings the cup to his lips. He's wearing a pair of sweats, and nothing else. His muscles flex as he takes a long draw of the steaming liquid.

My eyes are glued to those abs, and my tongue runs along my bottom lip. I want to lick the grooves of that damn six-pack he has going on there.

"Bree, stop looking at me like I'm breakfast. You need to eat. Sit down." He busies himself putting bacon, eggs, toast, and then baked beans on a plate, before setting it down in front of me. "Eat up, buttercup. We've got a busy day to plan."

"Do you have a food fetish?" I ask him. After he fucked the life out of me last night, he walked over to the kitchen and came back into the room with a shit-load of Chinese food.

"I have many fetishes when it comes to you, but food is not one of them."

"So, do you cook breakfast for all the girls you have sleep over?"

"Yes, I do," he answers.

I scowl and push the eggs around on my plate. Why the hell did I ask a question I didn't want to know the answer to?

"Breanna, before you get all stabby, you should know—apart from Ava and the twins—you are the only girl I've had sleep over."

"Really? You don't need to lie about your past. I mean, we both have them, right? We've both slept with other people. It's okay."

"I clearly didn't fuck you hard enough last night, if you can still remember someone else being inside you.

I'll have to try harder next time." Ash picks a piece of bacon off my plate. "Also, I wasn't lying. I've never had a girl wake up here, who wasn't my sister or my cousin."

"Remember when I was little, and insisted that if you were Dominic's cousin, then you had to be mine too. For years, I was convinced we were related." I laugh at the memory of when I was seven and followed Ash around, arguing with him over that fact.

"What changed your mind about wanting to be my cousin?"

"You got hot." I smirk.

"Thank fuck for that then." He reaches out for another piece of bacon. I pull my plate away.

"I will stab you if you take any more of my food."

"I believe you bloody would. Okay, I'll get my own." I watch him stand and walk around the counter. Every one of those overused "hot ass" sayings runs through my mind as I unashamedly stare at the fine specimen that is Ash.

I hate to see him go, but boy, do I love to watch him leave.

That's an ass I could bounce a quarter off.

"Ash, I'm going to need you to tone down the sexiness a little bit. My vagina will not cope with the frequency that I'm wanting to jump you and ride you like you're a bloody pony."

"I'm not going to object to you riding me like a pony. *Ever*, Bree. I'll make sure I have plenty of icepacks in the freezer. I'll even help you ice it." He winks.

"What are your plans for today?"

"To make use of those icepacks?" His response is more of a question than a statement.

"Sorry, as fun as that sounds, I can't stay around here all day. I need to go home."

"You could always just move in here. That way, you'd already be home."

I choke on my mouthful of eggs. He didn't seriously just say that. Once I've composed myself, and I'm pretty sure I'm not going to die from shock—or, you know, death by breakfast eggs—I look up at Ash, who is smirking.

"You good?" he asks as he sits next to me at the counter, with his own plate of bacon.

"Uh-huh." I nod my head. I have no idea what to say to him. He's joking; he has to be. Why am I suddenly sweating bullets?

"You know, when I picture you choking, the vision is of you on your knees with my cock in your mouth. Not sitting at the breakfast counter, eating eggs."

"Play your cards right, Mr. Williamson, and your hot new secretary might just turn that fantasy of yours into a reality."

We spend the next twenty minutes eating and chatting in an easy comfort. I like being around Ash. I'll admit, when I was sixteen, my crush was purely based on how bloody fine the man was. As I got older, that torch I've always held for him turned into more than just a physical attraction.

Everything about this man captivates me. He's loyal.

He loves his family. He's fiercely protective of those he loves. He's kind, generous, and funny. He's always been able to make me laugh. He started to tell random jokes at our family dinners. It took me a while to catch on, but they weren't random at all. He'd tell them whenever I was uncomfortable or nervous about something. Mostly, it was being around him that made me freaking nervous in the first place.

"You got everything?" Ash asks as we walk to the elevator.

"Yes. You know, you don't have to drive me home. I can get a town car or something."

"I like driving you. I also like driving into you, but that's not an option right now, so I'll settle for driving you home."

"Damn it, Ash, now my panties are wet," I deadpan.

"Want me to lick you clean?"

"Yes—no! Let's go."

***

The trip home consists of Ash trying to put his hand up my dress, and me trying to fight off the need to climb over the seat and attack him. By the time we arrive, I'm horny as all hell.

"Walk me in," I say as I get out of the car.

"You should wait for me to open your door. I want to open doors for you, babe."

"I don't need you to open a car door for me. What I need from you right now is to help me sneak you into my bedroom. Then, I have a *need* only you can fulfill. "

"You want me to be your dirty little secret now?

Okay, lead the way." Ash adjusts his crotch in his pants, making no effort to hide his actions.

Opening the front door, I listen for any sign of my parents being around. How ridiculous is it that I'm twenty-two, and currently sneaking a boy into my bedroom? Maybe Ash is right... It might be time for me to move out... to find my own apartment in the city somewhere.

The coast is clear. I pull Ash by the arm, racing up the stairs before either of my parents or any of the staff see us. I've got my hand on the bedroom door, about to tug Ash into my room and have my dirty little way with him, when the voice behind us locks me in place.

"Breanna, nice of you to remember where you live. Ash, I'd like to think you are not attempting to sneak into my daughter's bedroom right now."

"Ah, nope, was just walking her to her door, Josh. I'm a gentleman like that."

"Well, in the future, you can be just as much of a gentleman and walk her to the front door instead. I'd hate to see you have a terrible accident, where you were thrown—I mean *tripped*—down the fucking staircase."

"Daddy, stop! Oh my God, Ash, I'll see you at the club tonight." I don't lean up and kiss him goodbye like I want to. But that doesn't stop Ash from smirking at me, before taking my face in his hands and kissing me gently on the lips. It's probably the most PG kiss he has ever given me. Yet, at the same time, the fact that he has done this in front of my dad makes it feel all the more forbidden and dangerous.

I pull back and smile at him, ignoring my dad's growl coming from behind me.

"I'll pick you up at eight," Ash says. "Josh, pleasure to see you again."

"I'll meet you at the club. I do know how to drive, you know," I call to Ash's retreating back.

"I'll pick you up at eight, Bree." He makes his way down the stairs.

I turn to face the lecture I have no doubt I'm about to hear from my dad.

"I want to see you in my office in twenty minutes," he grumbles, leaving me in the hallway.

Great, maybe I should have just stayed at Ash's all day.

***

"You can't dictate who I do or do *not* date!" I yell.

"Watch me, Bree. He's six years older than you. How long, exactly, has this thing between you two been going on?" Unlike my own, my dad's voice is calm and quiet.

"Two days. You know, I asked Ash not to tell anyone. I wanted to give us a chance to see where we were going, before everyone else interfered in our lives. You're the only person I told how I felt about him. So how is it that everyone seems to know?"

"I didn't tell anyone, Bree. You made your feelings pretty clear last night at the station, which is another reason why he's not good enough for you."

"He's not good enough for me, because he defended his cousin? Yeah, that's a real horrible trait to have in a boyfriend, Dad."

"Why the hell are you in here yelling?" My mum walks into my dad's office. Great, now it's the two of them against me.

"Because Dad here thinks he can tell me who I can *and can't* date. I'm twenty-fucking-two years old. I can and will see whomever, whenever, I want to."

"Breanna, calm down." My mum walks around to my dad, who hasn't moved from his desk. She picks up his hand. "Josh, what would you have said if your mum told you that you couldn't date me?"

"What? I would have told her where to go. Obviously."

"Right, so, what do you think *you* telling *Bree* she can't date Ash is going to do?"

"Make her see sense and cut ties with the little fucker?" My dad smirks.

"No, it's not. It's going to push her away. And it's Ash—we've known him since he was five years old. Come on, you know he's a good person."

"Not good enough," my dad grumbles.

"He's good enough for me, so you can either get onboard with the idea, or I'll go find my own apartment, so you won't have to see who I'm bringing home at night."

"You're not moving out! Breanna, you can't leave, please. I'm not ready to let you go yet." My dad's eyes plead with me; he looks like he's in pain. The thought of me moving out hurts him. My mum glances between the two of us, before silently begging me to ease my dad's suffering.

Walking around to the vacant side of him, I pick up his other hand. "I'm not moving out yet, but you do know I can't live with you guys forever."

"I know, but I just need more time to get used to the idea of you growing up."

"You've had twenty-two years, Dad."

"It's not enough time."

"Okay, well, now that that's settled… We're happy that Breanna's dating Ash, aren't we, honey?"

I send up a silent prayer, thankful that at least my mum is on my side. Even if my dad isn't there yet.

"I wouldn't go as far as saying *happy*. However, I guess… we can see how it goes. But, if he hurts you, if he so much as makes you shed one fucking tear, I'm ripping his fucking heart out."

"Don't worry, Daddy. If he hurts me, I'll rip his heart out myself." I smile.

"Nobody is ripping out hearts. Come on, Bree, I need a shopping partner. Do you have any idea how hard it is to pick out gifts for this family? Everyone already has everything."

"Sounds fun. I need to finish my own Christmas shopping, and Daddy's black card is suddenly burning a hole in my pocket."

"Breanna, we're not having another Bugatti Christmas," my dad warns. Geez, it was one time. I was pissed at my dad for something. I can't even remember what it was we were arguing over. What I do remember is walking into Bugatti when I was eighteen and swiping that McKinley credit card to buy myself a little gift.

"It was one time!"

"It was a two million dollar charge, Breanna. I should have made you return the fucking car. Emmy, keep an eye on that card."

My dad likes to pretend he was angry about my impromptu purchase, but he secretly loves the car. I was allowed to keep it, but I wasn't allowed to drive it for twelve months. That was my punishment for exploiting my card privileges.

My mum has never been a big spender. She'd happily shop the sales and grab a bargain. Sometimes I think she forgets just how wealthy she is. She wasn't raised with money though. Me? I was born a McKinley. There isn't a thing I've ever asked for that I haven't been able to get. Am I a bit of a spoilt brat? Yes, but I blame my dad for that. He made me this way. I do wonder how Ash will handle the whole McKinley-money situation. Don't get me wrong, Ash's family is wealthy. It's just not the McKinley kind of wealth.

It's always been an issue with guys I've dated before. I really hope it doesn't become one with Ash as well.

CHAPTER 13

Ash

Fucking hell, of all the girls I had to fall for, it had to be the one with a psychotic father. I'm not afraid of Josh. I just know how unstable the fucker is. You'd be stupid not to watch your back if he's got it in for you.

Leaving the McKinleys', I head to Lily's house. I need to check on her... to make sure she's okay after last night's events. Both Lily and Hope have more than enough skill to defend themselves—they are Bray's daughters after all. My Uncle Bray was a cage fighter back in his prime. He was undefeated, and he'll be sure to tell anyone who will listen just how good he was.

My dad and Uncle Bray used to run the best underground fight club, in the basement of The Merge. The same place I now hold my poker games. I make more money through the weekly games I hold there than I do through my legitimate businesses. Chase is an accountant by trade; he handles my finances. He's fucking great at laundering the dirty money to make it appear clean. There's no one else I'd trust with my assets.

I guess I do take after my dad in a lot of ways. He was able to build up The Merge into what it is through the dirty money he made with the fight club. He only went clean after Uncle Bray was shot and couldn't fight anymore. From what I've heard, my dad made a lot of changes when he met my mum.

After the closure of the fight club, Uncle Bray and Aunt Reilly opened a chain of MMA gyms. He's made sure all of us kids know how to fight. He taught me that being the oldest boy in the family meant that it was my job to protect the younger kids. I guess I've never grown out of that frame of mind. I still feel like it's my responsibility to make sure my younger siblings and cousins are safe.

The fact that Lily was hurt in my club worsens my guilt over not getting to her sooner. She should be fucking safe in a family place of business. Nothing has ever happened to any of them in my club before. God, I wish I could beat the shit out of that fucker who hurt her all over again. Even with the legal ramifications, I'd still fucking do it twice over.

Most people around Sydney know not to fuck with my family. I wouldn't say we're deep-seated in the underworld, but we're not exactly clean either. My fingers tighten on the wheel as I think about the incident last night. Then the image of Bree hitting a fucking mammoth of a guy over the head with a chair plays out like a movie, and I smile.

She is one of the most fearless people I know. A trait I both love and fucking hate about her. I'll end up grey, well before my time, with the amount of worry she's going to cause. Yet, I wouldn't change her for the world. I know she can seem a little unhinged now and then, but she's my kind of unhinged. She's spoilt for sure; there is nothing she's ever wanted that she hasn't been given.

Well, for a while, there was me. I was the one thing she wanted and couldn't have. I wonder, now that she's had a fix of me, will her desire fade and fizzle out? Is it just the thrill of the forbidden, the untouchable, for her? Getting her hands on that one thing she's lusted over for years. And could never possess?

Fuck, the thought of her getting over her feelings for me is not fucking good. I'm going to have to make sure she's kept entertained, satisfied, so she doesn't get bored. I'm not prepared to part with her now that I have her.

Pulling into Lily's apartment building, I jump out and hand the keys to the valet.

"Keep it close. I won't be long," I instruct the kid.

"No worries, Mr. Williamson." He can't help the excited smile he has, at being able to drive my Maserati Ghibli. It was a twenty-seventh birthday gift to myself.

Lily lives in the penthouse. Punching her code into the keypad, I watch the numbers go up until the door opens. When I step into Lily's foyer, my best friend is the last person I expect to see lounging on her sofa.

"What the fuck are you doing here?" My voice echoes in the otherwise quiet apartment.

Chase waves a hand at the blankets on the sofa. "Put your murderous glare away, Ash. I slept on the fucking couch."

Lily and Hope both enter the room—they've clearly just woken up. "Nope, hell no. Turn around and go put some clothes on." I walk over to them, grabbing one arm each, and turn them around before escorting them back the way they came.

Lily's wearing a shirt. Just a shirt. No shorts and no fucking bra. My cousin's nipples are not something I need to see peeking through her fucking clothes. Hope is dressed even worse, in a little pair of what I think is meant to be shorts and a tank top. Again, no fucking bra.

When they both share a look, I know I'm in trouble. And before I can react, I'm lying on my back in the fucking hallway, with two angry looking redheads staring down at me.

"Ash, you're forgetting something. This is my apartment, and I'll wear whatever I goddamn want. If you don't like it, you can leave." Lily stomps back towards her bedroom. I smile. I know she's still going to put something else on.

"What she said. I need coffee," Hope says before walking out to the living area. I guess one out of two isn't bad.

"You know, a simple good morning would suffice!" I yell after both of them as I get up off the floor. I now need to make sure my best friend isn't staring at my cousin's fucking tits, which is exactly what he's doing when I walk into the kitchen.

Slapping him across the back of the head as I pass, I tell him, "No." I don't need to explain what I'm saying *no* to; he already knows.

"Wouldn't dream of it. Well, actually, I've dreamt of it often, but you know reality is probably never as good as the dream anyway, right?"

"If my hand wasn't already busted up from last night, I'd be hitting some sense into that idiotic brain of yours," I say, taking the coffee cup out of Hope's hand and bringing it to my mouth.

"Well, I can assure you, Chase, the reality would be way better than the dream." Hope smiles, flipping her hair over her shoulder.

"Hope, don't you have somewhere to be? Anywhere Chase isn't is a great fucking idea," I prompt.

"Nope, I've got nowhere. Lily and I are going Christmas shopping today."

"So are Mum and Ava. Why is everyone going shopping today? There's still two weeks until Christmas."

"Ash, you better not be last-minute shopping for my gift. I've given everyone the list. I know you got my list."

Every year, Hope sends out a group chat over messenger with her Christmas wish list. I've never bought her anything off it. Instead, I prefer to buy her a shit gift I know she's gonna hate.

"I read your list. It was stupid," I say. "*And* I've already got the perfect gift picked out for you."

"If it's not on my list, chances are I don't want it. Although, there is something else you could give me that I didn't have on my list," Hope says, while eyeing Chase up and down.

"Not happening. Ever!" I growl.

It's not that I don't love my best friend; he's a great fucking guy. He's just also the biggest slut I know. He sleeps with anyone who has a vagina and a pair of tits. My cousin is not going to be another notch on his bedpost.

"Well, that's a damn shame. I sure would enjoy unwrapping him," Hope says as she walks out of the kitchen with a new cup of coffee in her hands.

"Get that look off your fucking face. You are not going there with my fucking cousin."

"You heard her. Who am I to deny her the one gift she wants to unwrap for Christmas?" He smirks.

"You'd be a bloody dead man, mate. That's who you'd be."

"Meh, could be worth it." Chase laughs, ducking his

head so the glass I just launched misses and hits the wall behind him.

"Ash, you're cleaning that up," Lily says as she comes up and hugs me.

"Are you okay?" I ask, wrapping my arms around her, while watching Chase with a death glare.

"Well, I'm heading out. Lil, thanks for letting me crash on the couch." Chase puts his coffee cup in the sink.

"It's not like I had a choice. You wouldn't leave." Lily smiles at him.

"I'll see you tonight. What time are you getting in?" Chase directs to me.

"Ah, around nine. I'm picking Bree up first."

"Well, if you survive that, I'll see you at nine." Chase walks out, laughing at his own stupid joke.

Lily spins back to me, and I know an inquisition is coming. I'm also not sticking around for it.

"Well, if you're all good, I'll catch you later, cuz. I've got shit to do." I walk around her, hoping to make a speedy escape.

"Not so fast. What's going on with you and Bree?"

"Yeah, I'd like to know too," Hope adds, walking back into the kitchen, now dressed.

"Nothing's happening that either of you two need to know about." I fold my arms over my chest.

Both of them are standing at the only exit; they're not going to let me out of this easily.

"I don't know, Lil. I smell bullshit. What about you?" Hope looks to her sister, raising her eyebrows.

"Yep. Bullshit," Lily agrees.

They turn their gazes to me. Two against one? It never bloody ends well for me.

"You're both nosey-asses, you know that?"

"We do," they answer at the same time. This twin shit they have going on is bloody *Children of the Corn* scary at times.

"You're not going to get anything out of me, so you might as well give up."

"Huh, so you don't mind that I'm asking Bree to come on a double date with me this weekend. I met this guy—*Brad*. Anyway, Brad has a friend. I think his name's Chris, and he's hot. Not boring, boy-next-door hot, but more like Heath Ledger hot. I think Breanna would like him." Hope smirks at my obvious distress.

"I think you should call Bree now and ask her, Hope. You know, make sure she doesn't have plans already." Lily pulls her phone out and hands it to her lookalike.

Shit, what the fuck do I do? As much as I want to rip that phone out of Hope's hands, I don't. That's exactly what they want me to do. So, what *do* I do? Put on the best fucking poker face I can muster.

"Go ahead. Call her."

I watch with tiny bits of sweat running down my back. What if she agrees to go on this date? Fuck that, she can agree all she wants, but she won't be turning up. I'll tie her to my fucking bed all weekend if I have to.

Hope puts the phone on speaker. It rings five times before a breathless Bree answers.

"Hope, what's up?" Just hearing that voice does something strange to my heart. I've always fancied Bree. No, not fancied, I've always been in love with her. Not that I've ever admitted that until recently. But now that I've had a taste of her, I'm becoming near obsessed.

"Hey, Bree, so you know how I met Brad? Well, Brad has this friend, Chris, Hot Chris. We're double dating on the weekend. I need you to come with me."

"Ah, I already have plans on the weekend." Bree's answer makes me smile. *Yeah, plans of waking up in my fucking bed.*

"I'm sure you can spare a few hours for your best friend. Come on, Bree, I need you."

"I really can't. I promised Benny I'd go and be a referee at his parents' beach house. I'll be out of town all weekend."

What the actual fuck? I pull my phone out and fire a text to Bree. *Like fuck*, am I going all fucking weekend without getting my fix of her.

Me: Don't make plans this weekend. We need to fly to Perth.

I wait for a response that isn't coming through, although I know she's there.

"Oh, are you going shopping today? Maybe we could meet up. I've got Daddy's card burning a hole in my pocket. Maybe if we drag all the mums along, I can ditch mine and go buy something huge."

Hope and Lily both laugh. "What'd your dad do this time?" Lily asks.

"He tried to tell me I'm too young to date, then tried to tell me the guy I like isn't good enough for me."

"Oh, who's the guy? Do I know him?" Hope looks directly at me.

"I'm sure you do. He runs in our circle. But I gotta go. Meet me at the mall in about three hours."

"Deal, but if you're going Bugatti-level crazy with that card, count me out."

"Nope, I was thinking more like apartment shopping. I've got a realtor on standby."

She's looking for an apartment. *That's interesting.* Before I can stop myself, I send her another text.

Me: My offer to move in with me still stands.

"Okay, we'll meet you at the mall," Hope and Lily both say at the same time, before hanging up the phone and staring at me. *Looks like they still want answers they're not going to get.*

"I'm out. I've got work to do." I walk directly to the foyer. I need to get out of here. As soon as I get into my car, my phone starts going off with messages.

Bree: I'm not moving in with you. See you tonight. We'll discuss the weekend.

Lily: I know there's something going on. I will find out!!!

Hope: You know how you always say I can't have your best friend? The same rules apply, Ash. Bree is my best friend. Don't fuck with her.

Shit, they *are* fucking best friends. I never even

considered that, not that I fucking care. Bree is mine, and I don't give a shit what anyone thinks about it.

Bree: Your cousin wants to take me on a blind double date with some guy she calls Hot Chris. I panicked and said I was going away with Benny this weekend. If anyone asks, that's where I'll be.

I reply to Bree's message, ignoring my cousins.

Me: Good girl. xx

CHAPTER 14

Bree

ood girl? Is he fucking serious right now? That's it? He's just going to send a text message saying "Good girl"? I'm embarrassed how much those two little words affect me. The instant they popped up on my screen, my thighs clenched. There goes another perfectly clean pair of panties, thanks to Ash bloody Williamson.

Argh, what's the lady version of blue balls? Whatever it is, that's exactly the predicament that message has left me in. Well, fuck that. And fuck him. Two can play that game.

I step into my bathroom and strip my shirt off. Painting my lips with the brightest red lipstick I can find, I ruffle my hair up, sorting it so it hangs loosely over one shoulder. Then I situate my breasts higher in my black, lace, see-through bra. I don't need to do anything to my nipples. Thanks to those two words, they're already hard.

I sink my teeth into my bottom lip, and a subtle smile spreads across my face as I snap a selfie, angling my phone so the camera is looking down on my breasts. Perusing the image, I'm satisfied that I look hot as fuck. I mean, *I'd do me*. I was blessed with my mother's beautiful features, not that my dad isn't a good-looking fella in his own right.

I had to scare a few high school girls away who wanted to hang around me just to get a peek at what they used to call their ultimate DILF. *Gag*. After the third time I heard a girl say that to me, I lost it and smashed her face against the lockers. It's disrespectful to my mum. He's a married man, and not to mention, old. I mean, I get the whole daddy kink, just not with *my* dad.

Opening my messages, I send the image to Ash, along with a teasing text. If I have to have lady blue balls, then so does he.

Me: I'd much rather be your naughty girl. Tell me, Ash, what would you do to me right now if you

knew how naughty I've been? FYI: my fingers are
nowhere near as good as yours.

It takes exactly twenty seconds before my phone vibrates in my hand with his incoming call. I know, because I was silently counting in my head.

"Hey there, handsome. Miss me already?" I answer.

"I need you to meet me at the club. My office. Twenty minutes, Bree."

"Sorry, babe, no can do. I'm just walking out the door with my mum."

"Breanna, you cannot send me pictures like that and not be within arm's reach. I almost hit the car in the lane next to me when your tits popped up on my screen. I'm also fifteen minutes away from the club, which means I'm at least twenty minutes away from being able to do something about the raging fucking boner you just gave me."

"Sorry, not sorry. So, when you jerk off in your office, what will you be thinking about?" I ask.

"I'll be imagining you, bent over my desk. Your perfect ass on display, nice and pink from the spanking it just received. I'll be picturing myself on my knees behind you, licking up the juices you'll be spilling just for me. I'll be imagining my cock burying itself inside you, while my finger pumps in and out of your asshole. I'll hear your screams, your moans. Your scent will fill my nose." I hear him take a deep breath.

I clear my throat. Fuck, that *is* more appealing than a day of shopping. "Well, that sounds like a grand fantasy. Maybe we can play that one out tonight?" I ask, hopeful.

"Fuck, Bree, I don't remember a time I've been this fucking hard. Cancel your plans. I need to be inside you."

"I can't cancel my plans. Besides, it's only a few hours."

"It's eight hours away, babe. I'm picking you up at eight. It's only twelve o'clock now. What the hell am I supposed to do for eight fucking hours? It's bloody torture. I'd rather be locked in your father's shed than endure this right now."

I laugh. He's being overly dramatic. No one would want to be locked in my father's shed. Usually, the people he takes in there don't make it back out. The McKinley world is dark. I learnt that at an early age. When I was six, I walked in on my father while he was disposing of someone.

He was beside himself that I'd seen what he was doing. I didn't care though. I walked straight up to the pigs and petted them, while they were feasting on human remains. I think that's when my dad noticed just how like him I really was. We had a big family meeting. My mother was upset and hugged me tight the whole night. They made me sleep in their bed, between them, in case I had nightmares.

The thing is, I've never had a nightmare in my life. Once I'm asleep, that's it. I'm out. I do have the occasional dream, though they're usually of the X-rated variety and almost always involve Ash. Sometimes Chris Hemsworth or Joseph Morgan, but mostly Ash.

"Babe, you have no idea how many times I've woken up a needy, wet mess because of the dreams you invaded. Trust me, you can last eight hours. I gotta go." There's an awkwardness at the end of my sentence, like I want to say something by way of parting, but I can't bring myself to do it. Instead, I just hang up.

Throwing my shirt back on, I make my way downstairs. My mum's waiting with a coffee in a to-go cup for me.

"Thanks." I take the cup and swipe the keys to the Bugatti off the wall, before putting them back and replacing them with the Mercedes keys that were next to them.

"You can drive. Plus, we'll need as much room as we can get. I haven't bought a single gift for anyone yet."

It's not until we're out of the driveway, and past the gates, that my mum says, "So, Ash? Tell me all about it."

"There's nothing to tell, Mum," I try.

"Baby, you don't go up against your father, fighting for a guy there's no story to. What's happening?"

"I, ah, I'm working for him. Helping him out at the club. His secretary quit, and he needs help with the new location he's opening in Perth."

"I heard from Alyssa he fired the girl."

"Did he? I thought she quit." I shrug. I'm not lying—I did think she quit... until he inadvertently let the truth slip.

"Since when do you want to work in a nightclub?

You could be using the summer to help your dad at the office."

"I could, but my boss certainly wouldn't be eye candy."

"I want you to be careful, Bree. I don't want you rushing into anything. You're young, and you have the world at your fingertips. You can have and do anything you want. You can be anything you want to be. Don't waste your youth."

"I'm doing exactly what I want to be doing, Mum. Trust me. It's Ash. You guys have known him my whole life—you said so yourself. Why are you both so opposed to this?" I ask, curious.

"I'm not opposed, just worried. You've held a torch for Ash for a long time. I don't want him taking advantage of you."

I scoff at the thought. "You don't have to worry about that, Mum. I'd never let a pretty face and a nice set of abs blind me."

"Love makes us blind to a lot, Bree. Just take your time, go slow, and try not to give your father a heart attack in the process. He loses sleep on the nights you don't come home."

"I know. I'm sorry." I *am* sorry. I don't want my parents to worry. But I'm also twenty-two. I'm not asking for permission to have sleepovers at my boyfriend's.

"You don't need to be sorry. Don't worry about Dad. I'll help him process the fact that his little girl is probably going to leave the nest sooner than he wants."

"Thanks, Mum."

I really did need this girl time with her. I text Hope and Lily and tell them there's been a change of plans. I'm going to spend the day with my mum.

***

I'm bloody exhausted when we pull into the garage at seven thirty that night. I have half an hour to shower and get ready to go to the club. I somehow manage to sprint through the grooming process. I throw on a teal dress; it's silky and trimmed with black lace around the edges. I put a black jacket over it and slip into a pair of black Louboutins. I am a sucker for a red-soled shoe.

The doorbell rings just as I'm walking down the stairs. "I've got it," I call out. The house is quiet. I have no idea where my parents are. Just before I get to the bottom of the stairs, Lukas—our family's butler—steps out of nowhere. He nods his head and opens the door wider for Ash to step in. I'm not chancing another run-in with my dad. Taking Ash's hand, I pull him out the door.

"Thanks, Lukas," I call behind me, not wanting to be rude.

"Someone's keen," Ash says, following behind me.

"Someone wants to keep you breathing. The less time you spend around this house, the better the odds are you remain that way."

I reach out, placing my palm on the door handle, only to have it swiped away. Ash opens my door. "My lady." He tips an invisible hat at me.

I watch (okay, drool) as he walks around the front

of the car. When he gets in, I decide to mess with his head a little.

"You know, a lady wouldn't be so quick to jump between the sheets with you. Maybe I like the idea of being a lady. I should close up shop. Wait for marriage maybe," I suggest. If he wants to go all old school on me, and insist on opening car doors every damn time, I should probably act more like a lady.

"That's not even remotely funny, Bree. And if you insist on waiting for marriage, well, I suggest you get that fancy McKinley jet fired up, because we'll be heading to Vegas tonight."

"That's not happening. Ever. My parents would actually kill you if we ran off and got married without them."

"It'd be worth the risk." He laughs as he puts his hand on my upper thigh. I move it towards my knee.

"You know, a lady wouldn't be so quick to let you have your hand up her panties."

"Seriously? Fine. You win. You can open your own doors," Ash grumbles.

I reward him by moving his hand all the way up my thigh. He doesn't waste time; he somehow manages to get underneath the lace covering my mound. His fingers run up and down my slit before entering me slowly, agonizingly slowly. My hips move towards his hand, my body having one goal: chasing that high and jumping over the cliff. No, not jumping, soaring. Because that's what orgasms are like when Ash is giving them to me.

By the time we get to the club, he's made me come twice. My legs feel like Jell-o. At this rate, he may just have to carry me upstairs. The fatigue of barely sleeping the last few nights is finally catching up with me. I'm wrecked. I don't know how I'm going to work all night and be of any use to Ash.

Ash pulls in at the back of the club. He makes a show of licking his fingers before he gets out. I tug on the handle of the car, but it doesn't budge. The asshole smirks at me from outside before opening my door.

"What the hell, Ash?"

"I must have accidentally put the child-lock on. Sorry, babe."

"You're not sorry at all, asshole." I step around him and head into the club. I don't look back as I make my way through the kitchen, beeline for the elevators, and stab at the button.

Ash is two steps behind me the whole time. I can tell he's trying his hardest not to laugh right now and that just pisses me off more. When the elevator doors open, I step in and turn around. Ash crowds my space until my back is pressed against the wall.

CHAPTER 15

Ash

As soon as the doors close behind me, my hand wraps around the back of Bree's neck and my lips descend onto her mouth. I push my body into hers as hard as I can, without hurting her, and her back arches off the wall, pressing her soft tits into the firmness of my chest. My hands fall to the curves of her hips, finding their way to her ass.

She doesn't miss a beat as she jumps up and wraps her legs around my waist. An animalistic growl leaves my mouth as I devour her with my tongue. I've jerked off to the picture she sent me three times today, and I'm still not fucking satisfied. Not even close.

I grind my cock into her pussy. Judging by the way her body tightens, and how her moans echo off the walls, I've hit just the right spot. I repeat the motion again. And again. The moment the ping of the doors rings out, I drop her legs and pull her in the direction of my office.

"Get out," I yell at Chase, who is currently sitting on my couch with his feet up on the coffee table. He takes one look between Breanna and me, and smiles.

"Well, hello to you two kids too. I'll be downstairs, you know, *working*." The door slams behind him. I twist the lock before I turn and pick Breanna up, walking straight to my desk. I undo her jacket, throwing it across the room. Then, spinning her around, I push on the top of her back until she's lying face down, her perfect fucking ass right in front of me.

Bree lifts her head and looks at me over her shoulder, waiting, anticipating what I'm about to do to her. She bites into her bottom lip, just like she did in that fucking photo she sent me earlier.

Lifting the hem of her dress, I ball the fabric up above her hips. She's wearing a lace thong. Fucking perfect. I fill both hands with the globes of her round ass. Massaging. Squeezing.

"I've been thinking of nothing but this ass all fucking day, Breanna." I lean over and bite her ear. "You were a bad girl today. Are you ready to be punished like the naughty little girl you are?" I ask her.

She nods her head as a breathless "yes" leaves her lips. My right hand comes down hard on her ass, the sting sending shivers through me. I let my finger trail over the length of her slit; she's already drenched. I circle her hardened clit a few times, before removing my hand and bringing it down on her other side. The sound of skin hitting skin is music to my ears.

I don't give her time to adjust to the pain before I repeat the action. Again, and then again.

"You have no idea how fucking beautiful you look right now. Sprawled out over my desk, your ass reddened with my palm marks." I rub her globes, before dipping my finger down between the lips of her pussy. She pushes back against my hand.

"I think you might be enjoying this punishment more than I am. Do you like having your ass spanked like a naughty little girl, Breanna?"

"I think I like anything you do to me," she says, squirming as my fingers pump in and out of her.

I trail her wetness up to her back hole. "You're going to fucking love every dirty, forbidden thing I do to you. I guarantee it." I insert one finger in her ass. "And when I finally fill this hole with my cock, you're going to be begging me for more."

"I—*Oh, God.*" Her moans get louder as I kneel behind her, replacing that finger with my tongue.

"There is no part of you I won't lick. Bite. Devour. Fuck." Her screams get louder. I fucking love how she pants as my name leaves her lips. I circle my thumb around her clit as I continue eating out her ass. Within seconds, her body seizes up as she flies over the edge, her orgasm wrecking through her.

Standing behind her, I make quick work of freeing my cock from the confines of my pants. Then I slam into her, her pussy still convulsing with aftershocks. "Fucking hell, I'm never going to get enough of this. Your cunt was made for me to fuck, Bree. Hold onto the edge of the desk. Things are about to get rough." It's the only warning I give her as I take her from behind, pumping in and out as hard and fast as I fucking can.

***

Breanna is asleep on the couch. She crashed a few hours ago. I guess I'm not the only one running on minimal sleep the last few days. I've been trying my best to concentrate on my computer, instead of staring at her. But she's not making it easy. She looks so peaceful, so fucking beautiful, it hurts.

Chase strolls in, looking from the sleeping beauty to me. "What'd you do to her?" he asks.

I raise an eyebrow. *Like I'm going to fucking tell him a thing.*

"Okay, fine, don't share the details. I don't need you to. My imagination is plenty good at coming up with them anyway."

"Chase, best-mate status does not make you immune to my rage. Don't fucking push your luck," I whisper harshly at him. I don't need him waking up my girl.

"I've got you both booked on the two p.m. flight

direct to Perth on Friday, returning on the Monday redeye."

"Thanks, I appreciate that." It's not his usual task—that would be the job of my secretary. But I fucking fired her ass, so I'd have a reason for Bree to work with me. Turns out, she's definitely more of a distraction than I anticipated.

"I thought you were done in Perth for a while? Why you goin' back so soon?"

"Something came up," I say, not wanting to admit it was yet another spur-of-the-moment decision, revolving around Bree.

"Something, or *someone?*" he asks, looking back to the couch.

"Fine, someone. Hope asked her to double date with her on the weekend. Bree said she had plans to go away with Ben. I panicked and told her we had to go to Perth."

"Wait, back up. Hope has a date? Where?"

"I don't fucking know."

"Who's it with?"

"Again, I don't fucking know." She mentioned a name, but fuck if I remember.

"Fine, I'll find out for myself. Also, the new furniture's arriving next week. Contractors should be done with downstairs by Monday. I've opened the first game up on the 23rd."

"Good, let's keep that on the DL. The last thing I need is Bree finding a way to sneak herself into that game."

"Done. Anyway, I got shit to do, an asshole with a death wish to find, and money to make. Catch you tomorrow. I'm out for the night."

"Who's the asshole? Should I expect a call in the middle of the night to bail your ass out of a cell?"

"Nah, I'm too loveable for anyone to keep me locked up."

"Right," I deadpan. The sad thing is, he actually believes the shit that spills out of his mouth.

I work for another two hours before I shut everything down. Picking up my keys and wallet, I then grab Bree's bag and jacket, before bending down and scooping her still-sleeping form into my arms. She stirs, settling her head against my chest. I somehow manage to get her all the way to the car and seated before she opens her eyes.

She looks up at me. "I really fucking like you, Ash Williamson. Don't break my heart," she whispers, before closing her eyes and leaning against the headrest. I kiss her forehead as I buckle her seat belt in place.

"I wouldn't fucking dream of it, babe." I know she doesn't hear me. To break her heart would be to break my own. I can't stand the thought of hurting her like that.

***

The chorus of Saweetie's "Best Friend" song plays loudly through my bedroom. It stops, before starting again. "What in the ever-loving fuck is that?" I grumble as Breanna swipes her arm out, picking up her phone.

"Benny, why the bloody hell are you waking me up?" she answers.

Fucking Ben… of course, it is. I roll over, throwing my arm around her waist and pulling her body into mine.

"Well, obviously I'm not dead. If I were, you'd see that announcement all over the news, idiot."

I can hear the mumbling of the voice on the other end, but I can't make out what the fucker is saying. I'm only getting one side of their conversation.

My hand starts trailing downwards, like it has a mind of its own and is seeking out my own version of heaven.

"I'm out of town this weekend. I can't. But let's do lunch today." I look at the clock on the bedside. It's already one in the afternoon. Ben must be telling her as much, because she says, "It is? Huh, okay. Let's make it drinks. Usual spot. Meet me there at five. I gotta go, Benny. Love you."

My body tenses as she utters those words. An insane amount of jealousy overwhelms me at how easily they left her mouth for a guy who isn't me. Bree hangs up the phone and throws it down on the floor next to the bed. She rolls over to face me.

"What's wrong?" she asks.

"Nothing." I attempt to get up. I'm not about to tell her I'm jealous of her fucking best friend. However, I don't make the quick escape I was planning. Bree jumps up and lands on top of me, pushing me onto my back. My hands instantly go to her waist.

"What's wrong?" she asks again.

"Nothing," I repeat. "Well, my cock *is* fucking hard as concrete right now, begging to get a taste of heaven again."

Her laugh brings a genuine smile to my face. "I like it when you smile, Ash. You should try doing it more often." Her lips softly brush over mine.

"I love…" She pauses before continuing. "…how your cock fills me up. I love…" Again, she pauses, and I hold my breath, silently urging her to utter the one word I'm longing to hear complete that statement: *you.* "I love the way your tongue makes my body light up." She sits and looks directly into my eyes. "I love the way your arms hold me all night. I love how you make sure my every need, every desire, is met. I love the way you make me feel things I've never felt for anyone else. I love how you accept me for me, and how I don't feel like I need to pretend when I'm around you. I love you, Ash Williamson. And if you don't love me back, I might just stab your pretty fucking face right now."

Well, that sweet spiel took a dark turn. *Fast.* "Babe —*Breanna.* I fucking love you so much it bloody hurts. I've always fancied you, always desired your body. I've always loved you from afar, but the last few days I've realised something." My confession is much easier than I thought it would be.

"What's that?"

"I don't just love you. You aren't someone I just want. You are what I need. You're the other half of me.

You and me, we're fate, babe." I smile into her kiss as her hands cup my jaw, holding me in place.

"So, is my pretty face safe from your pocketknife?" I laugh.

"I wouldn't want to ruin that face before I've had the opportunity to sit on it and ride it like Hunter."

"Who the fuck is Hunter?" I growl.

"Hunter... *Oh, Hunter*. He's big, strong, beautiful." She smirks at the obvious anger boiling inside me. "He's also the horse I got for my thirteenth birthday." She laughs.

Within seconds, I pick her up, sliding my body under hers. She certainly does not need to fucking ask me twice to ride my face. That shit is. My. Fucking. Pleasure.

"Saddle up, babe. It's going to be a rough ride," I say as I bring her bare pussy down onto my mouth.

CHAPTER 16

Bree

The cocktails are going straight to my head, or is it the tequila shots? Who knows? Who cares? I'm having a blast. I always have fun when I'm hanging out with Ben. We really are two peas in a pod. We've been inseparable since primary school, when I decided I needed a friend and he was going to be it.

Lucky for me, Ben didn't suck and was half-cool. We've always had each other's back, playing the role of wingmen often. I know the look he gets when he's interested in someone. Right now, that look is directed at the brunette seated across the bar.

"So, are you going to sit here all night, staring at her? Or are you going to grow a pair and go talk to her? You never know… She could be the one." I throw back another shot, the liquid burning down my throat.

"She'd be the one… *for tonight* at least." He shrugs.

"Okay, well, if you're not going to hit that, let's get out of here. I feel like dancing."

"Where do you have in mind?" he asks.

My smile gives me away. I want to go to The Merge, obviously, but maybe that's not the best idea. If I end up there, I'm also going to end up in Ash's office doing a different form of dancing.

"Let's go anywhere that's not The Merge. Come on."

Ben and I make our way out of the bar, climbing into his waiting town car. "You know, I reckon he'd find you no matter what club you go to."

"Well, let the hunt begin." I smirk as I take a selfie and send it to Ash. His response is instant.

Ash: I can see you're having fun. Let me know when I can pick you up.

Me: I'm probably going to crash at home tonight. I'll see you tomorrow.

Ash: Let me know when you want me to pick you up. It's not up for negotiation, Breanna.

I choose to ignore his bossy ass and focus on my friend instead. "What?" I ask Ben, who is staring at me, confused.

"I know you've had the hots for this guy for as long

as I can remember. But you actually love him. Like love-love. Don't you?"

"Maybe."

"So, tell me, does he live up to all those fantasies? Does he make your kitty pulse?"

"Ew, do not ever talk about my kitty, Benny. Not ever. And, yes, he's so much better than I could have imagined. Best I've ever had."

"Really? That's an achievement, considering I know just how many you've had."

"Shut up. I was trying to fuck him out of my mind. Turns out, all I needed was him to fuck me until my mind's blank—which, FYI, he very much has. Multiple times." I smile.

"Good, I'm glad he finally manned-up and claimed your ass. I was starting to think it was never going to happen."

"You and me both, Benny."

The car pulls up to the club before we skip in front of the waiting patrons, receiving the usual glares aimed in our direction as we head for the door. I'm a McKinley. I don't line up.

"Hey, Tommy. Long time, no see." I hug the bouncer who has held my hair up for me on the sidewalk once or twice.

"Miss McKinley, great to see you back. Give me five, and I'll get you hooked up with table service." Tommy speaks into his wrist before opening the rope for us to enter.

"Thanks, Tommy. Appreciate it."

"Have fun, but not so much that your father turns up again," he says.

"It was one time, Tommy. One bloody time."

"It was a bloodbath, Bree."

I smile. *Yeah, it was.* I don't confirm or deny his statement. Instead, I take Benny's hand as I head straight to the dance floor.

We've been dancing—*drinking and dancing*—for the last three hours. My feet are fucking aching, but I'm so energized right now I don't want to stop.

Benny's eyes go wide as he watches something behind me. Great, I bet someone called my dad again. Benny's shit-scared of Dad. When a pair of hands lands on my waist and pulls my body flush against a hard chest, and a hard cock, I realize whoever is behind me is most definitely not my dad.

I know these hands, I know the scent that's engulfing me, and I know the fiery tingles that this man's touch ignites throughout my body. I push my ass against his crotch. My arms lift up and backwards, and wrap around his neck behind me. His face buries into my head.

"Mmm, I didn't know you danced so well, Mr. Williamson," I murmur.

"I don't, but when I saw you shaking this hot little ass around this dance floor, all eyes on you, I had to come over and make a public claim. Everyone in this club will now know that this ass belongs to me."

"Really?" I ask, spinning around. Everything that isn't Ash blends into the background, my body pressed up against his and one of his thick, muscled thighs firmly placed between my legs.

"Mmmhmm, did you have fun?" he asks into my ear while nibbling.

"I did, but the night's young. I'm sure you could find a way to add some spice to it."

"Spice, huh? That can be arranged."

"So, tell me, what is the owner of The Merge doing in a second-class club like this one?"

Ash laughs. "Remind me to tell Wes that you called his club second-class." My eyes go wide. He knows Wes? Fuck, how did I not know that?

"Ah, maybe we should get out of here and go to The Merge." I look around for Benny, and find him locking tongues with a redhead a few feet away. I pull him off her. Leaning into his ear, I yell that we need to go. He doesn't question, just follows my lead.

I take Ash's hand and head for the door. We're almost at the exit when Wes steps in front of us.

"Leaving so soon, Bree?" He leers at me. Argh, I can't believe I ever fucking slept with this douche. And why the hell did I choose his club to come to tonight, of all places?

"Sorry, I gotta go." I motion to step around him, but his hand reaches out and grabs my elbow.

"I think you should stay. We could revisit the meeting we had last time you were here."

"Get your filthy fucking hands off her now." Ash pulls me back behind him.

"What the fuck is your problem, Williamson?" Wes yells.

"Right now, you are. Move, Breanna. We're leaving." Ash takes my hand and walks straight past Wes, who does nothing but stare after us. Well, I guess that could have been worse.

When we're out on the curb, Ash's angry face turns to me. "Really, Bree, him? Do you have no fucking standards?" he yells.

"Well, I fucked you, so apparently my standards are pretty fucking low," I yell back. Ben's car pulls up. "Come on, Ben, you're giving me a lift home." I open the back door.

"Do not get in that car, Breanna. I'll take you home."

"No, you can go to hell, Ash." I get in the car and slam the door shut. The windows are blacked-out, so I know he can't see me through them. I watch as he exchanges heated words with Ben, before shaking his head and storming off.

***

I've been tossing and turning in bed for around two hours. I can't fucking sleep. I've slept in his bed for three nights, and he's already fucking ruined me. I get up and go to the kitchen in search of something: food, water, anything to help distract myself.

"Can't sleep?" My dad's voice scares the shit out of me. Where the hell did he come from?

"No," I say as I dig through the fridge, retrieving a block of hazelnut chocolate.

"What's wrong?"

"You really don't want to know, Dad."

"I wouldn't have asked if I didn't want to know. What's wrong, Breanna?"

"Ash fucking Williamson is what's wrong. I can't bloody sleep, because *somehow* my body got used to being in his bed. Three nights, and it's like I've never slept in my own bed alone before. What the hell is wrong with me?"

"As much as it pains me to say this, and believe me, it fucking does, you're in love with the asshat."

"Well, love can kiss my ass. I don't want it." I slump down on one of the counter stools.

"Yes, you do. Individuals like you and me don't get to feel these emotions for many people. When we do, you need to treasure it." My dad's words hit home. *Hard.* He's right. I've never had these feelings for anyone.

I pick up the keys to my Bugatti. Wrapping my arms around my dad before I leave, I say, "Thank you."

"Anytime. Of course, if he hurts that heart of yours, I'm feeding him to the pigs," he reminds me.

"Sure, Dad." I laugh, although I know he meant every word of that threat.

***

The whole apartment is quiet as I let myself in. Dropping my bag in the foyer, I slip out of my shoes and walk towards the bedroom. My heart pounds in my chest the closer I get. What if he's not alone here? Shit, what do I do? I should have called. I shouldn't have just assumed I could invite myself over to his place.

Opening the bedroom door, I'm greeted by a sight I wasn't expecting to see. Ash is sitting on a single sofa chair, a bottle of whiskey in one hand, his phone in the other. He lifts his head, and his glassy eyes meet mine.

"Breanna?" His voice is husky, quiet, almost like he doesn't want to say my name too loudly, in fear I'll disappear.

"Yeah, it's me." I make my way to him and drop to my knees. I take the bottle of whiskey from his hand; it's three quarters empty. "Did you drink this all on your own, Ash?"

"You left me," he says, as if that one statement holds all the answers.

"I didn't leave you. I went home to sleep. I could never leave you." I put the bottle down and rest my head on his thigh. I'm so tired.

"I was an arse. You were right to leave. I'm sorry."

"We were both asses."

I crawl up and place myself in his lap, curling my body around his.

"Mmm, you smell good. Like raspberries. You always smell like fucking raspberries," he says. "You always feel so soft. So good. So mine," he continues as his hands travel up my waist. "Don't leave me again, Bree. My heart can't cope."

"I won't," I promise him, hoping to God it's one I never have to break. "Come on, Romeo, let's go to bed. I'm tired, and you need to sleep off this alcohol."

"I couldn't get in the bed without you," he slurs as I pull him to his feet. He stumbles his way to the bed. I consider attempting the task of undressing his drunk ass, but I don't have the energy. Once he's lying down, I climb in and snuggle into his side, my head resting on his chest. This is where I needed to be. Before I know it, I fall into a deep sleep.

CHAPTER 17

Ash

I feel like my head is about to fucking explode. I go to lift my arm, only to find it weighed down by a mass of blonde locks. I smile. I don't remember Breanna coming here last night, but I'm sure fucking glad she did.

I slip out, careful not to jostle her too much. I go into the guest bathroom. I need a hot shower. I smell like a brewery. How Breanna managed to sleep next to me all night, I have no idea.

After a long, hot shower, I wrap a towel around my

waist and head straight for the kitchen. The sooner I get caffeine into me, the better. It's not until I get there that I think maybe I should have put some clothes on first. I'm so used to living here alone, I don't expect to see people sitting at my counter in the mornings.

"Ah, good morning." I head straight for Breanna, running a hand through her hair and kissing her forehead. It's not really how I'd like to be kissing her right now… But, considering Emily is sitting next to my girl watching my every move, I decide to keep it as PG as I can. Bree's dad might be a scary fucker, but I can assure you *her mother is worse.*

"Morning, Emily. How are you?" I ask, walking to the coffee machine and starting it.

"Good. Thanks. You?"

"I've been better," I say.

"Well, I made breakfast. I figured you'd be feeling a little sorry for yourself this morning," Bree says.

I look around the kitchen. It's spotless; there is no sign that she's been cooking. The intercom rings, and I watch Bree jump up to answer. I smile. She really is making herself at home.

"I'll be right back," she says. "Mum, be nice." With that, she whizzes out of the room with an energy I'm a little jealous of.

"So, Ash, tell me. What *exactly* are your intentions with my daughter?" Emily cuts right to the chase.

"I promise I only have the best intentions for Breanna." I don't back down from her intense stare.

"And I promise, if you break her heart, I'll put a

bullet through yours." She smiles sweetly at me. Fuck, these McKinley women are something else. I suddenly have a lot more respect for Josh. I don't know how he's survived the both of them for so long.

"Oh, and if you have any plans of running off and marrying her, don't. She might not admit it, but she's been planning her dream wedding since she was sixteen."

"Sixteen, huh? Interesting." I smile. That's around the same age Breanna started crushing on me.

"Don't be smug, Ash. It really doesn't suit you."

"I'm just going to, ah, get dressed. I wasn't expecting company. Sorry." I put my cup down and retreat to my bedroom.

I pick up a pair of grey sweats and a white shirt. When I walk back into the kitchen, Breanna has a smorgasbord of food set out on the counter, and Emily is nowhere to be seen.

"Did your mum leave?"

"Yeah, she only stopped by to drop off my suitcase. I left it at home yesterday."

"Are you expecting other guests?" I ask, waving a hand at all the food.

"Nope, I told you I cooked for you." Her smile lights up her face.

I tilt my head at her. I can't tell if she's serious or not. "Babe, you ordered in. That's not cooking. But I appreciate it just as much. This looks delicious."

"Ordered in... cooked... same thing, really. Here, load up." A plate gets shoved into my stomach.

"Sure, thanks, babe." I load a plate of waffles, bacon, and scrambled eggs.

I sit next to her and we eat in a comfortable silence.

"Out of curiosity, have you ever cooked a meal before?" I ask her.

Her nose screws up at me. "Why the bloody hell would I do that when I can order in? Besides, we have chefs at home. The stuff they make is way better than anything I can cook."

"Right, you have chefs." I laugh. Sometimes, being around her, I forget the lifestyle she grew up in.

"So, when I cooked you breakfast and you acted like it was good...? Fucking hell, you can't be that good at faking it. What else have you been faking?"

"No, I never fake it. And I loved your cooking. You know, if I woke up to that every day, I might just reconsider the whole moving in with you thing."

"Hold that thought." I open the drawer and pull out a set of keys. The apartment doesn't have a door key; it's a code you put into the elevator to get up here. The gesture is more symbolic. "Okay, you have yourself a deal. Here's your key. I'll cook breakfast for you every day for the rest of our lives. When should I arrange the U-Haul to rock up to your parents' house?"

"Ah, I said *consider*. And do not send a removal truck to my parents' house. My dad is only just coming to terms with the fact that we're dating—which, by the way, no one is even meant to know yet."

"I didn't tell a soul. That's all on you, babe."

"I know. I can't believe I lost my shit in front of your dad at the station. He must think I'm a loony."

"He doesn't. Also, I don't care what anyone thinks of you. I happen to love your lunatic ass, and that's all that matters." I lean over and hold her chin with one hand, tilting her head up so I can access those lips.

After losing myself in her kiss, I pull back. "I'd love to stay here all day and kiss these lips until they're red and swollen, but we have a plane to catch."

"Okay, let's do this. I'm excited. I haven't been to Perth in a while."

"I'm excited to get you to myself for a whole weekend… no family members randomly interrupting us."

"Sounds blissful," she murmurs as she pecks me on the cheek. I watch as she stands and walks out of the kitchen, leaving the mess of our ordered-in breakfast behind.

"It's okay, babe. I'll clean up," I yell after her.

"Thank you."

***

We've just walked into the airport and Breanna is looking around like a tourist. "Is it always this busy?" she asks.

"Pretty much, yeah. Come on, we have to line up here." I point to the first-class sign. There are only five people in front of us.

"We have to line up? What the hell for?" Bree asks.

"Have you never flown commercial, Breanna?"

"No, we have our own jets. I should have organized one to fly us. Next time, let me do the flight booking."

"Wow. Well, babe, welcome to how the other half lives." I laugh. We're flying first-class; it's hardly roughing it. But to her standards, it probably will be.

Once we're checked in, I take her through to the first-class lounge and get her a wine and some snacks. She's still looking around in awe.

"This isn't so bad. I don't know why people complain about flying."

"This is first class. If you want the economy experience, I'll have our returning flights downgraded for you."

"No, I'm good. I saw that line. I can't believe people have to stand there for that long."

"You really are a tad spoilt, Breanna."

"It's not my fault." She folds her arms over her chest.

"It's cute." I shrug.

"Come on, Ash, it's not like you're poor. We aren't living worlds apart here." She does have a point. We're just not fancy-private-jet rich, although I have been on that McKinley jet plenty of times when we've holidayed with Aunt Ella and Uncle Dean.

"So, are you a member of the mile-high club? If your answer is anything other than *no*, lie to me."

She laughs. "No, I'm not." She smiles.

Fuck, now I can't tell if she's lying or not. "Maybe we could rectify that?"

"Sure. But if we get arrested by the airplane police for indecent exposure, I'm telling my dad it was your idea."

"Shit, babe, you'd really sell me out like that?" I

place a hand over my heart, acting way more wounded than I actually am.

"If it's you or me, yeah."

"It's a good thing I'll always choose you too. So, feel free to sell me out to save yourself."

The announcement for our flight is called, and we make our way to the gate. I've always hated flying. But now, having Bree with me, I'm suddenly looking forward to the five-hour flight.

Once we're seated, we're served champagne. The hostess doesn't hover—that's a first for me. They usually always fucking hover. "Maybe I should bring you on my trips more often." I clink my glass with Bree's.

"Why's that?" she asks, looking around the cabin.

"This is the first time—in as long as I can remember —that I haven't been hit on in the airport, or by the flight attendants when I board."

Bree's eyes squint at me. "Are you serious? They hit on you?" She sends murderous glares to the hostesses.

"Not these specific ones, but usually, yes. Why? Is that hard to believe?"

"Well, no, but that doesn't make me want to gouge their eyes out any less." She's still looking around at the hostesses. I take hold of her hand, just to make sure she doesn't follow through with her thoughts.

"Relax. You have absolutely nothing to worry about." I bring her hand to my lips and kiss each one of her knuckles.

"Okay, so what do you do to pass the time on these flights?"

I lean in and whisper into her ear, "Well, on this particular flight, you're going to put this blanket over your lap, take off your panties, spread those pretty thighs of yours, and let me play with your pussy." Bree gasps as her face reddens, and she looks around the cabin to see if anyone heard her. I unfold the blanket and place it over both of us. "When the plane takes off, I want those panties in my hand, Bree."

"Ash, you can't be serious. People will know," she hisses.

"People will only know *if* you can't be quiet. You're going to have to be a good girl, babe, and very quiet. Think you can do that for me?"

Her chest heaves with her heavy breaths. "Yes," she whispers.

"Mr. Williamson, we're about to take off. Can I get you anything else?" the hostess asks.

"No, I'm good. Babe, do you need anything?" I look at Bree while answering.

"Nope, I have everything I need right here." Bree smiles as she leans in to kiss me.

Why does it feel like she's making a public statement here? Claiming me as hers... And why does that fucking turn me on so much? I know I shouldn't encourage it, but I fucking love a jealous Bree. It's one of the few times her mask falls, and the true Breanna comes out.

"I love you," I say into her lips.

"I love you more," she replies.

The plane takes off, and I patiently wait for those panties to appear. Just when I think I'm going to have to remind her, she looks around. Then her hands vanish under the blanket and she shimmies, before triumphantly smiling at me with her undergarments closed in her fist. I take the red lace and tuck it into my pocket. I know she's expecting me to start playing with her right away. That's not what I do though. I reach through my bag and remove my iPad.

"Ah, what are you doing?" Bree asks.

"I need to answer a few emails." I feel like an ass, dismissing her like this, so I pull out a file. "Here, can you do me a favour and highlight all the transactions on these statements marked HFD?"

"Sure, what's HFD stand for?"

"I'm not sure I should tell you that. You did steal thirty K from my club." I smirk.

"I offered to pay it back. I can still pay it back. If I had known the boss would be such an ass, I wouldn't have taken the job in place of payment."

I laugh. "You love that asshole. Also, I didn't hear you complaining the other night... when you were bent over the boss's desk."

"Nope, no complaints. Although, if that boss does not make good on his promises soon, I might excuse myself to the ladies and do the job myself."

My laptop falls to the side. "Do not stop highlighting," I tell her as my hand moves under the blanket.

"Is this tight little pussy of yours feeling needy, Breanna?" I lean in and bite at her earlobe.

"Yes."

As soon as my fingers reach her clit, and start circling, she drops the papers to her lap. I remove my hand. "Keep working, Bree. If you're not working, neither are my fingers, and your greedy little cunt is going to starve."

She quickly picks up the papers. I make her task easier and pull down the table in front of her. She puts her pile on the tray and starts highlighting. As soon as she does, my fingers find her clit again and move in slow figure eights. She gasps, and her eyes roll back in her head.

"You're being a very good girl, Bree. Remember: not a single sound." My tongue travels up the side of her neck.

CHAPTER 18

Bree

*H*oly shit, is he serious right now? How the hell am I meant to focus on these statements, when his fingers are playing my body like Beethoven plays a piano. He's a damn genius. "Oh, God, Ash," I hiss, very aware that I need to be quiet. I hold his arm in place, my finger digging into his skin.

The highlighter falls to the table with a loud *thunk*. I glance around the cabin to check if anyone is looking my way. They're not. I can't really see any of the other passengers; we're pretty secluded in these cabin seats.

That knowledge does not make my panic, or distress at the thought of being caught, any less. Although, if I'm honest with myself, it also makes it that much more exciting.

"Pick up the highlighter, Breanna." Ash's gravelly demand sends shivers throughout my body. How can I be turned on from a voice? This isn't normal; it can't be. With a shaky hand, I pick up the highlighter. The moment I do, Ash starts circling his finger around my clit again.

His movements are slow. So damn slow. And soft. Every time I try to lean my pussy into his hand harder, he pulls back. I'm desperate for more pressure. I'm desperate to be filled. My core is pulsing, weeping, and so empty. I'm going to combust, scream this whole plane down, if he doesn't let me come soon.

This is torture... It's like he's keeping me on the precipice, letting me view the drop-off, but not permitting that final leap from the ledge. I want to take the bloody leap. My grip on his arm tightens. "Ash, I need you to make me come—now." My eyes send daggers at him.

"You know, I'd love to make you come, Bree, but you forgot one thing." His face is smug. Handsome, but so smug. If my hands weren't already occupied, I'd probably slap the smugness off him.

"What's that?" I ask, playing along. At this point, I'd do anything to feel the bliss I know is so close.

"Beg, like the good little girl I know you are. Beg,

Breanna. Beg me to make your pussy gush all over my fucking hand," he whispers in my ear.

I'd do *almost* anything. As soon as those words leave his mouth, I drop the highlighter. If he thinks I'll beg him for it, he can think again. I do not beg. He stills, then looks over at me, confused.

I pull his hand from between my legs. "I think you've forgotten who I am, Ash," I say proudly. "I'm Breanna fucking McKinley. I do not now, nor will I ever, beg a man for anything. Especially something I can do my damn self."

With those parting words, I get up and make my way to the bathroom. *Fuck him*. Who does he think he is, asking me to beg? Is he trying to prove a point? That he can have me squirming and needy? That he can control me with just a touch of his fingers?

Locking myself in the bathroom, I look around at my lack of options. I didn't realise the space would be so small. But I'm not one to give up on a challenge. I'm still so worked up from Ash's fingers I know it's not going to take me long to finish.

Lifting one leg onto the tiny counter, I rub my clit before plunging two fingers as deep into my opening as I can manage. My palm grinds down on my sensitive nub as I pump in and out. I close my eyes and imagine that it's Ash's hand. That he's in here with me, getting me off.

It doesn't take long. Before I know it, I'm coming hard. Opening my eyes, I look in the mirror, satisfied that I've got that fresh-orgasm glow. I clean up a bit before I head back out.

Once I'm seated, Ash looks to me, then to the bathroom I just exited. "Are you okay, babe?" he asks with concern.

"I am now." I smile proudly at him with my best *screw you* face.

He smirks before leaning into me. "You might have just gotten yourself off, but you and I both know… it was nowhere near as good as what you would have gotten from me."

I bloody hate that he's right, and I hate that he knows he's right. I press my lips together and pick up the highlighter. "Maybe, but I guess you'll never know for sure. I, on the other hand, very much *do* know."

***

Feather-light kisses bring me out of my slumber. I swat at the face disturbing my sleep. My hand gets caught in a strong grip. My eyes shoot open to see Ash's stunning smile greeting me. "What are you doing?" I ask him, pulling my hand free and rubbing at my eyes.

"We're here, Sleeping Beauty. I thought you might want to get off the plane." He laughs.

"How long was I out?" I remember closing my eyes and pretending to be asleep, so I could escape Ash's scrutiny. He's pissed that I took care of things myself. I'm pissed that I had to. I can still feel the tension between us, many unspoken words I'm sure will come flying out as soon as we're behind closed doors.

"About three hours. You slept right through the turbulence, landing, everything. You must have needed it. Unless you're sick. Fuck, you're not sick, are you?" He brings his hand to my forehead. I swat it away.

"I'm not sick. I just have an asshole boss who likes to keep me up all night." I unplug my seat belt and stand, stretching out my stiff limbs.

"That asshole boss appreciates your dedication to the job." Ash smirks. He leads me off the plane with his hand on my lower back. That simple touch does strange things to both my heart and my vagina.

I follow the path that leads us out to a large foyer. This airport doesn't seem as busy as Sydney's. I stop and look around, having absolutely no idea where I'm going. "What do we do now?" I ask Ash.

He takes hold of my bag. "We go collect our luggage from the arrivals terminal. Come on, princess. I've got you."

"Shut up. You know it's much easier when your bags just get loaded straight into your waiting car." I cringe when I hear my own words. *Bloody hell, I am a spoilt princess.*

"I'm sure it is." He takes me towards a turn belt with everyone's suitcases going round and round. People are scrambling... pushing into each other to reach for their luggage when they spot them. I look at the crowd, horrified.

"Wait here. Don't move. I'll get our bags," Ash says as he walks towards the masses.

I stay put on the spot, observing the chaos. I do love

people watching. I wonder what they're all here for. Are they holidaying? Returning home? I smile when I see people being greeted by their waiting loved ones. I've watched this happen in movies, but I've never actually seen it, or experienced it first-hand. I want that.

I spot Ash walking back towards me, and I can't help myself. I run and jump into his arms. He doesn't miss a beat as he lets go of the baggage in each hand. His arms circle around my back, holding me securely to him. My mouth meets his, and I kiss him like I haven't seen him in months.

It's not hard. I feel like it's been way too long since I've had his tongue in my mouth. As our tongues duel for domination, my hands tug at the back of his hair. "Mmm, I missed you." I smile as I pull back from his kiss, his lips following mine like they're being drawn by a magnetic force.

"I was only gone for a minute, but I missed you too. If this is the greeting I'm going to get, let me walk away for another minute."

I untangle myself from him, not caring in the least about the number of eyes that stare our way. "I was watching all these people, and it occurred to me that I've never met anyone at an airport before. I've never had anyone waiting for me to arrive. I've never waited for anyone to arrive. I wanted to see if the whole 'run and jump into the person's arms in the airport' is as good as the movies make it out to be."

"And was it?" Ash asks, with no mention of my

embarrassingly vulnerable confession.

"It was, but maybe that's just because I really like kissing you."

"Probably not as much as I like kissing you. Come on, let's see what other firsts we can cross off our lists this weekend."

"Other firsts?" I question.

"In the car, we're making a list of all the things we've never done and always wanted to do. We're going to get through this list together."

Swoon—that one word repeats in my head. Well, I can mentally cross that one off. I don't know how he does it, but this man makes me swoon. I go to grab hold of my suitcase, but Ash shakes his head at me and starts walking, giving me no choice but to follow him.

Asshole—another word that often pops up in my head when I'm around Ash Williamson. He may be a bossy ass, but he's *my* bossy ass. If I'm truly honest with myself, I wouldn't have it any other way.

Outside, there are a few cars lined up, waiting to collect people. Ash leads us to a sign that reads: Uber. After he speaks to the driver and hands our bags over, Ash holds open the door for me.

"Whatever you do, never mention to my dad that we took an Uber," he says as he sits in the back seat next to me.

"Why not?" I've never really had many conversations with Ash's dad. He's the silent brooding type, so I don't see how a discussion about Ubers is ever going to come up with him.

"He has a thing about public transport. He doesn't trust it. His parents were hit by a train."

"Shit, that's horrible. How did I not know this?" I knew Ash had no living grandparents. But shit, to be killed by a train, that's rough.

"It's not something they talk about much."

"Well, I knew that your dad raised Aunty Ella from when she was young, but I never really questioned why."

"So, let's start on this list." Ash changes the topic, clearly not wanting to discuss family.

I remove a notepad and pen from my bag. "Okay, what's something that you've never done that you really want to do?" I ask him.

His eyebrows wiggle at me as he takes the items from my hand, not letting me see what he's writing down. When he passes them back, I read the words. *Fuck Breanna's virgin ass* is scrawled across the page.

"Really?" I ask him, trying to ignore the fact that my face is now redder than a beetroot.

"Really. Now, what's something on your list that you want to do?"

I smile, deciding to mess with him a bit. I write on the page: *To be shared by two men at once*.

I hand him the notepad and watch as his jaw tightens, and his eyes bore into me. He plucks the pen from my fingers and crosses out what I wrote.

"That's never fucking happening, Breanna. Forget it," he growls.

"Okay, then neither is this." I take the pen and cross

out his item from the list. I'm actually really curious about that act though, and I do want to try it. But I'm stubborn.

"You can cross it out, babe, but it's happening." His confidence just pisses me off.

"Okay, let's keep this PG, shall we? Here." I jot down: *Cook bacon and eggs for my boyfriend in the morning.*

He smiles at my item and thinks for a moment, before he adds one of his own. He silently hands the list back to me. My heart swells as I read: *Play a game of poker with Breanna McKinley.*

"You've always wanted to play poker with me?" I ask curiously.

"I left out the part about it being strip poker. And in my fantasies, you were very much the loser."

I laugh. Of course, I'd be naked in whatever he fantasized. "Well, we can play, but I can't promise I won't win. I'm really good at poker," I say proudly.

"No, you're really good at cheating. There's a difference, Breanna."

"Care to wager on that?" I'm all for showing this ass that I can win just the same without cheating.

"What's the offer?"

"If I win, you have to find a way to deliver on my fantasy. If you win, I'll let you have me in that spot you really, really want to take."

"Deal," he says all too quickly. He doesn't know what he just agreed to. But either way, it's a win-win for both of us.

CHAPTER 19

Ash

The car pulls up to the Crown Casino. I've booked us in the penthouse suite here. All I can think about is getting Bree alone in that suite. *And naked.* I've been fucking hard since we boarded the plane almost seven hours ago.

"We're staying at the casino?" Bree asks excitedly as she gets out of the car.

"Yeah, I booked the penthouse. Come on, let's check in."

"So, what's on the agenda for tonight? When do you

need to be at the new club building, or meeting, or whatever it is we had to come here for?"

"Tonight is all ours. We'll head over to the building at some point tomorrow and meet with the contractors. But most of the weekend will be free to cross things off our lists." I should admit I didn't really need to come here for work. I just panicked at the thought of not having her all weekend.

As we approach the check-in counter, the guy behind the desk smiles as he stares at Bree. "Well-well, look what the cat dragged in. Miss McKinley, it's been a while." He's already pissed me off with the familiarity with which he addresses my girl. But what agitates me more is the squeal that leaves Bree's mouth as she flings herself over the counter and wraps this douche in a tight bloody hug.

"Daniel, what the hell are you doing here? Last I heard, you were holidaying with a new bride in the Greek Islands." She steps back and waits for his answer.

"Ah, yeah... Well, that marriage was annulled. Grandfather's not doing too well. Thought I'd come home and help out a bit."

"Oh, I'm sorry to hear about your grandfather." Bree uses her well-practiced *I feel empathy for you* tone. I watch as she interacts; she doesn't give a shit about his grandfather. She's just bloody good at faking it.

"So, what happened with Alecia, or was it Amanda? I never can keep up with the names," Bree asks as she easily climbs back over the counter, not caring who sees her. I, on the other hand, very much care, considering I just got a full view of her bare pussy.

I step in front of her, holding her by the waist and pulling her the rest of the way down. As soon as her feet are on the floor, my hands swipe over her dress, ensuring it's in place properly. She squints her eyes at me but doesn't say anything.

"It was Amanda, and let's just say she wasn't a fan of sharing me with Eve." This Daniel douche really is a fucking idiot.

"Oh, I can't see why? Daniel, any girl would be so lucky to have an unfaithful ass for a husband," Bree sasses back.

"Well, what can I say? Unless it's you I'm married to, Bree, how can I stay faithful when there's just so much else out in the world tempting me?" Yep, I'm gonna kick his ass.

Bree takes a firm hold of my hand. "Daniel, meet my fiancé—Ash," Bree says.

I smile and wrap an arm around her. "Looks like you're going to be needing a divorce attorney on retainer, mate, because Bree is very much spoken for. Now and forever, right, babe?"

"Now and forever," she repeats as she leans up and kisses me, putting on quite the show. Who am I to say no? If she wants me to publicly lay claim on her, I'll oblige every fucking time.

"Wow, didn't think you'd ever settle down," the douchebag says. "Wait, this is Ash, as in *the* Ash?" he asks.

"Shut up, Daniel. We're here to check in. Check us in, please." Bree's reaction to his question has me even more curious about their history.

"How do you two know each other?" I ask.

"Oh, we went to school together. I've got you booked in the penthouse suite, Mr. Williamson. If I had known you'd be here, Bree, I would have had it more prepared for a princess," he says.

"Do you need a reminder of just how well this princess can kick your ass, Daniel?" Bree crosses her arms over her chest.

"So, you went to school together? How is it you know who I am?" I ask Daniel, and feel Bree cringe beside me as she stares daggers at him.

"Ah, babe, I really need a shower. Let's get our key and go. We don't have all day to stand around dillydallying. There are much more important things we need to be doing."

"I promise I'll run you a hot shower as soon as we get to the room. I'll even wash your hair for you. But first, I'm intrigued. So, Daniel, how do you know who I am?"

"Oh, Bree's only had the hugest crush on you since I can remember. She used to doodle *Breanna Williamson* all over her books. She even went as far as to write your name over her heart every day, believing it'd draw you to her somehow. Guess it worked."

"Yeah, guess it did." I smile down at her. She's clearly embarrassed, but I fucking love hearing about her high school crush on me. Call me egotistical. I don't fucking care.

"Okay, you're all checked in. Let me know if you need anything else. I have to go make sure security is aware that I've got a hit out on me now. Catch you around, Bree. Maybe I'll see you at the tables tonight."

I lead a very quiet Bree over to the lifts. As soon as we're inside, I can't help myself. I have to say something. "So, the future Mrs. Williamson, huh?"

"Oh my God, Ash. Ignore everything Daniel said. He's an ass, obviously. He can't be trusted. He's also an idiot."

"Babe, I don't care what you doodled on your books in high school. I mean, don't get me wrong, I fucking love that it was my name you scribbled down. But you just introduced me as your fiancé, so if that was your twisted way of proposing to me, I accept." My grin is huge and genuine. I'd fucking marry this girl tomorrow if I thought her parents wouldn't kill me for it.

"What? No, that was not a proposal. That was... I don't know what that was. It's just… Daniel and Benny used to make fun of my crush. I guess I wanted to rub it in Daniel's face that you're mine now. Besides, he's an incorrigible flirt. If he thinks we're engaged, he won't flirt with me anymore. He's a cheat, but he has this weird thing about having an affair with a woman who's married or in a committed relationship."

"But he has no problem being the cheat? That makes no fucking sense. Also, I'll tell anyone you want that we're engaged. We will be eventually, anyway. You having my last name, that's going on my list of things I need to do."

The doors open into the penthouse. Bree walks straight through to the bedroom—she's obviously been here before. She strips out of her shoes and then her dress as she goes. I follow behind her like the lost fucking puppy I am.

By the time we make it to the bathroom, she's naked. I don't think I've ever removed my clothing so fucking fast, but when a naked Breanna McKinley is in front of you, you don't waste time.

Before joining her in the shower, I head back to the bedroom where I left her bag. Plopping it down on the bed, I open it and find her toiletries. What I don't expect to see in her toiletries bag is a fucking box—a box containing a pregnancy test. What the actual fuck? I have so many fucking questions about that, but I choose to ignore it. Grabbing her shampoo and conditioner, I go and meet her in the shower.

Surely if she were pregnant, she'd tell me, right? I'd know if she were pregnant. Maybe it's just one of those things girls carry around with them, like fucking tampons and shit. They just always have it in their toiletries. That has to be it. She's not fucking pregnant. Because if she is, it's not mine. We've only been fucking for a week.

As I step into the shower, my eyes drift to her flat stomach. There's no way. Bree's hands fall to my chest, running along my abs. When she reaches down and wraps her fingers around my cock, all thoughts of a possible pregnancy leave my mind.

"You know, if you play with him, he's likely to want to play back." I smirk at her.

"I'm counting on it," she says as she sinks to her knees.

"Fuck me. You are a fucking wet dream. On your knees. Water running down your body." Breanna licks her lips as her mouth moves closer to my cock. Her tongue darts out, licking my tip. Fuck me, she's barely touched me, and I'm ready to shoot my seed down her tight little throat.

"Mmm, I think you might be my new favourite flavour," Bree hums as her mouth closes around my cock. She hollows out her cheeks and sucks me right down to the back of her throat. My hand tangles in her wet strands of hair, holding her head in place, before I loosen my grip and allow her to ease off. She inhales loudly, sucking me all the way in again. Fucking hell, I'm going to come really soon. I pull her back and look down at her, my thumb tracing around her swollen lips.

"Do you trust me, Bree?"

"Yes."

"Good, because you're going to need to hold on to that trust as I fuck your mouth. Are you ready to be a good girl again?"

The arousal in her eyes. The moans vibrating her vocal cords. That perfect picture of submission. It all eggs me on to push her further. "Open your mouth,

Bree, and let me fuck it."

She drops her jaw and parts her pouty lips. I smirk down at her. Taking my cock in my hand, I pump it twice as I line it up with her mouth. "Good girl," I say as my thumb gently strokes along her cheek. She leans into my touch, taking just as much enjoyment out of the praise as I do in giving it.

"Wider," I demand as I push my cock forward. "Ready?" I give her one last chance to back off. To stop this.

She nods her head, not taking those gorgeous blue eyes off me. I don't need any more reassurance. I push my cock in and out of her mouth. Holding her head still, I tip mine back as I fuck her face more ruthlessly than I should. The sound of her gagging on my cock only encourages me to go harder. Faster.

I feel my balls tighten, tingles running up my spine. "I'm going to come down your throat, and you're going to swallow every last bit," I warn her, right before I come. I ease back a bit, giving her room to swallow my seed as it squirts into her mouth. Her name leaves my lips in a harsh grunt as my climax continues running through me. I must have closed my eyes. Because when I open them, I look down at Bree, who is still sitting on her knees in front of me.

"You're fucking perfect, you know that?" I pull her up, claiming her mouth with my tongue, tasting myself on her, when right now I'd much rather be tasting *just her*. I push her back, until she's sitting on the bench seat at the other end of the shower. "Spread those legs for me, Bree. Show me your greedy little pussy."

She does as she's told. Her fingers go to the lips of her pussy and she parts them, giving me an uninterrupted view. It's fucking perfect. "I've never seen anything more beautiful," I tell her. "Don't move your fingers. Keep yourself open wide for me." My tongue licks from her hole up and around her clit. Her back arches off the wall, but she doesn't move her hands.

I insert two fingers into her. "You're so fucking wet. So fucking tight," I growl as I fuck her with my hand. I close my mouth around her clit and suck. The moment I do, her body freezes and she squirts all over my mouth. All over my fingers.

"Ah, God. Oh my God. Ash, stop. No, don't stop. Fucking hell!" she screams. Her hands move to my head as she holds me in place, rubbing herself on my mouth as she rides out the final waves of her orgasm. When she finally relaxes, her face lights up. "What the bloody hell was that?" she asks me, shaking her head.

"That was the best thing I've ever seen. I wish I had a video camera, because that vision of you is the best spank material I'll ever have."

"Well, stick around, Ash, and you won't need a spank bank." She laughs as she stands on wobbly legs.

CHAPTER 20

Bree

*I*f I could lie in his arms like this forever, I would. I've never been more comfortable than when I'm wrapped up in him. After our shower, where he delivered on his promise to wash my hair, he went about drying it for me as well. I'm curious as to how he got so good at blow-drying. I wasn't going to ask though. We ordered room service and put on a sappy rom-com.

He says it was for me, but I think he likes the movie just a little too much for that to have been true. I'm more of a horror film kind of girl. Rom-coms have never been my thing. I feel like he knows that and is just torturing me with this nonsense.

A knock at the door gives me an excuse to get up. "Did you order something?" I ask him.

"Yep. I'll get it. Wait here." He throws on a pair of sweats before heading to the door. When he returns, he's holding two black paper bags.

"What'd you get?" I ask.

"It's a surprise for later. But for now..." He pauses as he puts the bags down next to his side of the bed. Pulling out a deck of cards and a box of chips, he says, "It's time for that poker game. I really hope you're prepared to deliver on that bet, Miss McKinley. Because, I assure you, I fully plan to claim my prize." He smirks.

"I'm prepared, but are you?"

"Sure thing, babe. Whatever you want." I watch as Ash removes the cards from the deck. He then hands me the box of chips. "We'll start with one thousand each. Split them," he tells me.

"Sure thing." I smile sweetly, all the while wondering how the hell I'm going to win this game. I know I'm good, but it's really more about luck than skill. Something tells me Ash is going to be able to read each of my tells.

"We're playing Heads-up. You know the drill?" Ash asks.

"Yep." I don't tell him that I've been playing this game with my mum since I could recognize numbers.

"Ready? I'll go first as the dealer. After each hand, we'll swap." He starts by placing the small blind.

I put out the big blind. I win the first hand with a straight, beating Ash's set of pairs. He grumbles something about beginner's luck.

As it turns out, it was more than just beginner's luck because after four rounds, I've collected all of his chips.

"Maybe I should be taking you downstairs to play. Tell me, why the hell do you cheat with Ben if you can play this well?"

"Because we can." I shrug, not really having an answer for that question.

"Okay, well, you win, babe. How about we deliver on your little fantasy of having both holes filled at once?"

Is he serious? I begin to panic. What the actual fuck? There is no way he's planning on sharing me with anyone else, is there? Shit, maybe I should have let him win. As that thought crosses my mind, I wonder just how easily I actually won. He bloody well folded twice. I didn't even see his cards. The asshole let me win.

"Ah, Ash, in case you haven't noticed, it's just the two of us here. You're missing a whole other person." I smile, feeling damn proud of myself for finding my loophole.

"Who said anything about another person? Let me make this clear, Breanna. I will never fucking share you with anyone else." He leans over the bed and picks up the black bag, tipping the contents out onto the bed.

My mouth falls open in shock. A huge bottle of lube and a dildo fall right in front of me. My mind is trying to come up with what he could possibly have planned for that. But I got nothing. Okay, I've got images, but surely not…

"That robe needs to come off," he says, getting up and walking out of the bedroom. He comes back in with a full glass of wine in one hand and the remainder of the bottle in the other. Meanwhile, I'm still staring down at the items in front of me.

"Bree, why is that robe on?" Ash questions, putting the glass and bottle on the bedside table closest to me.

"Ah, because it's cold?"

"Good thing I'm here to heat things up for you then." His hands undo the tie at my waist before spreading the robe open. He pushes me back so I'm lying flat. His mouth goes straight to one of my nipples, while his hand finds its way between my legs. Within seconds, he has me squirming and wanting more.

He spends his time moving from one nipple to the other and back again, as he slowly drives one finger in and out of me. I can feel my juices coating my inner thighs. "Ash, I need more." My words are barely a whisper, but he hears me.

He flips me face down and settles me on my hands and knees. I look over my shoulder to see him squirting the bottle of lube over me, his fingers rubbing it in everywhere. I freeze when I feel one finger probe my back entrance.

It slides in easily with the lube. He pulls out and

adds another digit as he goes back in. Those two fingers circle around. I find myself grinding my ass into his hand. I don't know what I was expecting, but this is not it.

I feel full, so full. It's dirty, forbidden, and exciting. All at the same time. I hear the vibrations before I feel them. He rubs the pulsating dildo over my clit, setting my body alight instantly. It's too much, yet not enough.

His fingers pull out of me, and I feel him lining up the tip of his cock with my back entrance. I glance over my shoulder. He looks so damn intense right now, his jaw tight, his gaze laser-focused on the hole he's about to claim.

He makes eye contact with me. "I won't hurt you, Bree. Just breathe. I'll go slow. We'll take this at your pace, okay?"

"Okay." I nod my head. It's easy for him to say, but seriously, does he not know how bloody big his own cock is? And he's going to put that in my... "Oh." I feel the tip go in just a little bit. He starts rubbing the vibrator on my clit again, and I can't help but push back.

He enters me slowly, stretching me out. My mind and body are experiencing things I've never felt before. There's a slight sting and a subtle burning sensation as he stretches me. But I want more. I push back as hard as I can, and he bottoms out.

"*Fuck me.* Bree, stay still," Ash curses as he holds my hips in place. He continues to tease around my clit. After a few minutes, the burning is gone. I need to move. My hips fight against his hold and start rocking slightly.

"You feel so fucking good. Too fucking good. I don't know how long I can last like this, babe," Ash grunts from behind me as he begins to fuck my ass, thrusting in and out slowly.

"Ash, fuck me already," I groan, urging him to pick up the pace.

The vibrator moves down from my clit and pushes at my entrance. He slowly fills my pussy as his cock is fucking my ass. "Oh, fuck. I can't. It's too much." I shake my head even as I push back on him and the vibrator. I've never felt so full. This is next-level intense.

"You can take it. *And you will.* Look at you, Bree. Such a good girl. Your greedy little pussy is full and so is this beautiful fucking ass. Is it everything you thought it would be? Having both holes filled at the same time?" Ash asks, as he holds the vibrator, still buried deep within me. He starts to thrust his cock faster and harder. "You're so fucking tight. So fucking good," he groans.

"Fuck, yes. Ash, don't stop. I'm so close."

"I'm going to count, and when I get to five, I want you to come, Bree. I'm going to fill your ass with my cum. I want to fill every hole of yours with my seed before the night's out."

"Ash... I..."

He cuts my sentence off. "One." Thrust. "Two." Thrust. "Three." Thrust. "Four." Thrust. "Five." His hand comes down on my ass, the sting sending bolts of electricity through me. I come on his count. My body seizes up, and I feel him squirt into my ass, the sensation drawing out my own release.

We both fall to the bed, our chests panting as we catch our breath. "That was..." I roll to my side and look at him. "...intense." I finish my thought.

"That was fucking amazing." He smiles as he pulls me into his arms.

"Ash?"

"Yeah?"

"Did you let me win?" I ask.

"I'd say we both just won, Breanna."

"Yeah, we did." I lazily raise my hand. He meets mine as we high-five, our exhausted arms falling back down.

"What's next on this list of firsts?" I ask, because that was bloody amazing. If every first experience is going to be like that, then count me in. I want more.

"I don't think we got very far on the list. I believe there was something along the lines of you wanting to cook your very loveable, sexy fiancé breakfast." Ash smirks.

"Huh, I'm pretty sure it was to cook my *tolerable boyfriend* breakfast." I laugh, getting up on shaky legs, before I head into the bathroom and shut the door behind me.

"You know you don't need to shut the door. After what we just did, I think we're beyond being coy," Ash yells.

"Ash, you are not watching me pee. Ever," I yell back. I turn the tap on in the basin to further tamper the sound of me peeing. Some things are best left unheard. And unseen.

I can hear Ash's laugh as I pee. I decide to turn the shower on and quickly wash myself off properly. All that bloody lube he squirted over me is sticky as hell. After a quick shower, I wrap a towel around myself and walk back out to the bedroom. Ash is sitting on the bed with two bowls of ice cream. He's wrapped in a towel as well, appearing freshly washed.

"Did you just shower?" I ask, a little disappointed he didn't join me.

"I did. I used the other room. Thought you'd want your privacy," he says, lifting a shoulder.

"In the toilet, yeah. Not the shower. I missed out on seeing the suds run down those abs. That's a crime, Ash. Are you trying to punish me?"

I sit on the bed and lift the bowl of vanilla ice cream; it's covered in chocolate sauce and raspberries. A lot of raspberries.

"You really like raspberries, don't you?" I ask him around a mouthful of delicious dessert.

"At my twenty-second birthday dinner, I hugged you and got the strongest smell of raspberries from your hair. Ever since, I've always made sure I eat as many of them as I can. They remind me of you." He says this so nonchalantly. Like it's not the most romantic thing I've ever heard.

"Well, apart from the fact that I was sixteen, and

you were lusting over a minor at the time, that has to be the sweetest thing anyone's ever said," I confess.

"You might have been sixteen, but you sure as fuck didn't look it. You already had all these curves in all the right places. You were wearing a little black dress that night. I was so fucking pissed off at Josh for even letting you out of the house. Then you purposely sat across from me, flashing me glimpses of your cleavage all fucking night."

"Well, I wore that dress, hoping you'd notice me."

"Oh, I fucking noticed. But I noticed you long before that night."

"When was the first time you felt an attraction towards me?" I ask curiously.

"It was around your sixteenth birthday. I don't know when it happened. But I remember how fucking hard it was to be around you. I started to avoid going to family events so I wouldn't have to see you. I felt like a fucking creepy predator, lusting over a teenager."

"You weren't a predator, Ash. We're obviously meant to be. Do you believe in past lives? I think our souls have been connected before. We're probably lovers in every life we live."

"Ah, sure," he agrees, but looks at me sceptically.

"You don't have to believe me. I don't care. You'll see. You won't be able to live without me."

"I already know I can't live without you. How much time do you think your parents really need?"

"For what?"

"To get used to the idea of us being an *us*. For us to

get engaged for real, to get married, have babies. The whole fairy tale."

I freeze when he mentions having babies. I should probably confess that there is a very small possibility I might be pregnant now. I don't want to ruin what we have though. I don't want to ruin this weekend.

"You don't want kids? I'm pretty sure you're not freaked out over the whole marriage thing," Ash asks, his eyes examining every part of my face.

Does he already know? He can't possibly know. The worst thing is, if I am pregnant, it's not with his baby. I had a one-night stand about six weeks ago. I know the guy; I've known him for a while. Would I want his kid? Absolutely not. I'm praying that when the time comes for me to take that test, it's negative.

"I want kids, just not yet. I want us to be *just us* for as long as we can be. I'm not good with sharing, Ash. I'm also not good with loving people. What if I had a baby and couldn't love it?"

"When you have kids, I have no doubt that you are going to be the best mother there is. You think you're not good at loving, yet the way you love me is like nothing I've ever seen or experienced. That's a rare kind of love, Bree. You're more capable of it than you give yourself credit for."

"Well, I don't have to try with you; it's just there. But with other people, I have to really try. I shouldn't be telling you this. You don't need to know the ins and outs of my messed-up brain."

"I happen to love your messed-up brain, babe. You

can tell me anything. I know you, Bree. I know you pretend. I know when you fake having empathy or feelings for someone you really couldn't care less about. *I know.* Which is why I will never take your love for granted. I know just how rare it is that you truly give it out."

I pick up my phone and open Google. "What house are your parents at right now?" I ask him.

"Ah, I think they're probably home, in Turramurra. Why?"

"I need to send your mother some flowers. To thank her for raising you right. For creating a man as perfect as you are." I smile at him.

"You do realize, if you do that, she's going to know there's something going on with us."

"Like you said, I think the cat's out of that bag already." I shrug.

CHAPTER 21

It's been a week since our trip to Perth, and I still haven't come up with a way to ask Breanna about that damn pregnancy test I found in her bag. I have been watching her carefully. She sips on her wine, but her glass is never any emptier. She seems fine. She's not sick. She's eating normally.

I don't know what to make of it, and it's driving me fucking crazy. We're going to be surrounded by family all weekend, and this will just eat at me until I know one way or the other. I've come to terms with the fact that if she is pregnant, it doesn't matter that the baby is not mine. I'll raise it as my own. It's hers, and that's all that matters to me. I might have Josh help me destroy the fucker who knocked her up, but she won't have to know that.

I'm picking up my little sister and driving her out to my Aunt Ella's beach house. Breanna drove with her parents; they have their own house just a few doors down from Aunt Ella and Uncle Dean.

I'm standing in the audience, waiting for my sister to finish her performance. I always get chills watching her dance; she's a bloody natural. She's so beautiful up on that stage, and she knows it. She was born to be in the spotlight.

When the lights dim, signalling the routine is over, I make my way to the stage door. There's a young guy in a military uniform there, with a gift and a bunch of flowers, waiting for one of the other dancers. I stay back, not wanting to crowd him or ruin the romantic gesture.

The door opens and Ava comes up, still dressed in her leotard and tights. She's at least thrown a jacket over the top. She's also let her hair down. I'm about to step forward when her face lights up with a huge-ass smile—only it isn't directed at me. It's aimed at the guy in the uniform. He rocks uncomfortably from foot to foot.

Ava takes a step forward. The closer she gets, the more her smile faulters. She starts shaking her head, tears streaming down her face, as she throws her arms around this guy. What the fuck?

"Ava?" I call out, emerging from the shadows. She either doesn't hear me or ignores me.

"No, you're not leaving. Tell me you're not. You can't." She hits the guy's chest. He stands there and takes every blow. Ava might be a tiny little thing, but she can still throw a good punch.

"I'm sorry, A. I don't have a choice. I have to."

"Ava, what the fuck is going on here?" I'm losing my patience.

"Ash, nothing is going on. Noah was just leaving." Ava steps back and folds her arms over her chest.

"I'm sorry, A. I really am. If I could change this, I would." The guy, Noah, says as he steps back. He stops, looking me dead in the eye as I wrap my crying sister in my arms. "Can you make sure she doesn't open this until Christmas day? Please. Look after her for me."

"A, I will come back to you. I promise." He walks away.

"You can't promise that, Noah. You can't *know* that," she yells after him.

"Ava, what the fuck? You better start talking before I go kick the ass of one of our soldiers. I'd really fucking hate to do that. But for you, I will."

"No, you won't. Don't worry about it. Whatever it was, it's gone now. He's leaving. I'm fine. Let's go. I'm ready to hit the beach." In true Ava form, she pulls out a compact mirror and touches up her face as we walk out to my car.

It's not until I open the boot that I notice I'm still holding the small gift box. I throw it in. I'll just get rid of it later, although the thought that my sister might want to see what's in that box will more than likely make me give it to her on Christmas Day.

The drive out to the beach is quiet. The one thing going round through my mind is: *Ava has a fucking boyfriend, and I didn't even know.* She's fucking eighteen; she shouldn't be having boyfriends who are in the military and making her cry. *She's fucking eighteen.*

"Ava, honey, you know you can come and talk to me about anything. I'll always be here for you."

"I know," she says quietly.

"So, Noah… Who is he, and how do we know him?" I ask her.

"You don't know him. I don't even know him. Not anymore. I thought I could talk him out of joining. I thought I would be important enough for him to stay. Guess I was wrong."

"How long have you known him, Ava?"

"We went to school together. He was two years above me. I've known him since I was thirteen, Ash. But in the last few months, we started dating. I just didn't… I don't know. I didn't expect he'd actually do it."

"Do what?" I ask.

"Sign up," she says, looking away.

"It's a noble job, Ava. Also, what the fuck? Why didn't I know you were dating? Do Mum and Dad know?"

"Ah, no, they do not, and you're not going to tell them. Besides, it doesn't matter. He's gone now."

"Yeah, well, it kind of sounded like he had plans of coming back. Where they sending him anyway?"

"He's... I'm not meant to say anything. I'm not even meant to know."

What the actual fuck? What's so classified that she shouldn't even know where he's going? "Sweetheart, you know whatever you tell me will never leave this car. You need to talk to someone, otherwise it's going to eat you up inside, and you'll end up a crazy old cat lady."

"A crazy cat lady sounds good. At least her heart would be safe from being broken."

"Is your heart broken, Ava?"

"Right now, it feels like it's beyond repair. How can he just leave like that?" she asks.

"I don't know, honey." I reach over and squeeze her hand. "I do know that if you're in the military, you don't really have a choice where they send you."

"But that's just it. He didn't have to go and apply for the bloody special forces. But no, not Noah fucking Hunt. He has to be the best of the best. Always."

Special forces. Fuck, that's big. And she's right. She shouldn't know that. *I* shouldn't know that. "Ava, you really can't tell anyone. You could get him in a lot of trouble for knowing that he's special forces, or going to be."

"I know. But I hate him so much right now... Maybe you should go kick his ass for me, Ash." She smiles.

"I'd love to, sweetheart. Maybe after the Christmas break. I'll track him down for you and do just that."

"Thanks, Ash, you know you're my favourite brother today."

"Anytime, sweetheart."

After a while of driving in silence, I ask the question that's been eating at me. "Hey, Ava, can I ask you something?"

"Sure, if it's about that party that was reported in your penthouse last weekend, that wasn't me. I'm blaming Axel."

"It's not about that party. I already know that was you. Do you honestly think I don't have video surveillance, Ava? I saw your little slumber party with a heap of girls. No, I was wondering... pregnancy tests... are they something girls just carry around all the time? Like tampons?"

"What? No, Ash, don't be daft. Unless you think you're pregnant, and need to pee on a stick to make sure, you wouldn't just carry them around." Ava laughs, then stops and looks at me.

"Oh my God! Did you knock someone up? Oh, God, it's Bree. Josh is going to kill you, Ash. We should just keep driving and run now. Maybe get a head start."

I'd like to think she's joking; she's not though. Ava is wise beyond her years. "I didn't' knock anyone up, Ava, and I'm never fucking running. I just saw one in a friend's bag and was curious. That's all."

"Oh, it's Hope, isn't it? Lily is way too smart to get knocked up, but Hope would for sure be the kind."

"It's not Hope. You don't know them. Forget about it." Thank God we're almost at the beach house.

"I might just drop you and run. I need to check into my rental real quick before I come back here."

"Okay, sure."

***

I'm sitting on the balcony of my rental. I sent my parents a message to say I'd be around tomorrow, that I was exhausted and headed to bed early. I sent the same message to Breanna. The only issue is… I can't fucking sleep without her in the bed. I pull out my phone and dial her number. I should care that it's nearing midnight and she could be asleep, but I fucking need her.

"Hello, Ash, are you okay?" Her voice is quiet, but not groggy.

"I can't sleep without you, Bree." I sigh.

"Okay, do you want me to come over?"

"I want you to never leave."

"Give me five. I'll be right there."

She hangs up the phone. I put my glass in the dishwasher and head into the bedroom. Not even five minutes later, Bree is walking through the door and climbing into bed. I wrap my arms around her.

"Don't ever leave my bed again," I whisper into her ear. My arms hold her tight.

"I didn't leave. You told me you needed an early night. I thought that meant you didn't want to see me."

"I'll never stop wanting to see you."

"Everyone was asking where you were at dinner."

"I had work to do."

"No, you didn't. You were avoiding people. Why?"

"I'm not avoiding people. I'm just tired. Let's go to sleep. Tomorrow is going to be a huge day."

"Yeah, it is." Bree rolls over in my arms. "Can I tell you a secret?" she asks. My heart stops. This is it... she's going to tell me she's pregnant with another man's child.

"You can tell me anything. Always."

"I hate Christmas. I hate the gatherings, the fakeness, the happiness. Sometimes I go shopping just to wave that fancy McKinley card in front of everyone. When most people see that name, they get scared. I know I shouldn't, but I really like it when I see fear in their eyes."

She watches my face for a reaction. I'm relieved that she's not doing the whole *I'm pregnant* speech. "Babe, I already know how much you hate Christmas. I also know about the fear thing. I don't care what quirks you have. Fuck, I don't care if your hobby is spending time feeding the pigs with your dad. I love you. In saying that, when we build our own place, we are not buying any fucking pigs," I tell her.

"Deal, and I don't feed the pigs, FYI. My dad would never let me get my hands that dirty." Bree smiles. I lean in and kiss her, wanting to stay in this moment. In this bubble.

"Goodnight, babe." I kiss her forehead and run my fingers through her hair. I fucking love playing with her hair.

"Goodnight? So, this really was just to sleep, not a booty call? Are you getting old on me, Ash?"

"No, but we're both tired. I promise I will ravish the fuck out of this sweet little body of yours before breakfast."

***

I wake up and stretch out, reaching for Bree, only to come up empty. The bed where she's meant to be is cold. She's gone. I shoot straight up. Her bag is still thrown in the corner of the room. Then I hear a whole heap of shit banging around in the kitchen.

Fuck, she's in the kitchen. I need to get my ass in there. Bree and kitchens do not mix well. I throw on a pair of shorts and a shirt. I step over the threshold and instantly know I'm too late. The place looks like a disaster zone. How can one person make so much mess?

"Ah, babe, what are you doing?" I ask from the doorway, not even sure if it's safe to walk into the space. There are pots and pans lining the counters. There is flour from floor to ceiling. I look up. No lie— it's on the fucking ceiling. There's a broken egg on the counter.

But when she turns around and smiles at me, I can't even be a little bit mad at my beautiful disaster. "I'm making you breakfast," she announces proudly.

"Oh, it looks… interesting," I say, peering into a pan with what I think is meant to resemble pancakes.

The doorbell rings out through the house, and I'm literally saved by the bell. "I'll get it." I turn the knobs on the stove off before I head out of the kitchen. I'm lucky she didn't burn the place down while I was asleep.

I open the door and find my mother on the other side. Fuck, why couldn't it have been Aunt Ella or even Aunt Reilly? They, at least, know how to cook. "Hey, Mum, is Dad with you?" Please say yes. For the love of God, say yes. "Yeah, he's just grabbing breakfast out of the car. I thought we'd come have a quiet brekkie with you."

"Perfect, you're just in time. You've probably saved my life right now." I hug and kiss her.

"Why? What's wrong? Are you sick?" she asks, concerned.

"No, but I probably would have been if you didn't turn up." My dad walks through, carrying a few trays. I take some off him.

"Hey, Dad."

"Hey, yourself." He sniffs the air. "What the hell is that smell?"

"Shh, don't make a big deal about it. Pretend that it looks great. If either of you make her cry or feel bad, I'm gonna be pissed," I warn as I walk them through to the kitchen.

"Make who cry?" my mum asks, like she doesn't already know.

"Oh. Good morning, Breanna. I didn't know you'd be here. But don't worry, I packed heaps of extra. I'll set the table. Zac, Ash, put those down over here. I'll find the plates." My mum busies herself.

"Good morning, Breanna. Busy start?" Dad asks her.

"Oh my gosh, Mr. and Mrs. Williamson, I'm so sorry. Ash didn't tell me you guys were coming. I would have been more ready. Crap."

"Bree, it's fine, and why are we suddenly Mr. and Mrs. Williamson? You can call me Alyssa, like you always have." My mum hugs her.

"Ash, get the cutlery out. Sorry to interrupt your breakfast, Bree. It looks like it would have been great. But how about you save this for tomorrow? Or another day?" Dad suggests.

"Ah, sure. I should just go home. I'll see you later, Ash." Bree moves to step past me.

"You're not going anywhere. Sit down. We're eating breakfast." I wrap an arm around her and lead her to the table.

"Are you sure, Ash? Your parents are here?" she whispers.

"I noticed, but my mum brought food, and she'd be upset if you ran out now. So will you stay, please?"

I don't miss that my parents are watching our little interaction with way too much interest.

"Okay." Bree sits down. "This looks great, Alyssa. Maybe you could give me cooking lessons one day."

"God no! Babe, my mother is great at many things, but cooking is not one of them. Either Aunt Ella or my dad made this food," I tell her.

"It was me, after I saved Aunt Ella's kitchen from looking like yours does right now."

Bree glances over, but I swear she's blind to the mess.

"It's fine. It's just a few dishes," I say, dismissing my dad's comments.

"Oh, want me to get the cleaners to come over?" Bree offers innocently.

"No, babe, it's fine. I'll sort it out."

"Are you sure? I just… I mean… I guess I could help you?" she questions.

"Bree, when was the last time you cleaned a kitchen?" I ask her.

"I-I don't know, but how hard can it be? I've seen the maids do it heaps."

"How the other half lives." I laugh.

"Leave her alone, Ash," Mum says, dishing up everyone's plates.

The rest of breakfast is comfortable. Bree is extra polite and watches what she says more than she ever has around my parents. I squeeze her leg under the table, trying to reassure her that she can be herself. She doesn't need to try to make my parents love her; they already do.

CHAPTER 22

Bree

$\mathcal{A}$sh has been acting weird all day. We're now sitting near the bonfire on the beach, out front of Aunt Ella's house. I feel like I've been waiting all day for the other shoe to drop. Has the reality of being with me kicked in? Or maybe the excitement of the forbidden has worn off, now that we're basically out in the open with our relationship?

Whatever it is, I'm over feeling like shit because I don't know what he's thinking. "Okay, what the hell is wrong with you? And don't tell me *nothing,* because I will shoot you."

"I… it's noth—" Ash shakes his head and then looks at me. "You know I'd stand by you, no matter what happens. There is nothing I wouldn't do for you."

"Okay, thank you?"

"Bree, I saw the pregnancy test in your bag last weekend. Why do you have that?"

That's what's bothering him… He thinks I'm pregnant. "Well, Ash, usually girls buy them when they think there's a slim possibility they're pregnant."

"And… *are you?*" he asks me, point-blank. At that moment, Lily walks up and plops down on a chair opposite us.

I choose to ignore Ash's question. He can suffer a bit longer, before I put him out of his misery. "What's wrong with you?" I ask Lily.

"Have you ever met someone and just wanted to screw their brains out, but you literally have no idea who they even are?" she asks.

"Ew, no, just fucking no, Lily," Ash chokes out.

"I have." I smile and look at Ash. "But I always knew who they were, so I guess not."

"Argh, I just can't… Shit, he's coming. Pretend I didn't say anything," Lily hisses.

"Who's coming? Oh, yeah, I get it. You're screwed, Lil." I laugh as Ash's hand tightens around my waist. He pulls me closer to him, as he sends daggers to the hot guy who just sat next to Lily. I wonder if Ash knows who this sexy stranger is. *Because I do.* I don't know

Alex personally, but I have played a few games with him sitting at the tables. I've also heard the rumours saying he's the king of Sydney's underworld.

It's not long before Alex is following Lily into the ocean.

"You know exactly who Alessandro Mancini is, don't you?" I question Ash.

"Doesn't everyone?"

"Apparently not Lily. I don't care who he thinks he is, or how many goons he thinks he has. If he hurts her, I'm feeding him to the pigs."

"I'll help you."

"Come on, dinner should be nearly ready." I leave him sitting there. I know he'll make his way up soon enough.

***

Everyone's already at the table. Axel comes and sits next to me—in the chair I was hoping Ash would occupy. I don't know where he's gotten to. He's clearly pissed I never answered his question earlier.

When he does show up to dinner, he looks at Axel. "Move. You're in my chair."

"I don't see your name written on it," Axel smarts back.

"How about I write my name on it with your blood, after I knock your fucking teeth out," Ash grunts.

"Ash Williamson, stop it. You are not hitting your brother. Axel, get up and move. Stop stirring him." Alyssa raises her voice from the other end of the table.

Axel stands and takes a different seat. "I didn't want to sit there anyway," he grumbles.

The moment Ash sits down, his open palm lands on my leg, and he squeezes my thigh just a little. I wrap my fingers over his hand and hold it under the table.

Dinner's going really well. Turns out, Alex's sister, Mia, and his niece, Tessie, are great company. The kid is cute as hell. Even my dad seems smitten with her. The food is delicious and I'm starving. I fill my plate so high it's nearly tumbling over. However, afterwards I feel like I'm in a food coma.

"I need grandchildren already. Ash, when are you going to bring me home a baby?" Alyssa asks while smiling at Tessie's excitement.

Ash and I both still; we probably look guilty as fuck right now. Shit, I glance over at my parents. Three, two, one...

"Someone better start fucking talking!" Dad yells, glaring at us. "What the fuck did you do?"

Ash shoots out of his seat. I follow his lead and stand right next to him.

"First, you don't speak to her like that. Second, I don't have to tell you shit. Until you start acting like a human, instead of a fucking rabid dog," Ash yells back at my dad. Oh shit, that's not good. I know my dad, and exciting him—challenging him—is not how we get out of this in one piece.

Dad pulls out a Glock, from God knows where, and aims it right at Ash's head. Fuck. This is stupid. I go to open my mouth. To tell the idiots that nothing is happening. That I'm not bloody pregnant. But I choke on my words when Ash moves like lightning, shoving me behind him. Well, he attempts to anyway. I duck out of his hold and jump onto the table in front of him. I have no doubt my dad will shoot Ash, but there's no way he's going through me to do it.

"Dad, put the gun down. You are not shooting him," I demand. Ash, the fucker, reaches out and picks me right up and off the table, putting me back on the ground.

"Do not step in front of a fucking gun, Bree," he growls at me.

"Oh, please, he's not going to shoot me. You, on the other hand, he very much will!" I yell.

"Well, considering I'm not the one pregnant, I can handle being shot," Ash yells back.

My eyes go wide as I look around the room. Great, now everyone thinks I'm fucking pregnant.

"Okay, this has gone far enough. Josh, put the fucking gun down," Aunt Ella yells.

"Josh, honey, give me the gun," Mum says, holding her hand out. *Oh, this is bad.*

I watch, unable to move. It all happens so fast. Dad hands Mum the gun. I try to stand in front of Ash, but he shoves me back, his grip on my arm firm.

The gun goes off. Ash grunts out a curse. A heap of men in suits run up and surround Alex.

"Mum, stop!" I throw myself in front of Ash, giving him a quick once-over. He is still standing. Maybe the bullet missed him.

"Put the fucking gun down. *Now*," Zac growls out as he walks around the table, placing himself between his son and the other end of the barrel.

"You knocked up my daughter? You could have at least had the balls to date her in public, Ash," Mum says in a quiet voice.

I need to fix this shit. Put a stop to this madness. If anyone would just listen to me... "He didn't... he wasn't the one. I'm not..." I try to explain.

"Bree, stop. It was me, okay. I got her pregnant. And guess what?" Ash says to everyone. "I'd do it again." He smiles. Damn him, I can feel little tears form at the corner of my eyes. Why would he claim a baby we both know wouldn't have been his?

"Joshua, get Emily out of here now," Uncle Dean says.

Alyssa comes running out of the house with a first aid kit. "Ash, do not move. You need to be still. Someone call a fucking ambulance."

"I barely scraped him; he'll survive," Mum says.

Alyssa glares at her. "You just shot my son. I'd be very quiet right now if I were you."

"He got my daughter pregnant. She's only twenty-two." Mum shrugs as if that's reason enough to shoot someone.

"Yeah, last I heard, it takes two people to get pregnant," Zac grunts as he walks around the table to where Ash and I stand.

"I'm not bloody pregnant, you idiots!" I yell.

"Wait... you're not?" Ash asks me, confusion all over his face.

"No, and if you listened to me, instead of hearing one word and going crazy, you would already know that." I take a breath in and stare my parents down. "Also, if I were pregnant, like I thought I might have been, it wouldn't have been Ash's. We've been together for two weeks. Do the bloody math."

Alyssa fusses over Ash, and he swats her hand away. "Mum, I'm fine. It's just a scrape."

"You're not fine, Ash. You just took a bullet to your leg. We're leaving. Come on." Alyssa walks into the house, calling out, "Ava, Axel, go get your stuff. We're not staying here."

"Shit. Ash, you good? I've got to go talk to your mum. You should go back to your place. I think everyone needs to calm down," Zac whispers to Ash before following Alyssa into the house.

"Yeah, I'm good," Ash says.

My parents are awfully quiet as they stare at me. I know their disappointed glare; it's not the first time I've experienced it. I also know they want to have a family-style interrogation. I'm not sticking around to endure that right now.

"Ash, take me home." I walk through the house, without a backward glance.

I'm waiting at Ash's car. I have no idea what's taking him so long. Hope comes out, and I cringe.

"So... that was a little intense," she says.

"Just a little." I smile.

"Look, Ash is obviously head over heels for you. He wouldn't be standing in front of bullets if he weren't. But if you hurt him like this again, I will find a way to hurt you back."

"I'm sure you will." I'd never underestimate Hope. We've been close friends for as long as I can remember.

"Okay, so now that that's out of the way, help me devise a plan to get Chase between my sheets. I know he wants in, but he's so damn loyal to Ash. He keeps saying he'd be breaking the bro code or some bullshit." Hope rolls her eyes.

"Hope, you are not hooking up with my best friend. Find someone else, or better yet, *don't*," Ash says, coming around and opening the car door for me.

"Why the hell not? You're clearly sleeping with *my* best friend," Hope huffs.

"I saw Bree first. That makes her more my friend than yours." I think Ash actually believes his weak reasoning.

"No, it doesn't. I don't care what you say, Ash. Bree, I'll call you later."

"Okay, thank you." I hug her before getting in the car.

Ash silently starts the engine. He doesn't say anything as he pulls out of the driveway, and directs the car towards his house just a few streets over.

I wait for him to break first, but I don't think he's going to. I should just let him process whatever it is he's thinking about, but I can't handle the silence. I have a lot of self-doubt creeping in right now, and I don't bloody well like it.

"Are we just going to pretend that the whole ordeal didn't happen?" I ask.

"What do you expect me to say, Breanna? I just stood there and claimed a baby in front of our whole family. A baby who: one, wasn't mine, and two, didn't even fucking exist. Why didn't you just tell me you weren't fucking pregnant?"

I flinch. "I never asked you to claim anything that wasn't yours, Ash. That was all you. Don't you think, if I were pregnant, that I would have told you?"

"I don't know. I panicked, okay? I saw a pregnancy test in your bag and I panicked... Not because I thought you were knocked up. I panicked because I thought I was going to fucking lose you."

"You're never getting rid of me, Ash. I'm stuck to you like a bad rash now; there's no getting away from me. Also, why'd you say it was yours?"

"If you were pregnant, Bree, whether or not it was mine, I'd claim that child as my own. No one would have to know any differently. If it's a part of you, I'd love it just as much as I love you."

Well, fuck me. I was not expecting that. "I appreciate the thought, Ash, but I'd never put that kind of responsibility on you. Also, we're both so young. We have plenty of time to make babies of our own. *Together*. You know, in around ten years' time."

Ash laughs. "Babe, I'll be nearing forty in ten years. I'm not waiting that long to knock you up. Wait, are you on birth control? Because I don't know if you've noticed, but we've been going at it like rabbits without any protection."

"I'm good. I'm on birth control."

"How do you feel about not being on it? I kind of like the thought of you being knocked up."

"Charming." I smirk at his choice of words. "How about I finish my master's degree first, and then we can revisit this conversation."

"Fine… And I guess there's no more hiding now. I'm pretty sure the whole family knows that your ass is mine."

"I think what they know is that your fine ass is *mine*, Ash."

"Let's hope we can get through the rest of Christmas, without anyone else getting shot." Ash pulls into the driveway of his rental house. It's not until now that the exhaustion of the day finally kicks in.

CHAPTER 23

Ash

I t's Christmas Eve. Everyone's back at Aunt Ella and Uncle Dean's beach house. My parents and siblings ended up staying there last night, after my dad talked my mum off the cliff she was on.

I'd be lying if I said things weren't a little tense still. My parents are pissed at Emily. Bree is giving her parents the silent treatment, and I've observed her on her phone, ordering shit with that black credit card she keeps pulling out of her pocket. She likes to make sure her dad sees her using it every time she does.

I've asked her about it, but she just keeps insisting she's ordering last-minute Christmas gifts. I keep in mind to try not to piss her off. I feel like that's an expensive lesson I don't want to learn.

Before I left last night, Josh and Emily stopped me. They both apologized for how they reacted. Josh asked if I knew who the other guy was. I fucking wish I did. I have no doubt that he'll find out by the end of the day. As much as I'd like to bury the fucker, I'm more preoccupied with figuring out just how I'm going to get Bree to agree to move in with me.

We're all sitting at the dinner table together, out on the patio again. There's a lot of talk about the house next door; we used to hang around the kids who grew up there.

"Remember the little secret rooms we'd play hide and seek in?" Hope asks. I recall every nook and cranny of that house. It was the best place to store the shit we didn't want our folks to find.

"Yep, that house was fucking awesome. I heard you're looking to sell it, Alex? Maybe I should buy it," I say. I don't mention how odd I find it that he's looking to sell a house he only just purchased.

"He's not selling it to you. Hope and I are buying it," Lily yells at me.

"I think I'd rather see it burned," Alex grunts.

"Well, looks like you're not the only one." Bree points towards Alex's house, where there is currently a heap of smoke billowing out from the windows.

"Fuck." Alex jumps up. He starts towards the blaze,

then stops. I watch as he turns around and yells, "Mia, sugar!" Mia jumps up quickly, grabbing Tessie and throwing her under the table. Alex turns to the rest of us. "You all need to get down. Right the fuck now!"

I don't waste any time. I take Bree down with me, throwing my body on top of hers. I look around at the rest of my family, now all crouched on the ground. My dad is covering my mum's body, while Axel and Ava are right next to them. Ava's trying to push Axe off her, but he's not budging. Thank fuck.

Josh stares back, his eyes on Bree. I can see how much he wants to pull her out of my arms and be her shield. *Like I'm going to let that happen.* The next thing I know, Alex is jumping on top of Lily, right as an explosion rings out. Loud crashes and fallen debris follow the initial blast. I get up, pulling Bree to her feet. My hands run all over her body, checking that she's still in one piece.

"Ash, stop. I'm fine. What the hell was that?" she asks.

I have no idea. The patio is crowded with men in suits, guns drawn as they surround Alex and Lily.

"We need to get out of here. Have the cars pulled around front. I've got a place not too far. You're all welcome to come."

"I'm not fucking going to your place, Alex," Josh grunts, as he drags Emily over to where Bree and I stand.

"Dad, Mum. Please just come with me," Lily pleads

with her parents. I watch as Uncle Bray looks around. He wants to argue, but he doesn't.

"Sure thing, princess. Reilly, Hope, go pack an overnight bag." Uncle Bray turns and has a quiet conversation with my dad.

My dad then announces that Christmas is being moved to the Mancini house. Aunt Ella glances from Uncle Dean to Josh. "We're going with them. We're not being separated on Christmas morning," she declares before heading inside.

"Ash, are you going with your parents to Alex's?" Bree asks me.

"I have to, babe. It's Christmas. I'll understand if you don't come. I won't like it, but I get it. You should be with your parents for Christmas."

"Ash, you clearly underestimate just what my parents will endure for me." She smirks at me before turning on her heel to face them.

"I'm going with Ash. You're both coming with me. Unless you want your only daughter, sleeping in a mobster's house without you there to protect her."

Well, shit, when she puts it like that, maybe we should all be rethinking our decision. But as I look at Lily, I know she's going with Alex. And none of us are about to let her go alone either.

"Okay, but there better be lots of fucking bedrooms in this house. Lots of *separate* bedrooms," Josh says, directed at me. I just smirk. I'll let him think that Bree is safely tucked away in a bed. *Without me*. There's no fucking way that's happening though.

***

"Ash, Jesus Christ. You have a fucking death wish, don't you?" My dad's voice booms through the room, dragging me out of my sleep. I'm fucking tired. Bree and I were up late last night.

"Why the hell are you yelling at me?" I groan.

"You're lucky it was me who came in to wake your ass up. I'd say you have about five minutes before Josh figures out Breanna is not in that room he thinks she's sleeping in. *Alone.*"

Bree stirs in my arms. I look down, her mass of blonde hair falling over my chest. She has the blankets tucked up to her chin—thank God—because she's very naked under here.

"Ash, I know you're fond of your dad, but I'm considering ripping his balls off so maybe his voice won't be so damn loud," Bree mumbles.

"It's scary just how much you're like your mother, Breanna." Dad laughs. "Ash, get your ass downstairs. It's Christmas morning."

"Sure, give me five. I'll be down."

I wait until the door clicks before I roll Bree over, landing on top of her. "I'm not sitting through Christmas morning without the taste of you on my tongue. Lie still. Let me get my fix in." I kiss my way down Bree's naked body. Her legs fall open, an invitation I have no intention of turning down.

I slowly drag my tongue up her centre. Circling around her clit, I draw out little infinity symbols.

"Mmm, God, I'm never going to get enough of you," I say into her mound as my tongue pushes into her tight, little, wet hole.

Her hands pull at my hair. "Oh, fuck, Ash. Keep doing that. Don't stop." She grinds her pussy into my face. Holding my head still, she fucks my tongue. Before long, she's coming all over my fucking mouth.

I make my way back up her body. "That's a much better way to wake up." She smiles.

"You know, if you move in with me, I'll wake you up like that every day of the week. And *twice* on Sundays," I promise her.

"That's tempting, but I'm still not moving in with you, Ash." She laughs. "Although, I might move in on Sundays only."

"Deal," I say quickly. "Now I just have to wear you down enough to agree to the other six days of the week."

"Come on, if we don't get up, they're going to come looking for us again."

"I know."

***

The morning has consisted of unwrapping gifts. I remember that I've still got that box for Ava in my car. Everyone seems busy either cleaning the mess, or playing with Tessie, Alex's five-year-old niece. I think my parents, aunts, and uncles just adopted her into the family—even Josh got her a fucking pony.

He's always over the top with gifts. For my thirteenth birthday, he gave me thirteen thousand dollars in stocks. I still have them; they're now worth over three hundred grand. He told me it was an investment for the future. At the time, I just thought it was a weird gift. Now, I think it's the best thing to give a kid.

"Ava, come outside with me for a sec."

I walk her to the boot of my car. Opening it, I remove the little gift box. She recognises it straight away.

"No, I don't want it, Ash. Throw it out."

"Ava, trust me, you want to open this, sweetheart. If you don't, you're going to regret it, always wondering *what if.*"

"If Noah wanted to give me a Christmas gift, he should have been here to give it to me himself." She folds her arms over her chest.

"Ava, the kid might be entering into the special forces, but he wouldn't have survived ten minutes here trying to be your boyfriend." I smirk at her. I don't know what it was, but there was something about the way he looked at her before he left, like it physically pained him, that makes me root for the kid. It'd be different if he were around. It's easier to like someone when they're not in your proximity.

"Ash, I can't open it."

"Yes, you can. Here, I'll stay with you." She takes the small box, slowly removing the lid.

I can't help it. I peek inside. There's a letter and a small jewellery box—*there better not be a fucking ring in that box.* Ava takes the letter out and tucks it into the pocket of her shorts. She then removes the Tiffany-blue box, letting the outer packaging drop to the ground.

I can see the tears in her eyes as she pulls out a rose gold chain with a ballet slipper pendant on it. She turns the pendent over and tears fall down her face. Something is engraved on the little slipper, but I don't ask her what it means. I pull her into my arms and hug her tight.

"It's going to be all right, Ava. I know you don't believe that now, but you're young and you have your whole life ahead of you."

"I'm going to buy a cat. If this is what love feels like, then I don't want anything to do with it." She wipes at her face before turning her back to me. "Help me do this up, please."

I fasten the chain around her neck. If I knew this was going to make her so upset, I would have thrown the fucking thing out.

"Ava, tell me what I can do to fix this for you. I'll do anything." My heart is breaking for her.

"Nothing. There's nothing anyone can do. Just don't tell anyone, please, Ash."

"I promise I won't tell a soul, sweetheart. Come on, let's get back in there and get this whole Christmas thing over with."

"Yeah. We still have to make it through Boxing Day at the McKinley Ranch," she reminds me. Fuck, I forgot about that. Every Boxing Day, we all get up at the crack of dawn and fly down to the McKinleys' ranch in the Hunter Valley. For the past few years, I've made excuses as to why I can't make it, but I won't be missing it this year.

CHAPTER 24

Bree

*A*sh and I left Alex's yesterday afternoon. Ash made up some excuse about having work to do. I had a message from my dad not long after—to say they'd be at their place and that the plane was taking off at seven thirty a.m. It's now six thirty and I'm scrambling to get myself ready. The airport is a good forty-minute drive.

"Bree, come on. Hurry up. We're going to be late," Ash calls out for the millionth time.

"Okay, I'm coming. Hold on." He doesn't get it. We're going to a private airport—the same one we go to every Boxing Day morning. The press will be swarming the gates; my photo gets plastered all over the social news sections every year. I will not allow them to get another bad picture of me. I still cringe, remembering the one year I didn't bother with my appearance. I looked like a damn hot mess boarding that plane.

The paparazzi went wild with speculations: I had mental health issues, or a teenage pregnancy. I had been abducted and only just rescued.

Obviously, none of it was true, but that shit went around my school like wildfire.

Ever since, I always ensure I'm properly dressed and that my hair and makeup are flawless. I make my way out of the bedroom, my heels tapping on the tiled floor as I go. Ash turns around when he hears me coming.

"Holy shit, Breanna. Fuck. You look... wow... fuck." His mouth gapes open, then closes as his eyes roam up and down my body.

I'm wearing a red pencil skirt; it has a zipper that runs up the middle at the back. The fabric is tight and hugs my hips. I've paired it with a see-through, sheer, black lace blouse with a black lace bralette underneath. My black Valentinos finish off the outfit perfectly.

"I thought we were just boarding a plane? Am I missing something?" Ash asks.

"We *are* just boarding a plane, but that airport will

be swarming with paparazzi, Ash. It's the same every year." I look him up and down. He's wearing a pair of black distressed jeans and a white t-shirt. He looks absolutely scrumptious.

"Ah, I feel a little underdressed. Should I change?" he asks me.

"Nope, you're fine. They won't scrutinize every bit of your outfit. Only mine."

"You know, no one believes what they write in those magazines. You don't have anyone to impress, Bree."

"I know. It's just… if my photo is going to be plastered everywhere, I'd rather it be a good one." I shrug.

"It's impossible for you to have a bad photo. You look fucking great in anything you wear."

"Well, I'm glad you think so, because as soon as we get to the ranch, this outfit is coming off."

"I'll help peel it off you." He raises his eyebrows up and down.

***

We step out of the car at the airport, and the flashes immediately start. My name is called out over and over again. I turn and wave, smiling politely as I let them get their pictures. I watch as my mum and dad are waiting at the bottom of the jet's stairs. Ash looks over the crowd of paparazzi. I can't tell what he's thinking with his eyes hiding behind his aviators.

"Want to give them something great to write about, babe?" he asks me.

"Like what?" I turn and look at him. His arms go

around my waist; one hand comes up to my hair as his lips descend on mine. *Holy shit, talk about coming out publicly.*

I return his kiss, getting lost in the sensation. All the flashes. The name calling. It fades into the background, until I hear my dad clear his throat behind us. Shit, how did I forget my parents were there? I pull away from Ash, his face smiling down at me.

"Ready?" he asks.

"Yep."

We both turn towards my dad's stormy glare and walk up the steps of the jet. The rest of our family is already onboard. Everyone is silent as we make our way to the back of the plane. My parents file in behind me, and the only other empty seats are those opposite us. Great, now we have to spend the next forty minutes sitting under their scrutiny.

"Was that really necessary, Ash?" Dad asks.

"*I* thought so." Ash smiles. He has no sense of self-preservation.

"Sometimes I wonder if Bray landed one too many hits to that head of yours," Dad grumbles, referring to their training days. I can see he wants to say more, but he holds back.

"Well, I think it was sweet—*romantic* even. I wish someone would kiss me like no one else is watching," Mum adds, and I gag.

"Emmy," my dad says, right before taking my mum's face in his hands and kissing her just as she described.

"Gross, stop. Just stop. Okay, you've both made your point. I won't ever kiss anyone again," I plead.

"Don't make promises you can't keep, Bree," Ash whispers from beside me.

My parents finally tear themselves off each other and look at me. I should be used to this. My dad is always all over my mum.

"Ash, how long can you stay at the ranch?" Mum asks.

"Ah, I'm not sure." Ash turns to me. "How long are you planning on staying there, Bree?"

We haven't discussed this yet. I usually stay until the day before New Year's Eve, preferring to spend that night in the city.

"Ah, probably until New Year's Eve." I look for Ash's reaction.

"I can stay until then," Ash informs my mum.

"Right, next time, I'll just ask Breanna, shall I?" Mum laughs.

"Probably."

"Oh shit," I call out, suddenly remembering both of my grandmothers will be at the ranch waiting for us. I love my grans, but Granny McKinley is going to have a wedding planner on retainer the moment she finds out I'm dating Ash. She's been planning my wedding since the day I was born. *She told me so herself.*

"What's wrong?" All three pairs of eyes land on me.

"Granny McKinley is going to be there," I huff out.

"Oh, I love your grandmothers. They're the best," Ash says with a smile. He would say that;

they both dote on him whenever they see him. They feel like it's their job to be surrogate grandmothers to him because he doesn't have one of his own.

"Yeah, just wait. You're going to change your mind once she pulls out her wedding planner—which she's going to do the moment she finds out we're dating. Shit, she probably already knows." My eyes widen. "How about we go back to pretending we're just friends?" I suggest.

"Not happening," Ash grunts. "Your grandmother is not planning our wedding, Bree. Relax."

"She will be." My dad laughs.

"Well, I mean, it's not like I'm going to say no." Ash shrugs.

"Ah, wait, you're serious. Ash, let me know when you're going to pop the question. I want to help pick out her ring," Mum says.

"Mum, you literally shot him two nights ago, because you thought he knocked me up, and now you want to marry me off to him? What kind of dowry am I worth?"

"Breanna, I didn't shoot him. I shot *past* him. If I wanted to hit him, I would have. And he was fully prepared to raise a child who wasn't even his. That is a man in love."

"There was no child, for the love of God."

"But if there had been, Ash stepped up. Not many men would do that, Bree," Dad argues.

"Wait, you're on Team Ash now too? What

happened to you wanting me to try out dating girls before I settled for men?"

"Is that an option? Because I'll still one hundred percent support that," Dad says.

"No, it's not a fucking option." Ash's words come out harsh.

"Okay, well, if you have to end up with someone, Ash isn't the worst you could do." Dad shrugs.

***

Once we get to the ranch, I make a hasty escape up the staircase, heading straight for my bedroom while pulling Ash along behind me.

"Babe, if you wanted to get me all alone in your bedroom, you should have just said so." The cocky smirk that greets me when I look back at him sends butterflies to my stomach.

Surely, I'm too old to be getting butterflies still. Yet Ash manages to make me feel like I'm a horny, lovesick teenager way too easily.

"Shut up, I need to get changed. And we need to stay far away from Granny McKinley."

"I'm all for hearing about her grand wedding plans. The only thing I'm putting my foot down on is the cake. It has to be chocolate. I don't care about anything else. Just the cake." I shake my head at him. There isn't going to be any cake *any time soon*.

The moment the bedroom door closes behind him, Ash spins me around and pins my back to the door. His head drops to the crook of my neck, his lips leaving feather-light kisses in a trail along my collarbone.

"Mmm, do you know how many times I thought of you doing exactly this? In this very room?" I ask as my fingers comb through his hair.

"Tell me… did you used to lie on that bed and touch yourself thinking of me? When you closed your eyes, did you imagine my hands were rubbing all over your body? My fingers entering that tight little pussy of yours?" His hands drag along to the waistband of my skirt. "This zip has been driving me crazy all day." My skirt falls to the floor.

He lifts his head and looks down at me as he undoes the buttons of my blouse. He releases one, then another. "There are too many buttons on this thing," he declares, right before his fingers grip the material and tug on each side. Buttons go flying around the room. Why was that so bloody hot?

Ash traces down my arms as he removes my blouse. I'm left standing in front of him in my black lace bra, matching panties, stockings, and garter belt.

"Fucking hell, if I had known this was hiding underneath that skirt, we never would have made it out of the house." He picks me up and throws me on the bed.

"Mmm, Ash, I need you. *Now.*" My legs wrap around his waist the moment his body comes down on top of mine, my heels digging into the back of his thighs.

"This is a big house and all, babe, but you really need to be quiet. I don't want to get shot while I'm naked and fucking the life out of you. Although, if I have to go, buried balls-deep inside you would be the ideal way."

"Ash, too much talking. Not enough doing," I demand, grinding my pussy up into the hardness of his cock.

My fingers squeeze between our bodies and I undo the fly of his jeans, freeing that beautiful cock of his. My hands tug up and down, his precum coating my fingers each time they reach the tip.

"Argh, fuck, Bree, even your tiny little hands feel like heaven on my cock." Ash pulls my panties to the side, then lines himself up with my entrance. "This is going to be quick, hard, and fucking fantastic," he warns, right before he slams into me in one hard thrust.

He bottoms out, his cock hitting parts of me only he has ever reached before. He repeats the action, then he pulls out. A whimper escapes my lips. I watch as he picks up two pillows from next to my head. "Lift up," he orders, tapping my hip. I do as he says, and he places the pillows underneath me.

My body's now angled with my pussy pointing directly up at him, and he thrusts forward as my eyes roll back in my head. "Fuck, Ash. Fuck," I yell, not caring who hears me. This angle, bloody hell. I thought he was reaching new heights before, but this? This is insane.

Ash's hand comes down to my throat before closing around like a vice. My eyes snap open at the same time my pussy clenches and gushes. "Shh, you need to be a good girl for me, Bree, and very quiet. Otherwise, we have to stop. Do you want me to stop, Bree?"

His hand squeezes tighter. I feel like he's actually asking if I want him to stop choking me, not if I want him to stop fucking me. My head shakes no. I can't explain it, but my body is alight in a way it has never been before. His cock relentlessly fucks my pussy, my legs dig into him, my mouth opens, and I scream inside my head as the orgasm of all orgasms washes over me. I feel his movements stiffen. He bites down on my shoulder as he groans out my name, his cum squirting against the walls of my pussy.

Ash releases my throat as he falls next to me on the bed. He reaches out and wraps his fingers around mine.

"That was good," I huff.

"Just good? I must be losing my touch. I'll try harder next time." His fingers tilt my head to face him, his eyes examining my neck.

"I'm not sure you could possibly go any harder."

"Challenge accepted." He smirks.

"Wasn't a challenge, Ash. I'm jumping in the shower. Go and keep our mothers from killing each other." I rise up and head for my bathroom. "Oh, and stay the hell away from Granny McKinley," I warn him before slipping through the door and locking it behind me—so he's not tempted to follow.

"You know, a lousy door lock will never keep me from getting to you, Bree," he calls out. I wait and listen as his footsteps fall away, and I hear the click of my bedroom door closing.

Taking a large lungful of air, I stare at my reflection in the mirror. What the hell is he doing to me? I barely recognise myself. I look happy. Content. Or maybe it's just how someone looks after they've been thoroughly fucked by Ash Williamson.

CHAPTER 25

"Ash, it's been so long. I'm so glad you're here." Granny McKinley approaches me with wide arms. I lean into her hug and kiss her cheek.

"How are you, Granny McKinley?" I ask.

"Not getting any younger." She smiles.

I see Josh walk into the room, spot his mother, and walk straight back out—his eyes clearly telling me: *it's every man for himself.*

"Well, you don't look a day over forty." I wink at

her. I've always loved the attention Bree's grandmothers lavish on me.

"And you're as charming as ever. Come and sit. I want to run through a few things with you." I don't have any other option but to follow her to the sitting area. She pulls a big white book off the coffee table and holds it on her lap. "Tell me, what are your intentions with my granddaughter, Ash?" She cuts right to the chase.

"I intend to love her to the best of my ability," I tell her honestly.

"Good. Now, I've been planning this day ever since she was born. I know your family has a habit of running off and eloping, but that's not happening for Breanna. We are having her dream wedding. And thankfully, you'll be the groom. For a while there, I never thought you'd pull yourself out of your own ass and make a move."

I'm shocked speechless. I don't even know what to say to that. "Ah, I don't... I mean, Bree and I have only been dating a few weeks, Granny."

"But you've been in love with each other for forever, so let's start with the venue. I was thinking a garden wedding. Breanna's not really one for churches." She looks at me expectantly.

"Honestly, when we do get married, I'll do whatever Bree wants. As long as the cakes are chocolate and she's saying I do, I don't care about any of the other details."

"Well, that's great. But can we negotiate on the chocolate cake?" she asks.

"Nope, non-negotiable," I say. "Sorry, Granny, I think I hear my mum calling for me. Excuse me."

I rush out of the room like my ass is on fire. Damn, she's good. I thought Bree and her parents were over-reacting about the whole wedding thing. Turns out, they know exactly what they're talking about.

My escape is short-lived when I run into Emily. "Ash, just the man I was looking for. Follow me." She turns on her heel and walks down a hallway. This house is a fucking maze of corridors and rooms. How anyone remembers where they're going, I have no idea. I always manage to get myself lost.

"Ah, Emily, where are we going?" I ask.

"You'll see." As soon as she opens the door, I hesitate. She's leading me into a damn indoor shooting range. "Come in and shut the door."

I swallow. I'd rather Josh be in here than Emily. I do what she says anyway, and close the door behind me.

"You need to learn how to shoot better, and you need to start carrying a weapon at all times… if you're going to be hanging around Bree. Did you know she's ditched her bodyguards every time she's with you?"

"Bree has bodyguards?" I ask, like an idiot. Of course she does.

"She's always had bodyguards. Being a McKinley comes with a lot of risk, Ash. People will do horrible things to hurt Josh or extort money from him. It's no secret. And Breanna happens to be his biggest weakness."

"I—fuck, is she in danger?" My heart races, and I

want nothing more than to run upstairs and handcuff her to me, never letting her out of my fucking sight.

"We're always in danger; we always have to be prepared. She's safe inside this house. You can relax."

"Well, that would be easier… had you not just told me the one thing I love the most in this world is in danger of being fucking kidnapped." The moment the words leave my mouth, I know I was too harsh. "I'm sorry. I shouldn't have spoken to you like that."

"Yes, you should have. You care; it shows in everything you do for her. Now, let's start your first lesson."

***

I'm exhausted by the time I leave Emily and find Bree on the veranda. She's sitting on a bench swing, looking over at the paddocks.

"Where have you been?" she asks as I sit next to her. I pull her against me, wrapping my arm around her shoulder, and I fucking love how she instantly rests her head on me. Like we've always done this. Maybe she's right. Maybe we were lovers in every past life. It's always so comfortable with her.

"Your mother thought I needed to know how to shoot a gun." I smile at her.

"Oh, God, she didn't?" Bree cringes. "I'm so sorry, Ash. I'll talk to her and tell her to pull back her brand of insane."

"Don't. She's just worried about your safety. Why didn't you tell me you're at risk of being kidnapped? Or worse?"

"It's not as bad as they make out. I don't want you to

worry. I also don't want you to decide that being with me is too much effort."

"Babe, being with you is the best thing I'll ever do. Don't hide shit from me. Now, tell me about these bodyguards you keep ditching," I ask her.

"Please, I don't ditch them. They're far too scared of my dad to ever let me out of their sight. I just make sure no one notices them. And that only so much is reported back to my parents. It's a balance of having them fear for their jobs... and their lives." I shrug.

"I'm not a fan of the thought of something happening to you." I hold her tighter and kiss the top of her head.

"Don't worry, I'm much tougher than I look." She smiles.

"Yeah, you are." I stare out over the paddocks filled with horses.

"Which one of these is yours?"

"That black one—that's Hunter. He's too old for me to ride now, but he's still my favourite." She points at a huge fucking beast of a horse.

"Okay, let's get this party started!" Hope yells out as she comes through the back door with a tray of drinks. She's closely followed by Axel, Dominic, Ava, Lily and Alex. I didn't expect to see Lily and Alex—guess he's a goner if he's following Lil out here.

"Yes, let's. Come on, Ash. Try to keep up." Bree laughs as she catches up with Hope; they're making their way to the treehouse. Holy shit, I remember when we were teenagers, the twins and I would hide out in there to get away from the younger kids.

"You do know it's only eleven in the morning, don't you, Hope?" I yell after them.

"It's five o'clock somewhere, Ash. Pull the stick out of your ass, and loosen up for once in your life," Hope yells back.

"Hope, Ash is plenty of fun. Leave him alone. It's not his fault he's so much older than us," Bree says for everyone to hear.

"Ah, why am I being called out as old? Fucking Alex here is older than me." I don't duck Lily's punch quick enough. She gets me right on my jaw.

"Fucking hell, Lil, what the hell was that for?"

"Don't call my boyfriend old, Ash. At least he knows how to have fun. Want me to tell you about the fun we had in the shower this morning?" She smirks.

"Not if you want him to keep breathing." I stare back at her.

"Okay, truce," she calls, holding her hands up in surrender.

The thing about these twins though: they play dirty. And they're always on each other's team—*like they can telepathically communicate.* Hope turns around. "You know, Ash, last night I snuck out and met up with Chase. The things that guy can do with his tongue…" She lets her sentence trail off, and I have my phone out, dialling Chase's number. He picks up straight away.

"Ash, what can I do for you? You do know it's Boxing Day, don't ya?"

249

"What the fuck did you do with my cousin?"

"Which one?" the fucker asks.

"What do you mean *which one*? Fucking Hope, asshole, what did you do?" I yell into the receiver. Lily and Hope are both laughing their asses off. I look to Bree, who is offering the twins her McKinley death stare.

"I haven't seen Hope for a few days. Why? What happened? Is she okay?" The concern in his voice has me faltering momentarily.

"Nothing. I gotta go." I hang up and glare at Hope.

"Sorry, did I forget to mention that after he did that thing with his tongue, I woke up horny as hell. That was one realistic dream. I wonder if the real thing will be just as good."

"I'm going to fucking kill you," I growl as I stalk towards her.

Alex goes to step in front of me, but Lily pulls him back. "Don't worry, he won't really hurt her. We're his favourite cousins."

"No, *you're* my favourite, Lil. I just tolerate Hope as an extension of you," I tell her as I storm past and catch up with her sister. Picking Hope up from around her waist, I plop her to the ground. Just when I think I've got the drop on her, she somehow ends up with her legs wrapped around my neck. She's got a tight fucking grip too. Uncle Bray definitely taught these girls skills he never bothered to teach me.

I'm covered in sticky alcohol (from the tray of drinks that went down with Hope) and rolling around on the grass, trying to get out of Hope's death grip. Then I remember she's fucking ticklish as shit. I rip the sandal off her foot. Locking her ankle, I run my finger-tips around in light circles. She immediately loosens her hold and tries to scurry out of reach.

"Ah, Ash, stop! Okay, you win! You win!" she pants as she tries to crawl away from me. I release her and stand, lowering a hand to help her to her feet.

"Someone needs to go and get more drinks. Not it!" Bree smiles, but it falls when I rip the soaking wet shirt over my head.

"Ah, Ash, why don't you go and get more drinks while you put some more clothes on?"

"I'm not getting more drinks. Ava, go fetch the drinks." I wrap an arm around Bree's shoulder and lead her to the tree house. It's been fucking years since I've been up in this old thing.

"Why me?" Ava whines.

"Because if you don't, I'm telling Dad about the party you threw at my place last weekend."

Ava doesn't bother arguing. Instead, she drags Dom back to the house with her.

Sitting down in the tree house, I pull Bree onto my lap. I bury my face in her neck, and the smell of rasp-berries assaults me.

"Okay, ew, Ash. Stop. That shit is just weird," Lily complains, sitting across from me.

"You know where the door is if you don't want to watch, Lil." I shrug.

"Really, that's how you want to play it? Fine." Lily

stands. "Alex, how opposed are you to PDA?" she asks as she straddles the guy right fucking in front of me.

"With you? Not at all. But if anyone sees those parts of your body meant only for me, I'll fucking rip their eyes out. Cousin or not." He glares at me over her shoulder. "Breanna, those pigs of yours eat eyeballs, don't they?" Alex asks.

"They do." Bree nods with a smile.

"Alex, shut up and kiss me like it's the last time you'll ever get to." Lily wraps her legs around him. I don't look. I turn around and stare at Bree. It's not like it's a hardship to look at her. But then, Lily amps up her little display, moaning and groaning, and I can't fucking take it.

"Okay, stop. That's it. I'm out of here." I get up and climb down from the tree house. I wait at the bottom, expecting Breanna to follow after me. Only... she doesn't. I hear her and Lily laughing—guess she's not coming.

I pass Ava and Dom on the way back to the house and swipe a beer. They're carrying an insane amount of alcohol. "Ava, I'll be checking on you in a bit. Don't drink too much."

"Yes, Dad!" She smiles at me—that innocent *butter wouldn't melt* smile. But I know her better than that. I'll be holding her hair back for her by the end of the night.

I find my dad and Uncle Bray on the deck. Dad hands me a beer.

"Thanks." I sit down on one of the chairs across

from them. They both stare at me. After a few minutes under their scrutiny, I cave.

"What?" I ask, bringing the bottle to my mouth.

"So, Breanna, huh? How long has this been going on? And that girl is like a niece to me. If you're not planning on marrying her, you best be disappearing real quick before I have to hurt you," Uncle Bray says.

"I'm pretty fond of Breanna myself. If you make her cry, I'll make you cry," Dad adds.

"Uh, hold up a fucking minute. You're my family. You're *my* father, yet you're placing her above me?" I shove my hand to my chest.

"No, I'd never put anyone above you, Ash—well, maybe Ava. But I won't stand by and see that girl hurt by you either."

"And here I was, thinking I was the fucking favourite child my whole life."

"You were my fav for three years… until the twins came along." Uncle Bray laughs.

"You do realise that one of your little princesses is in that tree house right now, getting hot and heavy with a mobster, don't you?" I smirk.

"Yeah, but better a mobster than her cousin."

"Breanna is not my fucking cousin. A cousin's cousin does not make her my cousin."

"Maybe not by blood, but you two grew up together, *like cousins*," Dad points out.

"*Like* cousins, but we're not fucking cousins." I shiver at the thought.

"How long have you been holding a torch for Bree?" Uncle Bray asks.

"Longer than I should have been," I answer. I'm not about to admit to lusting after a minor.

"And how long has this little love affair of yours been going on?" Josh chimes in, walking out from God only knows where.

"Fifteen days, three hours, and seven seconds," I answer, looking at my watch. "And for the record, I'm not the one who wanted to hide this. I was respecting her wishes."

"Like you fucking should," Josh grunts.

"You know there's a mobster in your daughter's treehouse. They're all in there, getting shit-faced right now. Why am I the one being grilled?"

"The mobster isn't dating *my* daughter." Josh shrugs.

"Or mine," Dad agrees.

"Well, mine happens to be in love with the fucking mobster, so what am I meant to do about that? Tell me, Josh, what would you do if you didn't approve of who Breanna was in love with?" Uncle Bray stares straight at me.

"I'd find a way to make the guy have a terrible accident. Faulty breaks. An unfortunate fall off a skyscraper... Who knows? The possibilities are endless."

"Well, I guess it's a good thing you like me more than you want to admit. Also, you'd never hurt Bree like that," I say with confidence.

"Maybe not."

"I should have stayed in the tree house," I grumble. It would have been much better than sitting around here with these three.

"Where's Uncle Dean?" He's usually on Team Ash. I could use someone on my side.

"Right here. I've got a bone to pick with you too," he grunts as he sits next to me. "My niece? Really, Ash, there weren't any other women out there?"

"Great, not you too. You know what? You can disapprove all you like. It's not going to change a damn thing. I will be marrying her. And I'll be the one growing old and grey with her, so you might as well get used to the idea of *Brash* because it's sticking." I chug the remainder of the beer.

"Brash?" Josh asks.

"Bree and Ash: Brash." I smirk.

"Fucking hell, you spent way too much time with this idiot as a kid," Dean mumbles, pointing at Uncle Bray.

CHAPTER 26

Bree

"Babe, we've got thirty minutes before we need to be at the club." Ash stands in the doorway of the bathroom. He's looking extra fine tonight, wearing a dark-navy suit that fits like a glove. His hair is a little lighter, his skin a little more tanned, after spending the last few days out in the sun on my family's ranch.

"Well, maybe we shouldn't have stopped on the way back here those couple of times. If we arrived earlier, I would have been ready earlier." My teeth sink into my bottom lip as I recall the reasons we stopped.

The first time was because Ash was thirsty, and not for the liquid you get from 7-Eleven. No, he had a craving for the kind of juice that's only found between my legs—his words, not mine.

The second time was because I apparently gave him *the look*. According to Ash, I have this look I get when I'm horny as hell, and he won't have his girlfriend left unsatisfied. I didn't argue with him, because he was right. *I was horny as hell.* But watching him drive... having his fingers trail up and down my bare thigh... Well, a girl can only take so much.

The third time he pulled over into a deserted rest stop, he said it was to stretch his legs, which he did... as he stood behind me while I was sprawled out on the hood of the car. If every road trip is like this one, I'm buying a bloody caravan. Maybe the Grey Nomads know something the rest of us don't.

"Babe, all those stops were necessary. Besides, I never once heard you complain." He smirks, so sure of himself.

I'm about to reply when a ringing echoes through the apartment.

"What the hell is that?" I ask, never having heard that sound before.

"It's the doorman. Are you expecting anyone?"

"No, everyone we know has the access code, Ash."

I continue curling my hair while I let Ash deal with the doorman. Ash doesn't leave the bathroom. He just presses a button on the wall. I never even noticed the intercom before.

"Hello."

"Hi, Mr. Williamson, I'm terribly sorry to disturb you, but you have a… uh… package down here."

"Just leave it to the side. I'll pick it up tomorrow," Ash replies.

"Well, you see, this isn't the kind of package I can just throw to the side, Mr. Williamson. I really do need you to come downstairs. Or it might be better if I just bring it to you. I'll be up in a jiffy."

The line cuts out and Ash meets my reflection in the mirror. "Is your doorman always so… unusual?" I ask him.

"No, never. Guess I'll go meet him." Ash turns to leave.

"Wait for me. I need to see whatever it is that has the old man in such a tizzy." I put my curler down, not caring that my hair is only half done up. I'm intrigued to see this package. *It better not be a finger, or a head, or something gross. I don't have the stomach for that shit right now.*

"Your imagination is crazy, Bree. It's not a body part," Ash says, laughing.

I didn't realise I said that out loud. We make it to the foyer just as the doors open and the doorman steps forward, pushing a stroller. Is it "bring your grandkids to work" day?

"I'm sorry, Mr. Williamson, but the lady said to

make sure I personally delivered her to you," the doorman says.

"Delivered what?" Ash asks.

"The baby." He nods to the stroller.

"Excuse me?" Ash asks.

"A baby?" I gasp. A baby... Some crazy ass just delivered a baby to Ash.

"Here, this is everything she said to give you." He passes Ash a yellow envelope. I watch as Ash opens it, pulling out a handwritten letter. His hands begin to shake. His face goes pale.

"Is this some kind of joke?" Ash's voice is harsh as he glares at the doorman.

"No, sir." The man steps back into the lift and presses the button, leaving the stroller—and the baby—in the foyer.

I snatch the letter from Ash as he stands there, staring into the stroller.

Dear Ash,

I'm sorry you had to find out this way. This isn't how a father should meet his daughter for the first time.

I thought I could do it. I really thought I could do it all myself and not have to involve you. Turns out, I couldn't. I really tried to love her, but I can't. I don't. When I look at her, I hate her. A mother isn't meant to hate her baby. A mother isn't meant to have visions of drowning her baby.

She's going to be better off with you. You'll be able to love her. And if you can't, you've got family who can help.

In this envelope, you'll find everything you need. I had an attorney do the paperwork. It's legit. I've signed over all of my parental rights.

I named her Faith, because at the time, I thought she would give me the faith I needed to be a mother. You can change it, but her legal name is Faith Lila Williamson. She's four weeks old.

Please take care of her, Ash. She should have at least one parent who loves her unconditionally. Who will protect her from the world.

TAKE CARE,

Hayley

"WHAT THE FUCK? ASH?" I look up, and he's still staring into the stroller. "What do we do?" I ask him.

"I don't know," he says quietly, without looking at me. At that moment, the baby cries out.

"Shit, Ash, we need to call someone. Your mum... we should call your mum. Or mine," I suggest, panic settling in more and more as the cries get louder.

Ash leans in and picks up the baby. Like he's done it a thousand times before, he cradles her to his chest and she instantly stops crying. *Yeah, he has that effect on girls,* I think to myself.

Holy shit, if this is legit, Ash is a father. Ash has a newborn baby. I can't even imagine what's going through his head right now. I want to help. I just don't have the faintest idea what to do.

"Shhh, it's going to be okay," he hums to the little girl in his arms. "Can you find my phone, Bree? I think I should call my mum."

"Ah, yeah, sure. Here, just use mine." I hand him my phone. "Do you want me to hold her while you call?" I offer.

"No, I got it," he grunts at me, as he walks through to the living room and sits on the couch. I follow, sitting opposite him. I wish I knew what to do. How to help him. Why the fuck don't I know what to do? I've never felt more helpless than I do right now.

"Mum, it's Ash." His voice is hoarse, like he's barely holding his shit together. I don't hear what Alyssa is saying on the other end of the line, but I'm listening intently to Ash's side of the call.

"Mum, I need you and Dad to come to the penthouse. Now. Please."

"No, I'm okay. I just… I need you to come over." He pauses and looks down at the baby, at Faith, and then adds, "Can you bring a doctor too?"

"Thank you." He hangs up the phone and hands it back.

"You should go home, Breanna." He's still not looking at me.

"Yeah, and you should try not to be an ass, but here we are," I retort. If he thinks I'm leaving him here, right now, he's got serious fucking issues.

"This is my problem. I need to deal with it. I'm not bringing you into this mess. Go home, Bree."

"This is a baby, Ash. She's not a problem to *deal* with. She's a living, breathing person—and apparently one *you* helped make. Now, I'm going out to that foyer, then to your office to scan in that paperwork, before I have one of my solicitors go over it to make sure it's legit." I stand and look at him. "I expect, that by the time I finish and return, you've pulled your head out of your ass. I will not let you push me away."

I pivot on my heel without so much as a backwards glance. I shouldn't be so hard on him. But *fuck him* for trying to send me home. I may not be able to help him with his emotions right now, but these documents, having them checked out, that's something I more than know how to do.

CHAPTER 27

*J*ust breathe. Take even, calm breaths. This is not the time to freak out. I may be screaming *What the Fuck?!* inside my head over and over. But on the outside, I'm trying to maintain my composure. I'm holding the tiniest fucking thing in my hands… No, not a thing, a baby… apparently *my* baby.

People are meant to have nine months to get their heads around the idea they're going to be a parent. It's not meant to be dropped on you. Like: *Here you go. She's all yours.* What the fuck?! What kind of person drops off a helpless newborn to a doorman? Someone I fucked evidently. It's good to know my standards are so high.

I can hear Breanna in my office, pacing up and down, her heels clicking on the floor. She said something about sending copies of the papers to a solicitor. I'll let her do it, but I need to find a way to get her out of here. I'm barely holding it together myself. I don't have it in me to hold her together as well. It's selfish. I know. Also, there's a baby snuggling herself into my chest at the moment.

To say I'm in shock would be a fucking understatement. But who the fuck wouldn't be? I may be twenty-eight, and have more than enough money to raise a child, but the nine fucking months to prepare would have been really bloody handy. I shouldn't be having an internal panic attack the first time I meet my daughter.

Oh, fuck me, my daughter. I have a fucking daughter. I can just hear God laughing at me now. I know that Bree wants to make sure those papers are legit. And I know my parents will want a DNA test done, which I'll go along with. *For their benefit.* So they don't have to live with that doubt.

The thing is, I don't need any of that. The moment she started crying in that stroller, my heart stopped beating. I didn't hesitate to lean in and pick her up. I didn't hesitate to hold her to my chest, cradling her and trying to reassure both her *and myself* that it's going to be all right. Something clicked inside me. I know I should be more wary that this could all be a fucked-up scheme some cunt is trying to play, in order to extort money out of me. But when I look at her, at Faith, I know she's mine. I also know that I will do whatever I have to do to protect her.

I'm tempted to call a solicitor now, a fucking judge even, to make sure those documents are ironclad. I won't have some fucking bitch come back trying to lay claim to her. What kind of mother leaves their child? Leaves a four-week-old baby? She didn't even have the decency to tell me herself.

I may not have liked the situation, but I would have fucking helped her... taken care of them the best I could. How can she want this little girl to grow up without a mother? No child should have to grow up without a mother.

I think about my own mother. There is nothing that could replace her love, her guidance, and her nurturing throughout my life. How can I do that for this little girl? I don't know shit about girls. Okay, well, I know plenty, but nothing that's useful for raising one.

My phone vibrates on the coffee table. Fuck, Chase. I'm supposed to be at the club right now. Carefully leaning forward, so as not to jostle the baby who seems content to snuggle on me, I swipe the phone up and answer it.

"Yeah?"

"Where the fuck are you, man? This shit is insanely busy tonight," Chase yells over the music in the background.

"I can't make it. I need you to take over for me tonight."

"What do you mean you can't make it? This is your fucking club, Ash. People are expecting to see you. It's New Year's Eve."

"I said I can't fucking make it. Deal with it, Chase. Do what I fucking pay you to do," I yell through the phone. I know I'm taking my frustrations out on my best friend. I also know the minute I stop and hear the baby cry that I just fucked up.

"Shit." I hang up the phone.

Bree comes running out of the office, looking panicked. "What happened?" She reaches over, takes the baby from me, and starts walking around while bopping up and down.

"I—fuck… I can't do this. Five minutes, and I already made her cry." I run my hands through my hair.

"Ash, I get this is a lot right now. But you need to harden the fuck up. And calm the fuck down. You absolutely can do this. And you *will* do this." She walks out to the foyer and I watch her with an eagle eye.

I trust Breanna one hundred percent. I know that rationally, but I also know how emotionally unattached she can be. And right now, she has my four-week-old daughter in her arms. Why the fuck do I feel like I need to go over there and take that baby from her?

My heart hurts, looking at the two of them. I always pictured us having kids together. Not me having one show up like the fucking stork delivered it. She's too young for this. How can I expect her to stay with me now? How can I let her throw away her youth to be tied down to a single father?

I'm no longer the nightclub mogul, frequenting Australia's most eligible bachelors' lists. No, I'm now the guy who comes with a whole heap of extra fucking baggage. And it's the kind of baggage I'm not prepared to lump Breanna down with.

I watch as Bree comes back over carrying a big-ass bag. The baby is... *Faith. I need to start referring to her as Faith, not the baby. Even if it is just in my own damn head.* She's still crying. I stand and reach out for her. "Here, give her to me."

Bree squints her eyes at me. "Are you calmer? Because if you're not, she's going to know. And it's only going to upset her. I won't let you upset her, Ash."

What the fuck? "Breanna, she's my daughter. My responsibility. Give her to me."

"Fine, but keep your voice down," she says, reluctantly handing Faith over.

As soon as she's snuggled back into my arms, her tears subside, until she's no longer crying.

"Huh, guess you have the touch," Breanna says as she digs through the bag.

"What are you looking for?"

"Found it. Thank God the chick you knocked up wasn't completely stupid and left some formula in here," she says as she retrieves an empty bottle and a tin. Without a word, Breanna heads into the kitchen.

"How do you know how to do that?" I ask, watching

her read the instructions and go about making up a bottle.

"I grew up on a farm, Ash. Baby animals drink formula too."

I count the number of scoops she puts into the bottle, and when she turns to add water, I snatch the tin up and scan the label.

"Don't worry, the very expensive education my folks paid for gave me the ability to read. But if you'd prefer to do it yourself, here." She holds out the bottle as she's shaking it.

"I know you can read, Bree. Did it occur to you that I was reading the tin so I'd learn how to make a bottle myself?" I ask, although I was fully checking to make sure she did it right.

"Oh, well, no, it didn't. Come on."

I follow her out to the living room again and sit down next to her. "Here, I may have hand-fed countless baby animals, but never a baby human."

I grab the bottle from her. I remember taking turns feeding Ava and Axe when they were little. For once, I'm glad for the huge age gap between me and my siblings.

I position Faith in one arm and press the bottle to her mouth. She takes it in and starts sucking. And the breath, held unknowingly in the depths of my chest, releases. Breanna and I sit there, watching my little girl drink. In silence.

"What am I going to do, Bree?" I ask her.

"First, we're going to get a DNA test, not that you

need one. That baby is most certainly a Williamson. Then, we're going to make sure those papers she came with are legit. You don't want someone coming around in a few weeks, months, years, realising the mistake they've just made."

"Bree, this isn't a 'we' thing. It's a 'me' thing. I'm not going to hold you back with all of this baggage. You really should go. I'm sure my parents will be here soon."

"Ash, shut up. If you weren't holding a baby right now, I'd knock you the fuck out." Breanna's quiet growl has me looking up and meeting her eyes... *finally*. I have been avoiding them. I wasn't ready for the rejection and disappointment I was certain I'd see there.

"Everything is an 'us' thing now, Ash. You can try to tell me to leave. You can try to be an asshole and make me want to. But I'm not going anywhere. So, get used to it. Also, if you ever describe her as baggage again, I will knock you out. She's a part of you, which means she's perfect." Bree's eyes get glassy as she stares down and rubs her fingers along the top of Faith's head. "I don't understand how someone could just walk away from something so perfect."

"Me neither." The sound of the lift alerts me to my parents' arrival. "Fucking hell, how do I explain this?"

"It's going to be fine. Your parents are fucking awesome, Ash."

"Yeah, it's not so much mine I'm worried about," I tell her.

"Ash, why is there a—" My mum's words trail off as

she enters the living room, her eyes locked on the baby in my arms.

"Ash, what's going on? Please tell me you two didn't commit a kidnapping," Dad says, leading Mum further into the room with a hand on her back.

"Nope, she was left with the doorman about half an hour ago." I'm at a loss for words on how to explain this.

"It seems Ash had pretty low standards, prior to me of course. He knocked someone up. That someone just dropped Faith off here with a note and a heap of paperwork, claiming she *couldn't do it anymore.*"

Fuck, the way Breanna explains it makes it sound like I was careless. "It was one time, and the fucking condom broke. I have standards, Breanna."

"Oh, so you know who the mother of this child is?"

"I'm pretty sure her name was on those legal documents," I answer her, not having a clue off the top of my head.

"Did you call the doctor?" I ask my mum.

"Yeah, he should be here soon."

"Ash, how sure are you that this baby is yours?" Dad asks.

"Pretty sure."

"Okay, well, let's order a DNA test to be one hundred percent certain. Where are these papers that you're talking about?"

"Oh, I left them in the office. I sent them through to one of our solicitors to get them verified already," Breanna answers.

"Okay. Wait—you sent them to a McKinley solicitor?" Dad directs to Breanna.

"Yeah, why?"

Before he has time to answer, the lift rings out again. "That's why," Dad says, pointing to one very pissed off looking Josh.

"Josh, stop. You need to calm down." Emily chases behind him, holding his hand.

"Nope, not happening." Bree gets up and pushes her dad out of the living room. I don't watch where they go.

"Can I hold her?" Mum asks, sitting down next to me.

"Um, sure. She's just about finished this." I don't want to hand her over. I want to wrap her up and keep her in my arms.

"I've done this once or twice before, Ash. I think I'll manage." Mum smiles.

My eyes don't leave Faith as Mum settles with her. "This baby is one hundred percent a Williamson," Mum murmurs.

"We should wait for the DNA test before we go around declaring that," Dad argues.

"Zac, come here and hold her."

Dad follows mum's instructions and picks Faith up. Mum places the finished bottle on the table. I watch my parents fuss over the baby. This is all a bit surreal.

"What the fuck am I meant to do now?" I ask them.

"Ash, whatever you choose to do, you are not alone. We'll do anything we can to help." My dad pauses as he looks down at Faith. "Your mother and I can take her home with us if you want. We can watch her until you're more prepared."

I'm on my feet within seconds, taking her back from him. "I may not know what I'm doing, but she's just had one parent give up on her. I'm not about to make that two," I grunt at him.

"Good, we didn't raise you to walk out on family. But we're here to help. Whatever we have to do, we'll do it. Maybe you should move back home for a few weeks?"

That's not a bad idea. My parents know how to look after a baby. What the fuck do I know about any of it? And, as if to reinforce just how little I know, white liquid starts spewing from Faith's mouth like something out of *The Exorcist*.

"What the hell is wrong with her?" I hold her upright, the front of my shirt now covered in chucked-up baby milk. "Shit, did I do it wrong? Bree and I both read the instructions on the tin."

I look up to my mum, who digs through the bag and hands me a towel. "She's fine, Ash. Relax. It's very normal for babies to burp up a bit of milk after a feed."

"That wasn't just a bit. When did you say the doctor was going to be here?"

"Huh, you know what? I think you're going to be just fine at this dad thing, Ash," my dad says.

"No, I'm not. I've had her for not even an hour and she's sick already."

The intercom on the wall chimes, and I hear Bree

answer it from the other room. The doctor's here. *Thank fuck.*

Breanna returns to the room with the doctor (and her parents) trailing behind her. "What happened? What's wrong?" she asks me, coming to my side.

"I don't know. One minute, she was fine. The next, she's projectile vomiting her whole bottle up at me. Doc, you gotta do something. That can't be normal?" I look from Breanna to the doctor.

"Ash, good to see you again. And who do we have here?" he asks, looking at Faith.

"This is Faith. She's four weeks old—according to the paperwork we got. Please, you gotta make sure she's not sick? Fuck, did I make her sick?"

"Here, let me take her. Ash, calm the fuck down. Babies throw up all the time, don't they, doc? I mean, they must. But you should probably do a whole checkup anyway, just to be sure."

I let Bree take Faith; she sits on the couch with my daughter laid out on her lap. The doctor positions himself next to her and goes to pick Faith up.

"You can check her from here. I'm sure you don't need to hold her." Bree stares at the poor man.

"Ah, sure, Miss McKinley. I need you to take off her clothes for me."

"What? Why? You're not getting your grubby hands on her. Dad, call another doctor, one who doesn't want to see an infant naked." Bree looks past me, and to Josh, who is standing off to the side with a smirk on his face.

"Oh my God, it's déjà vu," Emily says, smacking Josh

across the chest. "Breanna, it's very normal for babies to be undressed when doctors need to examine them."

"That can't be right. I go to the doctor all the time and don't have to get undressed," Bree argues.

"Bree, trust me—it's normal. Do you want me to help?" my mum asks her.

Bree looks like she wants to say something, but she stops herself and stares up at me for guidance—*guidance I really fucking wish I had*. But I don't.

CHAPTER 28

Bree

What am I doing? How do I make sure Ash and I get through this? This isn't a small bump in the road. This is something that has just changed the whole trajectory of our lives, of our relationship.

I had to make a stand tonight. To my parents. And to Ash. It's funny… I never thought my dad and Ash would be on the same page. For some fucked-up reason, they are both trying to get me out of this penthouse, and away from Ash. How quickly they all forget that only days ago, when Ash thought I was pregnant by another man, he stood there and proclaimed it was his baby. My parents were literally pointing a gun at him, and he refused to back down. All to protect me and my reputation.

Do I want to be a parent right now? No, absolutely not. But I'm not a parent. Ash is. What does that make me? The girl dating a single dad? The stepmum? I have no idea, but I know that I'm not about to give up Ash for anything.

Something I had to reiterate to my parents over and over tonight. As soon as I saw them walk in, I knew they were pissed. Well, pissed is an understatement. They were vibrating with rage, both of them ranting about my youth, and how I still had years ahead of me before I should be tied down with a child.

The conversation I had with them plays on repeat and the guilt eats at me. I've never spoken to my parents like that, never even considered a future they weren't a part of.

"Breanna, don't be stupid. You're smarter than this. You're going to throw your whole life away for him. For a fucking idiot. God only knows how many other surprise babies he's got out there." My mum paces the length of Ash's office.

"That's not fair, and I'm not throwing my life away. Ash is my fucking life," I argue.

"Bree, you need to come home with us. We're leaving now. Let's go," Dad growls.

"Feel free to show yourselves out. I'm not going anywhere."

"You're coming with us! If I have to throw you over my shoulder and carry you out, I will."

"Try it." I shrug. I know he will. But I'm not relenting.

"Breanna, please. Just come home. Spend a few days away from him, and let your mind get some fucking clarity." Dad runs his fingers through his hair, his frustration over my defiance evident.

"I'm not leaving. But if you two don't stop acting like I'm a fucking teenager you get to make decisions for, you certainly can. No one's stopping you. You have two choices: either you get onboard with the fact that Ash and I are in this together. That I don't care it's not my baby, because if it's Ash's, I will love it just as much as I love him. Or, if you can't, then I don't see any reason why you should be here."

Dad stares at me. No, stares through to my soul is a better description. For minutes, neither of us look away. Until he finally lets out a huff.

"Do you really believe you'll be able to love this baby as if it were your own?" he asks quietly.

"Yes." I don't tell him that I already sense a connection with her. When I was holding her, I felt a fierce need to protect her, to wrap her up and keep her safe from every-thing in this world that could hurt her.

"Okay," Dad says.

"Okay?" Both mum and I look at Dad like he's grown another head. He never gives in this easily.

"It's not ideal. And it's not what I want for you. But I'll do my best not to slaughter the asshole." He smirks.

I look to my mum, who has stopped pacing and is just staring at me.

"Breanna, is he..." She pauses, taking a gulping breath before she continues. "He's good to you, right? You'd tell us if he wasn't treating you right... You would come to us if you needed help, wouldn't you?" Dad wraps his arms around Mum.

"Emmy, I can't believe I'm saying this, but it's Ash. We know him. He's not like that."

"Mum, I promise, if I were ever in a situation like that, I would come to you." I don't tell her that I'd be the one to cut heads off anyone who tried to lay a hand on me. I've heard about her past before she was with my dad. She was in a very abusive relationship, one that took her years to finally escape.

"Okay, well, let's go meet this grandchild of ours, Josh."

"Thank you. I love you guys," I say, hugging them both.

Snapping out of that memory, I shut off the hot water. The place is quiet; Alyssa and Zac are staying in the guest room. We have Faith asleep in her stroller in Ash's room. Ash had a shower before I did, so we didn't have to leave her alone.

After drying off and slipping one of Ash's shirts over my head, I walk out into the bedroom. Ash is laid out on the bed with Faith asleep on his bare chest. I stand there and watch the scene. He's going to be a great dad; *that* I'm sure of.

I crawl onto the bed next to him, my fingers reaching out to hold onto Faith's little hand.

Ash turns his head to face me, bringing my hand to

his mouth and kissing my palm. "You okay?" he asks me quietly.

"Mmhmm, you?"

"I don't know. I'm scared I'm screwing everything up. I'm scared I'm *going* to screw everything up."

"Me too." I glance down at the peacefully sleeping baby. "I just don't understand how someone could not want her. Look at her… she's… perfect," I whisper the only word that seems fitting.

"I'm pissed that she didn't come to me sooner. I know the doctor said that everything looks fine, but what if she's been neglected for the last four weeks? How do we know what really happened to her?"

"We won't know. We can get a second opinion? Take her to a different doctor if you want?" I offer. I didn't like that doctor anyway.

"Do you think we should?" he asks.

"I have no idea, but it can't hurt, right?"

"You know, I won't hold it against you if you wake up tomorrow and decide to leave. I fucking love you, Breanna, but I don't want to drag you down."

"You need to stop telling me to leave. I'm not leaving, Ash. I love you. I'm not sure what else I need to do to prove that to you."

"Nothing. You don't need to prove shit, Bree. I know you love me, but it's not just me anymore. The path I wanted for our lives did a complete one-eighty on me."

"Sometimes the best things are the ones that aren't planned," I tell him.

"If we do this together, do you think you will be able to learn to love her, like you do me?"

Ash's words make my head spin. I know he gets me better than anyone, but that question has me realizing just how much better. I was surprised when I started developing feelings for Ash. At the time, I didn't know what was happening. But I was young. I'm older now, yet my feelings for him still have a way of overwhelming me to the point that I doubt my own sanity.

"I think I already might, Ash. I don't know how to explain it. It's different from how I love you." I think for a moment, trying to come up with a way to describe it, a way for him to understand. "Have you had something you wanted to hide away? Keep in a safe, so that no one else could get to it? Something you never wanted hurt, or broken?"

"Yes. But I've been told keeping women locked in a tower isn't very twenty-first century." The smirk he delivers sends shivers straight through me.

"Well, that's what it's like. When I look at her, I want to keep her safe. I don't want other people to touch her."

"You're an only child, Bree. You don't like people touching anything you've laid claim to." Ash laughs, the rumble of his chest momentarily stirring Faith, before her little body settles into place again.

"Well, it's not my fault my parents got it perfect on the first go," I counter.

"They really did create the perfect person." Ash

holds his arm out. "Come here. There's more than enough room on me for both of you."

I rest my head on his shoulder, my hand on Faith's back.

***

I jolt straight up when a piercing cry cuts through my sleep. The spot next to me is empty. Jumping out of bed, I follow the distraught sound. I find Ash in the kitchen, looking stressed as fuck as he walks around the space with Faith.

"What happened?" I ask, rushing over to him and holding my hands out to take Faith. He lets me pick her up without a fight.

"I don't know. She woke up crying about twenty minutes ago and hasn't stopped. What the hell's wrong with her?"

"Shhh, it's okay." I don't know if I'm trying to calm Faith, myself, or Ash at this point. "Is she hungry?" I ask.

"I've tried that. She finished a whole bottle. Should I give her another one?"

"No, I don't think so." I take a big breath in, trying to steady my nerves. Then it hits me. "Um, Ash, have you changed her?"

"What? No, why would I change her?" he asks, bemused.

"Grab the nappy bag. Bring it into the bedroom." I walk back to the room and lay Faith on the bed.

"Here you go," Ash says, placing the bag down beside her.

"Ah, nope, I don't know how to do this. You do it. I don't want to hurt her," I say. I might know how to make a formula bottle, from raising lots of baby animals, but changing nappies? Nope, I can't do that.

"I don't know how to do it either. Fuck, what do we do?" he asks, looking down at Faith, who is still crying on the bed. He bends down and picks her back up.

"Ash?" Alyssa knocks on the open door. Thank God. I forgot his parents were here.

"Perfect timing, Mum. She needs to be changed." Ash hands the disgruntled infant to Alyssa.

"Nice try, Ash. You're doing this. Come on, you have to learn some time." Alyssa laughs, before turning to me. "You okay, Bree?"

I must look like a mess. I nod my head yes. "I don't like her crying. She shouldn't be this upset, right?"

"It's perfectly normal. She's just letting you know she's not happy about something."

Alyssa lays Faith back on the bed. "Ash, come here. Unclip the buttons."

I watch as Ash follows his mother's instructions.

"Why are there so many bloody clips on this thing?" he grumbles.

"You'll get used to it," Alyssa says.

"Okay, what's next?"

I continue to watch, intent on learning along with Ash, as he follows the process.

"What the hell? This shit is not normal. How can something so tiny and fucking precious do this?" Ash grunts, as he opens her nappy to find it filled.

"Why is it green?" I ask.

"Trust me, it's normal. It will change over time, as she gets older. Now, grab the wipes."

I'm surprised how easily Ash manages to change Faith. As soon as she's dressed again, he picks her up and hands her to me. I go and sit at the top of the bed with her, rubbing little circles on her back and humming quietly.

"Okay, next time, I'll help you do it if you want, Bree," Alyssa says.

"Uh, sure. Thank you." Maybe I need to hit up a bookshop. There are books on parenting, and I'll read every single one of them.

Alyssa leaves and we end up lying back in bed. Faith is now fast asleep on my chest.

"It's wrong that I'm jealous of her right now," Ash comments.

"What?" I ask, confused.

"She's sprawled out on your tits, babe. I'd love to be sprawled out on them."

"That's perverted, even for you, Ash." I smile.

"Not my fault your tits are fucking perfect."

"Thanks." I'll take the compliment.

"We should probably put her in her stroller and try to get some sleep," Ash suggests.

"We should, but I don't think I want to let go of her yet."

"Okay, let's just lie here a little longer together."

CHAPTER 29

"*A*sh, wake your ass up. What the fuck is going on?" Chase's voice screams from my hallway. I jump out of bed with the intent of shutting his loud ass up before he disturbs Faith, who is finally sleeping peacefully on Bree's chest.

Correction: *was* sleeping peacefully. Faith starts crying. I pick her up out of Bree's hold. Maybe at least one of us can manage to sleep through Chase's rude awakening.

"Ash, can I cut his tongue out?" Bree mumbles as she rolls to her side, keeping her eyes closed.

"Unfortunately not, babe. Go back to sleep. I'll get rid of him." I walk out of the bedroom, in search of a best mate who's quickly losing that status. I find him in the living room with my dad.

"Chase, do you have any idea what fucking time it is? People are fucking sleeping. My wife is fucking sleeping. And you coming in here, yelling the place down, just woke her up," Dad seethes, looking as if he is barely containing himself.

"Sorry, Mr. Williamson. I obviously had no idea you were here." Chase holds his hands up in front of him, only to drop them—along with his jaw—when I walk into the room with Faith. She's already settled and back to sleep in my arms.

"What the fuck is that?" Chase whispers harshly, pointing towards me.

"This is the baby you just fucking woke up with all your screaming. What the fuck are you doing here?" I ask him.

"I can see it's a baby, but why do you have it? Whose is it?"

"This is Faith. She's mine." I smile.

"Here, let me take her for a bit," Dad offers, holding his arms out.

I hand Faith over and watch my dad walk back down the hallway with her. I don't turn around to face Chase until I can no longer see them. As soon as I do, he starts in with the questions I'm too fucking tired to answer.

"What do you mean *she's yours*? Who the fuck did you knock up? Oh shit, does Bree know about this? Fuck, what the hell, Ash? Why didn't you call me?"

I wait for him to finish before I raise an eyebrow. "I wasn't aware we were the *braiding each other's hair* kind of friends. I don't know who I knocked up, and frankly, I don't care. Faith was dropped off to the fucking doorman with a heap of paperwork and shit." I shrug, like I'm totally okay with tonight's events. When really, I'm fucking tired, emotionally drained, and fucking terrified that I'm in over my head.

"Are you sure it's yours?"

"She has a name, asshole. She's not an *it*. And I'm certain. I've already sent off a DNA test tonight with the doctor. Should have the results in a couple of days."

"Okay, what about the paperwork. Where is it?" Gone is the class-clown persona Chase likes to adopt ninety-nine percent of the time. And in its place is the serious, problem-solving, analytical mask he possesses on the rare occasion. I guess a surprise baby dropping on my doorstep warrants the sudden shift.

"In the study. Come on." I take him into my study and shut the door. "Want a drink?" I offer.

"It's five in the morning, Ash," he remarks.

"Like that's ever stopped you before?" I pour two glasses of whiskey from the bar.

"Well, I wasn't a responsible uncle before." He laughs.

"Shut up, idiot, and drink." Handing him one of the glasses, I down the other before making my way to the desk, where—in true Bree form—the papers have been left scattered everywhere.

"Did a hurricane come through your office?" Chase laughs.

"Yeah, she goes by the name of Breanna." I chuckle.

"She's here? And you're still alive after knocking up some random? Bloody hell, mate... Wait, is she sick?"

"No, idiot. Shut up." I pick up the first piece of paper I see, which is a birth certificate. I scan over the document.

Baby's name: *Faith Lila Williamson*
Mother's name*: Hayley Grace Hudson*
Father's name*: Ash Williamson*

The document looks legitimate. If it is a fake, it's a bloody good one. Then again, anyone can add a parent's name on the birth forms. I'm trying to pull an image of Hayley from my memory. I can barely picture her. I know I followed up around six weeks after that night the condom broke. She assured me she was not pregnant. She fucking lied right to my face. I never saw her again after that.

I hand the birth certificate to Chase. He peruses it before pulling his phone out. "What are you doing?" I ask him.

"Looking up your baby mumma. I need to know what kind of genes my niece inherited," he says, so seriously.

"She's not my baby mumma, fuckface. She's a

fucking lowlife scum who abandoned my four-week-old daughter. What the fuck do you need to look her up for?"

"So I know how big of a gun I need to invest in." He smirks. "You do realise she's a girl. That means boyfriends and shit."

"She's a newborn, Chase. Shut the fuck up." I sound like a broken record: Chase says something stupid, and I tell him to shut up. Over and over again.

"I know, but you can never be too prepared. Got it. This her?" He turns the phone around with a Facebook profile displayed on the screen. The woman in the photo looks happy. Normal. What the hell drove her to abandon her baby? My baby.

"Yes, that's her."

"Fuck, we're going to need a whole army for that little girl. This woman's smokin', bro. You couldn't have knocked up an ugly chick?"

I don't bother answering his idiotic question. Instead, I focus on the next piece of paper—some kind of form from a solicitor's office. Again, it looks authentic. I skim through the words, and the only ones that stand out are *give up all parental rights,* followed by my name listed as the sole custodian.

"You know this kind of paperwork takes time to process and organise. This isn't a spur of the moment decision a young mother who's had a bad night makes. She's put a lot of thought into this."

"Gee, I'm sure that's going to be comforting to Faith when she's older, and I have to explain to her how her

IGNITED BY HIM

birth mother is MIA, because she left her with the fucking doorman."

"That's not what I'm saying. It doesn't make sense. Why not just come to you and ask for help? It's no secret you're loaded, mate. Anyone who got knocked up by you would be set for life with child support payments. What is it that she wants out of this?"

"Or maybe she's just a shitty fucking human being and doesn't want to be a mother?" I suggest.

"Or... maybe she's got that postnatal depression or something, and will one day come to her senses and regret what she's done." Breanna's voice makes my head snap up. My eyes scan over her body. She's standing there in one of my t-shirts. I know she's naked under that shirt. I can see her nipples through the cotton. My eyes flick to Chase, who is also staring at her.

Walking around my desk, I slap him on the back of his head. "Stop fucking looking at her," I growl. "Show yourself out, Chase. I'm going back to bed." I stalk towards Breanna, with sleep being the last thing on my fucking mind.

"Yeah, sure you are. I'll see you later today," Chase says to my back.

I take hold of Breanna's hand and drag her towards my bedroom. I stop at the guest room and peek inside to see my mum and dad looking down at Faith, who is sleeping in the middle of the bed between them. I should bring her with us. A little bit of guilt eats at me.

"Do you want me to take her?" I ask quietly, not wanting to disturb her.

My dad looks up and shakes his head no. "No, go shower and shit. It's going to be a long day."

"Okay, thanks." I linger in the doorway before continuing to my bedroom. Pulling a very quiet Breanna into the bathroom with me, I switch the shower on and let steam fill the room.

I turn to Breanna, who has yet to utter a word; she's silently watching me while biting her lip. I walk her backwards, until her heels hit the wall, and cage her in, my hands landing on the tile above each side of her head. "What's wrong?"

"Nothing."

"What's wrong?" I ask again. I know something is on her mind.

"What if she comes back, Ash? Faith's mother... What if she changes her mind? What if... I mean, would you want to be with her?"

I'm stunned by her question. "Fuck no. Breanna, there is no one else I want to be with. You are the only one." I lean in to claim her lips, my tongue pushing into her mouth.

Her hands press into my chest. "You told me to leave *more than once* last night, Ash. I'm sorry if I find it a little hard to believe you right now."

Breanna is never this unsure, never this vulnerable. The fact that I've caused this doubt in her mind fucking shatters me.

"I'm sorry if I made you question how much I

fucking love you. I love you more than life itself, Bree. I know I'm a selfish fucking asshole, but I can't do this without you. You should go; you should run for the fucking hills. But honestly, I'd probably only chase you down if you did. I need you."

"You have me," she says, wrapping her arms around my neck.

"I don't deserve you. I'm messed up, Breanna. I don't know how to process all of this… what I'm meant to do…"

"Neither do I, but we can figure it out together."

"Thank you," I whisper before claiming her lips again. My hands drop to her ass, picking her up. Her legs wrap around my waist, and I push her back into the wall as I grind my hard cock into her bare pussy.

"Oh, God, Ash, maybe we shouldn't do this right now. Your parents are in the next room."

"Then I guess you should be quiet. Because we *are* doing this. My cock is fucking hard as stone, and your pussy is dripping wet. That's a winning combination if I ever saw one."

"Well, of course I'm wet. I'm wrapped around you. And, well, you're fucking hot. In case you haven't noticed," she mumbles.

"Huh, and here I was, thinking you liked me for my personality." With one hand, I pull my sweatpants down, freeing my cock.

"Eh, your personality could use a little work. But this body of yours? It's like God forgot to add flaws when he made you." Her hands run down my back, her nails lightly making their mark.

I line my cock with her entrance. "Hold on, babe. This is going to be a rough and fast ride."

I slam into her. Her walls convulse around me instantly, her hands dig into my back, and her teeth sink into my shoulder as she rides out an orgasm. I pump in and out, slowly, until she picks her head up.

"You good?" I know she's in that post-orgasm bliss, so of course she's fucking feeling good.

"Mmhmm." She nods her head with a huge smile plastered across her face.

"Fuck, I fucking love your pussy. It's like sliding into heaven every single fucking time." I pick up my pace as my palms squeeze the globes of her ass, probably leaving indentations on her pale skin.

"I'm pretty sure my pussy fucking loves you too." She laughs.

"Only pretty sure?" I lift one of my hands, wrapping it around her throat and holding her head still. "I'm going to continue fucking this pussy until you're one hundred percent sure that it loves my cock. Craves my cock. Fucking needs my cock filling it."

"It might take a while." She smirks.

"We've got all the time in the world," I grunt as I slam into her harder. The moment my hand tightens around her throat, her pussy clenches and her juices flood all over me.

"Fuck," I growl into her mouth. My balls constrict as I lose myself in her.

CHAPTER 30

Bree

There's a lot of commotion coming from down the hall, as Ash and I make our way out of the bedroom after another steamy shower session—one that sends a blush straight to my face even thinking about it.

"They mean well. Let's just keep in mind that we can't kill our family members," Ash says behind me.

Turning my head, I raise one eyebrow at him. "You might not be able to, but I could, and I wouldn't lose a wink of sleep." I shrug.

"Babe, we're parents now. We need to be responsible adults who don't go around maiming and torturing people."

My steps falter, causing Ash to stumble into my back. "What's wrong?" he asks, spinning me around to face him.

I blink as I look up at him. He just said *we're parents*. As in, him and me together. "I—do you mean that?" I ask him.

"About not maiming and torturing people? Yes, Bree, unless they really deserve it."

"No, not that part. The part about us being parents now."

"Um, you do remember the baby who was dropped on our doorstep last night, don't you?"

"Yes, but do you mean like: you're a parent now, and I'm just the sidekick, the girlfriend? Or like: we're parents, together?" I hold my breath, waiting for his answer.

"Breanna, if you want to do this with me, then we are doing this together. You are nobody's sidekick, babe. You're the fucking queen. What do you want, Bree?"

It didn't hit me until just now how much I want to be a parent to that baby. "I want to do this together. You, me, and Faith."

"Okay, you, me, and Faith. Now, let's go see why it sounds like the whole neighbourhood is in our penthouse."

"I'm going shopping today. I'm buying a house that no one else will have keys to." I smile up at him.

"You're not buying a house. If you want a new house, I can buy you one."

I can't help but roll my eyes at him. "Shut up, Ash. It's the twenty-first century. If I want to buy us a home, then I can. And I will. Also, there's the tiny fact that my net worth is at least ten times whatever yours is."

I wait to see his reaction. This is usually where guys get threatened by my family's wealth. Ash smirks. "Holy shit, I've scored myself a sugar mumma. And ten times is being generous; we both know your net wealth is at least one hundred times what mine is. Come on, Richie Rich, let's kick some assholes out of our home, then maybe we can go look at real estate together."

"Deal." I smile, spinning around and walking into the living room. The scene that greets us… well, I'm not even sure how to take it all in. First, there is pink. *Everywhere.* It's like a baby store threw up in Ash's apartment.

"What the hell is going on?" I ask, looking at my dad, who is currently cooing at Faith as he holds her out in front of him. There's no doubt in my mind that he had a hand in this madness.

"Don't look at me. It wasn't just me." Dad nods to Zac.

It's funny. You'd think it would be our mothers who loved to go crazy shopping. But, nope, it's the dads.

"Well, I can't very well let my granddaughter miss

out on a room fit for a princess. Don't worry, we'll get this all set up next to the master."

Ash walks up to Dad and plucks Faith from his hands. "Bree and I are heading out for a bit," he says as he steps around the boxes and bags scattered everywhere.

We get to the doors of the lift before we hear their laughter. "Should I tell 'em, or do you want to?" Zac says.

"You go ahead," my dad replies.

"Ash, you're going to need a few things if you plan on taking her out." Both Ash and I spin on our heels to face them.

"What do you mean?" I ask.

"Well, you're going to need: the nappy bag, bottles, formula, nappies, wipes, spare clothes…"

"Okay, so where is it?" Ash looks around.

"Oh, I bought you a new one." Dad pulls out an orange box.

"You bought a four-month-old a Louis Vuitton bag?" Ash questions.

Shit, is it wrong that I'm hella excited? I don't care. It's Louis Vuitton. Judge all you like, but I do have a penchant for designer bags. I take the box and unwrap it, pulling the large bag out.

"Ash, don't question it. Just accept it." I smile at him.

"Okay, well, is there like a list of shit we need to put in that? We're just going to be a few hours… how much crap do we really need?"

Once again, our dads burst out laughing. Ash and I look at each other, confusion mirrored on our faces.

"Here, swap." Ash hands me Faith while he takes the bag from me. "Mum!" His voice bellows through the apartment.

"In the kitchen," Alyssa yells back. Ash heads for the kitchen with the bag. I glare at our dads, who are still laughing.

"Ah, I think you are both taking this grandfather thing a little too seriously. I mean, did you really need to develop grey hairs overnight?" I ask them with my eyebrows drawn down. If ever there was a Kodak moment, this would be it. I fight hard not to laugh at their reactions, as they turn and leave me in the living room, probably in search of a mirror. I find a spot on the couch that isn't covered in bags, and take a seat. Resting Faith on my lap, I look down at her.

"You'll learn real quick that the men in this family are all extremely vain. Well, maybe not Uncle Dean, but he's gotta be the only one. All the others are vain as fuck," I tell her.

I probably should try to stop swearing around her. But it's not like she understands a word I'm saying yet. She really is a perfect little thing. The thought of someone not wanting her makes my blood boil. But maybe I should be thankful instead, because Ash and I can keep her to ourselves and not have to share her with anyone. I know it's a selfish thought. Faith shouldn't have been dealt a crappy-ass person for a birth mother.

"Your daddy is going to be the best daddy ever, Faith. Don't you worry about a thing. You will be just fine with us. I'm going to love you as if you really are mine. I promise I won't let anybody hurt you. I'm sorry you have a crappy birth mother, but I'm going to be the best—" I pause. What am I to Faith? Her stepmum? Her dad's girlfriend? I wonder if Ash will let me adopt her, so she can be mine too.

How would I even bring something like that up? Why am I even thinking this? I've known her for less than twenty-four hours. Maybe I need to slow my roll... Maybe this is all moving a little too fast... But when I look at Faith, I know that I already love this little baby. It's strange, because I don't love easily. Yet, she has somehow found a spot in my heart like she was always meant to be there.

Ash comes and squats down in front of me. "You are going to be the best mother, Breanna," he says quietly, not breaking eye contact with me.

"Do you really think so?" I ask him. He has no idea how much I needed to hear those words from him. Needed the reassurance that I wasn't just going a little crazy, or sprinting when I should be taking baby steps.

"I know so. When you love, you love with every-thing you have—*I'm a fucking lucky bastard for it.* And I know Faith is going to be the most blessed little girl around, because she gets to be loved by you too."

"Thank you." I lean in gently and kiss his lips. "We should probably try to stop swearing in front of her."

"Yeah, probably," Ash agrees, just as the sound of the

lift rings out. "We need to change the fucking passcode," he then grumbles, rising to his feet.

"Ash Williamson, how dare you not call me? I had to find out second-hand from Hope, who had to hear it from Chase."

A fuming Lily marches into the living room with Alex right behind her. When she spots me, she let's go of Alex's hand and rushes over to where I'm sitting with Faith. "Oh my gosh, look at her." Her voice quiets as she squishes herself next to me.

"She's so bloody perfect. Can I hold her?" Lily's eyes question me.

Shit, I'm not prepared for this. I know our parents have been holding her, but they're our parents. Should we really be letting everyone hold her? What if they're sick and they pass something onto her?

I look up to Ash; he can answer for us. I don't want to look like a crazy person when I say *hell no.* For once, I'm relieved that Ash can read my mind— that he knows the inner turmoil I'm currently having—because he ignores the question completely.

"What the hell are you doing here, Lil?" Ash grumbles, picking up Faith and holding her to his chest.

"Well, it's not every day that you become a second cousin. Did you expect me not to come? And you're welcome, by the way. Well, really, you should be thanking Alex."

Thanking Alex for what? It's never a good thing, needing to thank a mobster. I stand up next to Ash.

"What are we thanking Alex for?" I direct my question to the man himself.

"You don't need to thank me for anything, Breanna. I just had a baby capsule seat installed in a couple of your cars in the basement." He shrugs.

"How the fuck did you get into my cars?" Ash grunts.

Alex just raises his eyebrow, giving us a "bitch, please" kind of look. I roll my eyes. Breaking into cars is child's play; it's not that impressive.

"Thank you. I almost feel bad that I called them now." Ash pulls out his phone when it starts vibrating, ignoring the call before returning it to his pocket.

"Who'd you call?" Lily asks.

"Huh? Oh, don't worry, you're about to find out in: three, two, one." The lift doors open, and in walks four large men. My jaw drops. I haven't seen these guys since they were little kids, and we were all holidaying together in Hawaii. Damn, they grew up fine.

"I'm going to bloody smother you in your sleep, Ash Williamson," Lily grits out, before turning her charming smile on her other four cousins.

"Theo, Aunt Holly didn't mention you were in town." She calmly walks up and hugs him, kissing him on both cheeks.

"That's because she doesn't know we're here," Theo retorts.

"Ah, actually, she does now." Matteo, the second oldest of the brothers, says, answering his phone and walking off towards the kitchen.

I see Alex's hands clench as he watches Romeo and Luca take turns hugging and kissing Lily on each cheek. He's about to take a step forward when I stop him. Holding his arm, I whisper, "They're her cousins on her mother's side of the family." Alex sends me a thankful look that passes just as quickly as it came.

"So, I guess I can't cut their fingers off then?"

"Yeah, definitely not these ones." I don't think he has any idea who the hell Lily's cousins are. And I'm not about to break it to him. I will, however, get my popcorn ready to watch this show unfold.

"Theo, it's been way too fucking long." I smile and walk over to him.

"Breanna fucking McKinley, the pictures really do you no justice." Theo rakes his eyes up and down my body. I hear Ash growl behind me. Ignoring the tingles that growl ignites in me, I hug Theo.

"Why thank you. You haven't grown into as much of an ogre as I expected." I laugh.

"I heard you were shacked up with Ash. No one mentioned you went and had a baby. Did I miss the wedding?" Theo asks.

"No, you haven't missed it. Come meet Faith." I drag him by the hand over to where Ash stands.

Ash and Theo have always been great friends. It's no surprise that Ash called him to gossip about Lily dating Alex.

"Lil Pill, I didn't know you were dropping by." Zac walks back out with my dad next to him. Since when did those two become best mates? It's fucking weird.

"Uncle Zac, thank God you're here." Lily huffs out a breath. "Alex and I got those baby seats you guys wanted; they're in the cars."

"Hold the fuck up, buttercup." Matteo comes storming back into the room. Zac stops him with a hand on his chest.

"Matteo, you'll be best to remember that my grand-daughter is in this room. Save your bloodshed for another day," Zac grunts before letting him go.

"Don't worry, Uncle Zac, there won't be any blood-shed here. We're not heathens. We bought a warehouse for that." Luca smirks.

"TMI, Luca." My dad walks over and stands next to me.

"Lily, care to introduce us to your... friend?" Theo asks, looking Alex up and down, his disgust evident.

"You know I would, but we really got to go. Things to do. People to see. Tell Aunt Holly I said hi." Lily takes Alex's hand and drags him towards the lift.

Luca and Romeo are both standing in front of the doors, blocking her attempt at a quick escape.

"Ash, here's everything you need." Alyssa walks into the room, surveying the crowd of onlookers. "Oh, for goodness' sake, no. *This* is not happening right now. However, you four boys turned up at the right time. Come and help me move all this stuff into the bedroom."

"Ah, sure, Luca and Romeo will help you, Aunt Lyssa. Matteo and I are going to walk Lily out to her car."

"Great. Ash, here's the bag; everything you should need is in there. Are you sure you don't want me to come with you?" Alyssa asks.

"Thanks, Mum. We're good. We won't be long." Ash hangs the bag over his shoulder before taking my hand, the one that's not holding onto Faith, in his.

"Ah, Alex, think you can show us how these car seats work?" Ash walks towards the lift and presses the button. "Sorry, Theo, you'll have to save your fun for another day."

"That's okay. We'll be sticking around for a bit." Theo smirks.

"Wait, how long is a bit?" Lily asks.

It hasn't escaped me that she has yet to introduce Alex to her cousins. I don't blame her. If those boys were my cousins, I'd have Ash in hiding already. We'd have fake names, passports, and be on our way to a deserted island where no one could find us.

"As long as it takes," Matteo says.

"Great… Oh, did anyone tell you Hope's been trying to get this one's best mate, Chase, into bed?" Lily smirks at Ash.

"Trying and succeeding are two different things, Lil. Chase doesn't have a death wish." Ash looks to Theo.

"Matteo, call the car around. I think we have another cousin to pay a visit to today," Theo commands.

"Theo, no. Chase is family." Ash steps into the lift. Lily is quick to pull Alex in, before she presses the buttons to close the door.

"See you around, boys." Lily smiles as the lift shuts on them.

The moment we start descending, Lily's body slumps back and leans into Alex. She then turns her glare on Ash.

"What the hell did you call him for, Ash? Really, that's dirty even for you," she seethes.

"What's wrong? Not happy to see your cousins, Lil? I know I'm your fav, but still, they *are* family." Ash shrugs.

"You are my least favourite cousin right now."

"Anyone want to fill me in on what the hell that was?" Alex looks at all of us.

"That was Ash being a bloody gossip and not keeping his mouth shut," Lily growls. "Don't worry, I'm calling Aunt Holly. She will tell them they can't touch you."

"Can't touch me? Lil, I don't need your aunt to protect me from your cousins." Alex laughs.

"Eh, you just might," Ash suggests.

"Why?"

"Wait, you don't know who they are? Here I was, thinking everyone knew of the great Theo Valentino." I wait for it. The recognition. The sheer terror people emit when they hear that name. It's just like when someone realizes who I am. But the dread people have at the mere mention of the Valentinos is ten times more potent than the McKinley legacy.

Alex must be stupider than I gave him credit for, because the recognition comes, but never the fear...

CHAPTER 31

Ash

*I*t's been a week since Faith came into our lives. To say I'm fucking tired would be an understatement. I honestly don't know how I would have gotten through the last week without Breanna and the rest of our family, who have all insisted on barging into the penthouse and helping.

I'm sitting in my office at the club. Faith is sleeping peacefully in some sort of contraption my mum called a bassinet. Breanna should be here soon; she said she'd drop in with lunch. The envelope containing the DNA results is on my desk staring at me, taunting me, waiting for me to open it. But I don't want to, not without Breanna here. What if I'm not Faith's father?

I don't know if I'm more terrified that I am, or that I'm not. Don't get me wrong, from the moment I saw this baby, she stole a piece of my heart. I'd do anything for her. The lawyers tell me that all the paperwork is legit, that I do in fact have sole custody of Faith.

Chase has spent the last five days trying to find her birth mother. He thinks something is off about the situation. I have to agree. I get that it's fucking hard. I've only had Faith for a week, and I'm tired as fuck. I have experienced more stress in the last seven days than I've ever had to endure. But I wouldn't change it for anything. Nothing could possibly get me to dump her on a stranger's doorstep.

Part of me hopes to never find her, to never hear from her again. Another part wants the answers to the questions Faith might have when she's older. I need those answers for her. What kind of mindfuck will it be for a little girl to learn that her mother abandoned her when she was a newborn? How does someone even explain that to their child?

I have never been more grateful for my own parents than during this past week. I'm more than ready to have them leave my apartment, but I don't know how Bree and I would have gotten through it without both sets of our parents. I never thought I would be glad to see Josh, but he was in the kitchen the other night when I walked out to get Faith a bottle. He wordlessly took her from my arms, made her bottle, and sat there and fed her until she was asleep.

The conversation was... interesting. It was basically the same old routine: Josh threatening me if I ever hurt Breanna. Although, this time, he threw Faith into that mix. *Like I'd ever willingly hurt either of them.* He also mentioned something about Breanna wanting to adopt Faith, and asked what my thoughts were on that.

I honestly didn't know she was thinking along those lines. I don't have any issues with Breanna adopting Faith. I would, however, like to be married first. I want us to be a family. I want Faith to look at Bree as her mother. At first, I was worried that Breanna wouldn't be able to cope with a baby, and the responsibility of being a parent. That being said, I wouldn't want to do this with anyone else. It's fucking hard to accept that she's in this with me. That she is willing to take on someone else's child as her own.

But Breanna amazes me every day with the love and devotion she shows Faith. She has done everything, been with me every step of the way. Maybe that's why I'm feeling off right now. This is the first time Faith and I have been alone together since she arrived.

She's been asleep for the last hour. I can't help but look into her bassinet every few minutes to check on her. I thought, in coming here, I'd be able to get some work done. Chase has really stepped up and looked after the place in my absence. However, there is a lot of shit that still requires my attention. We don't just have the one club; we have ten locations across Australia.

The business doesn't stop just because my life took a one-eighty. I need to get this shit done. I open my emails again and start answering the ones that require an immediate response. I'm reviewing the latest report on the new build in Perth when I hear a click of heels approaching the door.

I'm expecting Breanna to walk in; she should be here soon. Instead, I get a feisty redhead pushing through the door.

"Ash, I think I might actually kill you." Lily plops into the seat across from my desk.

"Good morning, Lily. It's great to see you. What brings you by today?" I ask, sarcasm dripping from my voice.

"What, or who? Theo and Matteo. Call them off. They need to go back to bloody New York, Ash. I can't believe you reached out to them."

"They're your cousins, Lil, not mine. Also, last I checked, they're the legit fucking mafia. Even if I wanted to, I couldn't call them off from anything." I laugh.

"I know. But can't you talk to Theo and convince him that Alex is a good guy? I mean, just suggest that they take their macho bullshit and shove it up their asses?"

I don't think I've ever heard Lily curse so much. I'd expect this kind of rant from Hope, but not Lily. I squint my eyes at the redhead and examine her a little more closely.

"Nice try, *Hope*. Tell Lily to fight her own battles. What the hell did she offer you to come in here today?"

"Argh, I hate you." Hope stands up and walks around to Faith's bassinet. "But you do make beautiful babies," she says, staring down.

"I do, don't I?" I look at that fucking envelope still taunting me with whatever truths lie inside it.

"Okay, well, if Lil asks, tell her I tried and that you called Theo. I gotta go catch up with Romeo for drinks."

"Isn't Romeo only seventeen?" I question. I'm sure the kid is underage.

"Yeah, but he's like the mafia. I don't think a little underage drinking is the worst thing those boys have done." She winks as she leaves the room at the same time Breanna enters.

"Hope, hey, where the hell have you been?" Breanna asks.

"I'll fill you in later," Hope says, looking back at me.

"Okay, let me see this baby I can't stop hearing about." I groan as Ben follows Breanna into the room, walking straight up to the bassinet.

"Shh, don't wake her up, Benny," Bree hisses at him.

"Please, she wants to see her Uncle Benny, don't you, beautiful girl?" My eyes widen at his *Uncle Benny* comment. Breanna cuts me a warning look.

I shake my head and bypass my desk. Wrapping my arms around her, I bury my head into her neck, inhaling her raspberry scent. I knew I missed her over the last few hours while she met up with Benny for brunch. But damn, I didn't know just how much until now.

If I could keep her here in my arms for all of time, I would. If I could arrange it so that we never had to spend one minute apart, I would. "Mmm, I fucking missed you, babe," I whisper so that only she hears.

Out of the corner of my eye, I see Ben reaching into the bassinet. "Don't fucking touch my daughter," I growl, not moving my head from Bree's neck. My lips make a path up to her ear. I don't need to look to know he stopped reaching for Faith.

Breanna wraps her arms around my back, slipping them under my jacket. "I missed you too," she says.

"You were only gone for a few hours, Beebee. That's some unhealthy codependency shit going on there," Ben adds.

I lift my gaze and look Breanna in the eye. "Tell me again why I can't kill him?"

"Because he's my best friend, Ash. Don't worry, you'll grow to love him... over time." She smiles.

"Doubtful." I side-step my desk and return to my chair.

Breanna is quick to follow me, sitting her ass on my lap. One of my arms snakes around her waist while my other hand trails the letter A on her bare thigh, over and over. Do I want to permanently mark her as mine? Yes, I fucking do. If I could tattoo my name across her forehead, I would. I want nothing more than to have the whole fucking world know this woman is mine. And mine alone.

"Ah, yeah, Beebee, I gotta run. I'll catch up with you later. Nice to see you again, Ash."

"Thanks for brunch, Benny. I'll call you later," Breanna replies, not taking her eyes off me.

I wait for him to leave the room; he shuts the door quietly behind him as he does.

"Uncle Benny? Really, you don't think Faith has enough uncles without adding in randoms?" I grunt.

"Benny is not a random, Ash. He's my best friend, and of course he's going to be Uncle Benny to my children," Bree huffs. She goes to get off my lap but I hold her down.

I'm not going to lie. The fact that she looks at Faith as hers is fucking everything. This really could have been what destroyed us. Instead, the only thing Faith has done is bring us closer together.

"I want to get married," I blurt out.

Breanna tilts her head at me. "Is that a proposal? Because that wasn't a question."

"Breanna McKinley, will you marry me?" I ask her. This is not at all how I imagined proposing to her. But I can't seem to wait.

"I'll marry you, on one condition.".

"Name it," I say.

"You have to let me pay back that thirty grand I won, even if you're adamant I stole it."

"Babe, you cheated in that game. Cheating is stealing. And I don't need you to pay it back. What I need is for you to work it off, like we agreed."

Although, now that I think about it, Breanna has

successfully managed to get out of really doing much of anything at the club. At this rate, it'll take her the next sixty years to work off her debt.

"Okay, fine, I want to file paperwork for maternity leave then. I have a newborn now, so that means I'm entitled to leave." She stands when Faith starts to stir in the bassinet, and this time I let her go. *Reluctantly.*

Breanna picks up Faith and hugs her to her chest, and my baby girl settles right away. She comes back and sits on my lap while holding Faith.

"Okay, I'll approve the maternity leave." I laugh. Her working for me was never about the fucking money she stole; it was always just a way to keep her close to me.

"Okay, then my answer is yes." She smiles.

"Yes?" I repeat.

"Yes, I'll marry you, Ash Williamson. But be warned, I can't run off to Vegas. When we get married, it will be the event of the year. Granny McKinley won't let us have it any other way."

"I've seen Granny McKinley's wedding planner. I wouldn't dare deprive you of your dream wedding. As long as you are walking down the aisle and there's chocolate cake, I'll be there ready to shout *I do.*"

Holy shit, she said yes. We are doing this. I need to make a call to Granny McKinley, to tell her to go ahead and put a rush on that wedding she wants to throw. I can't wait to make Breanna mine.

CHAPTER 32

Bree

I pinch my arm. Yep, I'm definitely awake and not dreaming. I'm not going to lie. I've dreamt of Ash proposing to me a lot. I mean, I used to write my name as Breanna Williamson all over my diary during high school—as Daniel just had to point out during the trip to Perth.

In all of those dreams, I was never holding a baby, and we were never sitting in an office. Yet, this moment couldn't be any more perfect. Some may think it's fast, rushed even, but I've been in love with Ash for six years. I've tried everything to get him out of my system, to not be in love with him. Nothing's worked, which is why I can say yes to his proposal, without even a flicker of doubt in my mind that this is what I want.

This is the life I want. With Ash. And now Faith. Looking down at Faith, I couldn't imagine our lives without her. She's only been here for one week, but over the course of that week, I feel like I've bonded with this baby more than I've ever bonded with anyone else in my life.

I haven't brought up the topic of adopting her to Ash. I spoke to my mum and dad about it briefly. It's a big decision, but I already feel like she's mine. Honestly, I don't even need the piece of paper legalising an adoption, but it would be nice for Faith to know that I want her. That I'm *choosing* her.

I may not be her mother by blood, but I will be her mother in every way that matters. I get that I can't replace a birth mum, but when your birth mum abandons you, chances are you are better off anyway. There is nothing that I wouldn't do for this little girl. There is nothing that would make me abandon her.

Shit, if it came down to it and Ash decided he didn't want to keep Faith, I think I'd fight him to keep her myself. Not that Ash would ever not want her; he's besotted by her. I knew he would be a great father. After all, he grew up with the perfect fucking parents. He knows how to be a good father because his dad shows him every day what it means to be one.

It's hard. Parenting is not for the fainthearted. It's not about being perfect and never making mistakes, because I guarantee Ash and I will make plenty. It's about always putting your child first, always protecting them to the best of your ability, and giving them the unconditional love and guidance they'll need throughout their lives. I can do that. I *will* do that for Faith.

"Oh shit, I forgot. Jump up for a sec, babe," Ash says as he stands and plucks Faith out of my arms. His hands dig into his pocket and he pulls out a small, black, velvet bag.

I watch as he tips the contents onto the desk, and a huge diamond ring falls onto the table. Ash picks up the ring with his free hand.

"This is not how I was planning on doing this. You and I both know you deserve a better proposal. Nonetheless, I promise I will always love you, treasure you, and worship you. Will you marry me, Breanna McKinley?" He holds the ring out towards me.

"This is more than enough for me, Ash. All I need is you." I wipe at the tears falling down my cheeks.

"So, that's still a yes?"

"That's a hell yes!" I squeal as he slides the ring onto my finger. It's a perfect fit.

"Thank God. Because if you said no, I might have had to kidnap you, take you to a deserted island, and keep you there until you developed Stockholm syndrome." Ash smiles.

"Well, I mean, I wouldn't be opposed to the deserted

island idea. Oh, we should buy an island," I suggest. My family actually already owns one, but nobody outside of the McKinley clan knows it exists. I guess, once we're married, I can take Ash and Faith there for our honeymoon.

"It's a good thing you have a decent trust fund in place, because I'm not poor, but shit… I don't think I can buy you a fucking island, babe. Come on, sugar mumma. Come sit on the sofa. I need you to open this for me."

Ash hands me an envelope, then takes a seat as I turn the sealed paper over in my hands. It's from the DNA testing lab.

"Are you sure you want me to open it?" I question him.

"Yes, I can't do it. Just read it to me."

"Ash, no matter what this piece of paper says, Faith is ours now. I'm not giving her up."

What if it says he's not her father, and he doesn't want her anymore? Shit, no, Ash wouldn't do that. But what man wants to raise someone else's child? I know he said he'd do it for me, when the idiot thought I was pregnant, but that's different. If Faith isn't Ash's that means she isn't biologically either of ours. Would we even have the right to keep her?

"Bree, no matter what the paper says, I will make sure no one can take her away from us." Ash squeezes my hand.

"Okay, let's do this." I rip the envelope open and pull

out the single page. Scanning the document, I read the lines that matter out loud.

"The person tested IS ACCEPTED as the biological parent. The probability of paternity is greater than 99.9%."

I look up to see relief wash over Ash's features. "You really did knock up some random, Ash."

"I swear I didn't know, Breanna. I didn't know until Faith turned up on our doorstep."

"I know. Besides the murdery feelings I have at the thought of you sleeping with another woman, which I'm aware are irrational because it happened long before you and I happened, I'm glad you did. Because now we have Faith. It's not how I pictured life going, but I don't want to change a thing about it."

"The only thing I want to change is your last name." Ash smirks.

***

"Breanna, stop right there!" My mum squeals. "What the hell is that on your hand?" She grabs my left wrist and yells, "Lyssa, get out here now. Oh my God. It's happening."

Alyssa comes rushing in. "What's going on? What's wrong?" She stops short when she sees my hand firmly held up in front of my mum's face.

"Oh my gosh. Ash, you didn't tell me you were doing this. Let me see that." Alyssa takes my hand and inspects the ring before engulfing me in an uncomfortably tight hug. Once she lets me go, she turns to my mum and they both squeal together. "We're getting married," Alyssa screams.

"I know. Oh, God, this is going to be the wedding of the year," Mum screeches.

"Wait, hold on. I'm pretty sure that Bree and I are the ones getting married here." Ash screws his face up at our mothers.

"I guess you guys don't hate each other anymore then?" I question. Alyssa gave Mum the silent treatment for a while, after the whole shooting at Ash incident on Christmas Eve.

"Well, we're grandmothers now," Mum says, like that's all the explanation she needs to give for why they're best friends again.

"Oh, here, give me Faith. We'll take her for a walk through the park. And let you two have some time alone." Alyssa winks.

"Ah, that's okay. She's been out all day. We're just going to lounge in the theatre room with her," I suggest, not really wanting her to leave the apartment without me and Ash.

"Breanna, between us, we have raised four children. You two included. I think Lyssa and I are more than capable of taking a baby for a stroll through the park."

I turn to Ash. Surely, he can back me up. But when I look at him, the smoulder in his eyes tells me he has other ideas that do not include snuggling in the theatre room watching movies.

"Okay, fine, but make sure she has the cover up on her stroller and put some sunscreen on her. It's really hot out today. I don't want her getting sunburnt," I tell them as I lean into the stroller and kiss Faith's sleeping head.

Ash follows suit, whispering something to her that I don't catch.

"We won't be long," Alyssa says.

We both watch them go. "I've got a weird feeling that I should tell them to come back. That we shouldn't let her out of our sight," I whisper.

"Me too. Do you think it will always be like this? Maybe it's part of the whole parenting thing. This feeling of dread when you watch your daughter go out in the world without you," Ash comments.

"Maybe, but I'm going to need you to distract me, so I don't look like the crazy person I am and follow our mothers."

Ash smirks down at me. He leans into my ear, and his husky voice sends shivers through my body. "You have thirty seconds to be on the bed, naked, with that pussy of yours on display for me. Ready to give me my daily fix."

As he straightens, he starts counting down from thirty. I run into the room, tearing my dress over my head along the way. Who am I to deny him a taste? I might be crazy, but I'm not stupid. Ash has licked my pussy every day since we've been together—*sometimes twice*. He really is addicted. But honestly, it's one addiction I don't mind enabling.

Pulling my panties down, I jump on the bed just as he gets to five. I reach behind me, unclip my bra, and fling it across the room. He catches it on the number one.

"Impressive. Who knew you could move so quickly?" Ash stands at the end of the bed, looking down at me. He likes to look. I think if he could get away with hanging pictures of my pussy everywhere, he would, just so he could stare at it all day.

He takes his time as he slides his jacket off, folding it and placing it over one of the sofas. He then removes his cufflinks and walks over to the dressing table, dropping them in a little tray that sits on top. He's so agonisingly slow as he turns back to me and unbuttons his white dress shirt. I want to stand up and just rip that shirt open.

"Do you know how fucking perfect you look right now? Wearing nothing but my ring on your finger." He tilts his head, as his eyes roam over my nakedness, leaving a trail of goosebumps in their wake.

"I know that you'd look a lot better if you hurry up and lose the clothes." I raise an eyebrow in challenge.

"Are you in a rush? I like to savour the finer things in life, and this is… you are… the finest thing in my life, babe. Which means I'm going to take my time and savour every fucking minute that I get to drown myself in you."

Damn him and his sweet-talking. I can't wait any longer. His shirt hits the floor, all those tanned, toned muscles on display for me. My mouth waters at the sight. Maybe I should get a sculpture made of him; it would be the finest piece of art the world has ever seen.

My left hand runs down the middle of my body, his eyes following it. He really does love seeing his ring on my finger. My hand makes its way to my mound, and using my ring finger only, I rub circles around my clit.

"Fuck, Bree," Ash grunts as he strips his pants off and climbs on the bed, positioning himself between my opened legs.

I go to move my finger away. *He's here now. He can take over.* But he snatches my wrist and holds it in place. "Keep going. Don't stop until I tell you to." He smiles before he dips his head closer to my opening.

As I continue rubbing circles, his hands go under my ass and lift my hips to meet his face. His tongue swirls around my ass. It's not the first time he's done this, but it's just as shocking whenever he does. It seems like an act that is so taboo it's too bloody hot. And the fact that it sends sparks through to my core only adds to why I'm beginning to love it.

His tongue moves to the next opening and slides inside. I get lost in the feeling. My hand stops working my clit, instead reaching out for his hair to hold his head in place as I ride his mouth. The next thing I know, he's sitting up and spinning me around, positioning me on all fours. The slap that lands on my ass rings out through the room.

"I didn't tell you that you could stop," Ash growls, literally growls, as he lines himself up with my entrance. He slowly glides his cock into my pussy, while sliding his thumb into my ass. I push back onto him. I need more. I always need more of him.

"Your pussy's a greedy little thing, isn't it, Bree? Tell me... what is your pussy hungry for, babe?" He stills once his cock is bottomed out inside me. His thumb continues to slide in and out of my ass, the sensation of being filled overwhelming me.

"You, always you, Ash. I need you to fuck me. Now!" I order him. I told him I'd never beg, but I think I might just cave if he doesn't do what I need.

"Oh, I will be fucking you, Bree. I'll be fucking you every day for the rest of our lives," he promises.

I squirm, trying to push myself further onto him. I'm so fucking close to coming undone like this—my pussy impaled by his cock and his thumb fucking my ass.

"Oh, God, Ash, I'm going to..." My sentence trails off, my head dropping to the mattress below me.

"No, you're not. You're going to wait, and we're going to come together." He glides his cock out, until just the tip is left inside, then slams forward again. He doesn't hold back. He fucks me like I need him to, the double penetration of his cock and thumb forceful and unrelenting.

I don't know if I can suppress my orgasm any longer. I'm going to explode.

"Now, Bree. Come fucking now." I feel his cock pulse as he empties himself into me.

CHAPTER 33

Ash

Rolling over, I pull Breanna into my arms, both of us working on catching our breath. My phone rings out through the otherwise silent room. I would let it go to voicemail, but it's my mother's ringtone. Leaning over the side of the bed, I dig through my pants to find my phone. By the time I pull it out, the ringing has stopped, but then it starts back up almost immediately.

"What's wrong?" I'm up and out of bed, walking

into the closet and pulling on a pair of shorts when my mum's words finally sink in.

"Ash, I don't want you to panic, but you have to meet me at the hospital. Now." Her voice shakes a little.

"What happened? Is Faith okay?" I ask, removing a shirt from the shelf. When I walk back out, Breanna is already dressed and picking up a set of keys off the dresser.

I follow her out of the bedroom and straight to the lift, while listening to my mother.

"She's okay, Ash. She had an allergic reaction to something that bit her. Not a bad one, just a little localised swelling on her leg."

"What the fuck bit her?" I grind out. "Shit, Mum, I'll be there; I'm walking into the lift. I'll be there in ten."

"Ash, don't drive recklessly. She is fine. I just brought her to be checked out—that's all. It's nothing a dose of antihistamine can't fix."

"Okay, I'll be there as soon as I can."

I hang up the phone just as the doors close. Breanna grabs my hand. "What happened?" Her worried gaze meets mine.

"Mum said Faith had an allergic reaction to a bite on her leg. It's not bad, but they took her to the hospital to get it looked at. She's okay." I squeeze Breanna's hand. I'm not even fucking sure if I'm trying to reassure *her*... or myself.

"An allergic reaction? To what? Oh shit, Ash, what if she's anaphylactic?"

"Mum said there's just a little swelling. I'm sure it's nothing serious."

"Yeah, she's okay. She has to be." As soon as the door opens, Breanna heads to her Bugatti.

"I'm driving." I round the car and jump into the driver's side; she doesn't argue as she sits in the passenger seat.

The moment I see she has her seat belt clipped, I put my foot down and fly out of the garage and onto the street. Thank fuck the traffic isn't too bad at this time of day. I weave in and out of the lanes like I'm practicing for the Bathurst 1000.

I'd appreciate the drive more, if I weren't so hell-bent on making it to the hospital and getting to my daughter. Breanna has never let me drive this thing before.

Ten minutes later, we're pulling into the emergency room parking station at the hospital. Breanna and I both run inside, and straight away, I spot my mum talking to a doctor.

"Mum, where is she?"

"Ash, calm down. Faith's in the room with Emily. I'll take you back there. The doctor was just giving me an update. They don't know what it was that bit her, but the swelling is going down. We can take her home."

"Okay, let's get her." I nod, looking around.

"Thank you, doctor," my mum says before turning to me and taking one of my hands. "Come on." She then leads us through to the exam room.

"Something isn't right," Breanna says quietly from

beside me. I hate to admit it, but I also still have that sinking feeling in the pit of my stomach. I just need to get my eyes on Faith. Once I see her for myself, see that she's okay, I can relax.

"She's in that room there. I've just got to call your father back." Mum points to a door, and my feet pick up their pace as I walk across and push it open.

Breanna's gasp registers from behind me, then her scream pierces through my soul. "Mum!" Breanna shoves past the door and drops to the floor, where her mother is currently lying. I scan the room; there's an empty hospital bassinet where Faith should fucking be.

"Where the fuck is my daughter?" I scream as I spin around in a circle, searching every corner.

"Mum, wake up." Breanna stares up at me. "Ash, I can't wake her up." I'm at a loss right now. I don't know what to do. I'm standing here, fucking useless to everyone.

My mum runs into the room, looks down at the floor, and presses a button on the wall before kneeling on the other side of Emily.

"Breanna, she's okay. She's breathing; her heart rate is steady." The next thing I know, a heap of hospital staff burst through the door and tend to Emily.

"What the fuck is going on?" This growl comes from Josh as he stands at the threshold behind me. I have no words for him. His eyes shoot to Breanna, who is being held back by some fucking hospital attendant. That image snaps me out of my own head.

"Get your fucking hands off her now!" I bark, pulling Bree out of his grasp and holding her to my chest. Her sobs wreck through her body as she collapses onto me.

"Emmy! Somebody better tell me what the fuck happened to my wife. Now!" Josh yells, pulling and shoving the doctors and nurses away from Emily, who has been transitioned to a bed.

"Sir, you need to calm down. Someone call security," one of the doctors orders.

"Fuck off with your security. This is my fucking wife—*my life*—lying unconscious on this bed. What. The. Fuck. Happened. To. Her!!" The roar that leaves him is nothing short of animalistic.

I'm looking around the room, at the chaos, while trying to figure out where the fuck my daughter is. That's when I notice the small envelope in the now-empty bassinet.

As much as I'd like to be raging and lashing out like Josh is, that's not going to make Faith reappear. I tug Breanna over to the crib and pick up the letter. Before I can get it open, she rips it out of my hands and pulls a piece of paper out.

"I'm going to fucking kill the bitch," she seethes, handing the letter to me.

I read over the words. *Twice.* To make sure I read them right.

Sorry Ash,

I've reconsidered. I'll be taking Faith back. If you would like to keep her, I'd be open to a negotiation of sorts, in the sum of five million dollars. I want the money in cash, small bills.

You have forty-eight hours to arrange the drop, or I'll make sure you never see your daughter again. I'll send a text message tomorrow with a location.

Hayley

Fucking hell. That crazy-ass bitch. I'd happily hand over five mil to get my baby girl back. I don't think I can access that kind of cash in such a short amount of time though. Fuck.

"Ash, I-I'm going to get our daughter back," Breanna says quietly.

"I'll get her back. This is my fault, Bree. I shouldn't have let them take her out."

"It's not your fault, Ash. We'll get her back."

Breanna walks over to her dad, who has calmed down a little. The doctors are telling him something about Emily. I can't stop myself from following Bree. I'm lost, and she's what gives me direction right now.

"Daddy?" She reaches out and picks up one of his hands. Josh looks over; he immediately wraps his arms around her, whispering something in her ear that I don't catch.

I grab my phone out of my pocket and dial Chase. I don't know who else to turn to right now.

"What's up?" he answers.

"Chase, she..." I choke on the words. I can't get them out.

"Ash, where are you? What happened."

"I'm at the hospital. She took her. I have to get her back, Chase."

"Who took who?"

"Hayley... she took Faith from the hospital. I need to get her back."

"Don't move. I'm on my way. I'm jumping in the car as we speak. Is Breanna with you?"

I blink at his question. What does it matter who's with me? My daughter *isn't*... and she fucking should be.

"Ah, yeah, but her mum was unconscious when we got here. She's talking to the doctors with Josh now." I exit the room, my mum following me out with a worried gaze.

"Okay, don't go anywhere. I'll be there in fifteen minutes."

I hang up the phone and put it back in my pocket. Running my hands through my hair, I look up and down the hallway. Which way did she go? Does Faith have enough clothes? Nappies? Formula? Is Hayley going to take care of her properly? Would she really hurt her? There are too many fucking questions and not enough answers.

Leaning against the wall, I let my body sink to the floor. My head hits my knees and the tears stream down my face. I don't know when the last time I cried was, but I don't ever remember being this... helpless, scared, frustrated, and fucking angry. All at once.

I feel my mum's arms go around me as she sits next

to me. "Ash, it's going to be okay. We will get her back. Whatever we have to do, we'll get her back."

"I can't lose her, Mum. I only just got her."

"I know. We are not losing her."

"What the fuck happened?" My dad's voice has my head snapping up. He drops down in front of me, not caring that he's in the middle of the walkway.

"Dad, she took her." I pass him the letter I'm still clutching in my hands. His face hardens as he reads over it.

"Ash, I'll get her back. No one threatens my family and lives to tell the story."

Dad stands up and marches down the hallway, already talking on his phone. Breanna walks out of the room before her eyes land on me. She comes over and sits down on the side opposite my mum.

"How's your mum?" I ask her.

"She just woke up. She's pissed off. But other than that, she'll be fine."

"How are you?" My eyes roam all over her face. I need to be stronger right now. I can't lose my shit when everyone needs me to hold it together.

"I'll be better when I get our daughter back, and I'm feeding that no-good bitch to my dad's pigs." Tears run down her cheeks.

"I'll help, babe," I promise her.

"Ash, I-I'm going to get coffee. Do you want anything?"

"No, I'm good. Want me to come with? I'm waiting for Chase to get here. Once he does, we'll work on a plan. This isn't something we can do half-assed, Bree. We need to be smart. To find out where she is hiding out. If it comes down to it, I'll pay her the five mil."

"She didn't play that ransom very smart, because I'd pay five billion if it meant we could have Faith back in our arms right now."

CHAPTER 34

Bree

I hate doing this—lying to Ash. But what other options do I have? I need to get Faith back, and I'm not waiting around for them to come up with an idea. I know I can do something. I probably should have told Ash. But he's already got those assault charges dangling over his head. I don't want him involved when I end that bitch's life.

I don't care if she's Faith's biological mother. A mother does not use her infant as a way to extort money. She does not abandon her baby, leaving them with a bloody doorman.

As I drive to my Uncle Dean and Aunt Ella's, I devise a plan. I call Theo first.

"Breanna?" he answers.

"Theo, I need your help. *Family* kind of help," I tell him vaguely.

"Where are you?"

"I'm on my way to my Uncle Dean's. Can you meet me there?"

"Sure, sweetheart."

"Oh, and, Theo? Bring Matteo with you, but leave the twins behind." They are too young to be involved in this mess.

"Okay, we'll meet you there in ten."

"Thank you," I say, relieved. I knew he wouldn't ask questions on the phone, though I am sure he will have them in person. That being said, there's no doubt in my mind that they will help me.

The next call I make is to Alex—well, Lily actually, since I don't have his number myself.

"Hey, Bree, how's motherhood treating you?" Lily answers. I almost break down at her question. This is not me; I'm not a bloody crier.

Choking back a sob, I reply, "Uh, great. Hey, Lil, I was wondering if you were with Alex?" The question is rhetorical; those two haven't been separated since they met over Christmas.

"Yeah, he's just in his office. Why?"

"Do you think I could talk to him for a minute?"

Please don't ask me why… I know if I tell her, she'll be straight on the phone with Ash.

"Um, sure, is everything okay, Bree?" Her concern is evident.

"Yeah, I just need to ask him something."

"Okay, hold on."

There's a muffled exchange before Alex's voice fills my car.

"Miss McKinley, what can I do for you?"

Shit, I barely know this man. Should I really be asking him a favour right now? Can I trust him to help me?

"I need a favour?"

"People who call me usually do. I would appreciate it if you don't go through Lily to get to me again." His tone is harsh, but I get it. I'd probably be pissed too.

"Look, I wouldn't ever ask you for anything. But this… I—Faith has been kidnapped and I'm going to get her back. I don't need your help, but I would appreciate it."

"What happened? Who took her?" He sounds like he's moving around now.

"Her birth mother took her from the hospital today, left a note for Ash asking for five million if he wants her back."

"Okay, what do you need me to do? I'm pretty sure it's not to front the five mil."

"I need you to meet me at my Uncle Dean's. I know where she is. I just need backup, in case she's not alone."

"Okay, I'll be there as soon as I can."

"Also, you can't tell Lily. Ash doesn't know I'm doing this. And I need to keep it that way until after."

"I'm not lying to Lily for you, Breanna. If she asks, I will tell her."

"I'm not asking you to lie. I'm asking you to stall for a few hours."

"Okay, I'll see what I can do. I'll meet you at your uncle's."

The line cuts out just as I'm pulling into Uncle Dean's gated driveway. Entering the code in, I rush through and stop at the front entrance. Geoffrey, my uncle's butler, is already making his way down the steps towards me.

"Geoffrey, keep the car here. I won't be long. Also, I'm expecting a few guests. Can you show them down to the basement for me?"

"Will do, Miss McKinley."

"Oh, are my uncle and aunt home?" I ask.

"No, you just missed them I'm afraid."

"Oh, that's okay."

I walk through the quiet house, heading straight for the basement—that's where the family's armoury is. I will not let that bitch live to see another day. I won't live with the fear that she could take Faith from us again.

My phone starts vibrating. Pulling it out, I see Ash's name across the screen. Guilt crashes through me, but I decline the call. It's the fifth time he's tried to contact me since I left the hospital. A minute later, he sends a text.

Ash: Bree, where are you? Please, just tell me you're okay. If you decided this is too much, that's fine. I understand. Just let me know you're okay.

Me: I'm okay. I'll be back before you know it. I just had something I needed to do. Don't worry.

Ash: Bree, do not do anything on your own. Come back to the hospital. Chase is here, and we're working on the details.

Me: I'll be back in a few hours.

I turn my phone off. If Chase is there, I know he'll have my location pinged, and they'll both be hot on my trail. I type the passcode in for the safe room, pull the heavy metal door open, and step inside.

I'm browsing the weapons when Theo and Matteo walk in.

"Impressive. Want to tell me what was so urgent that we had to meet you here?" Theo whistles as he surveys the room before his eyes meet mine.

"Faith has been taken. I'm getting her back. You're here to help me?" I question.

"What the fuck? What do you mean 'taken'? And by whom?" This comes from Matteo.

"Her birth mother. She snatched her from the hospital today; she left a note asking for five million. I need to get my daughter."

"Where's Ash?" Theo asks.

"I'd also like to know why you're coming up with this plan without him?" Alex and Leo fill the doorway.

Leo is... Actually, I don't know who Leo is. I just know he works for Alex, purely based on the fact he always refers to Alex as "boss" whenever he's been around.

"What the fuck are you doing here?" Theo turns to Alex.

"You're either fucking stupid as fuck, or you have balls of steel," Matteo says.

Alex looks at Leo and smirks, before facing Theo and Matteo. Shrugging one shoulder, he says, "Funny, your cousin happens to love my balls."

Theo pulls a gun out from behind his back and aims it straight at Alex's head. Neither Alex or Leo flinch.

"Okay, that's enough. We all know you guys aren't going to shoot each other. Lily would never forgive any of you."

"It's a risk I'm willing to take," Matteo says.

"No, you're not. You either need to put your differences aside and help me get my fucking daughter. Or you can all go crawl back to the holes you came from, and I'll do it the fuck alone."

"Where's Ash, Breanna?" Theo asks again.

"I left him at the hospital; he's with his family."

"And he's okay with you going rogue? Going off on your own to get his daughter back?" Alex raises an eyebrow.

"He doesn't know, and she's my daughter too now, so are you helping or not?" I'm getting bloody frustrated. These idiots are wasting time.

"I'm helping, but I do want to know why you're

leaving Ash out of this?" Alex questions before adding, "Or should I just call and ask him myself?"

"No, you can't call him. He already has charges against him. I'm not about to let him get himself into any more trouble."

"What charges?" This comes from Matteo, although my eyes zone in on Leo, who is tapping away at his phone.

"Ah, just assault charges from a fight he was in a few weeks back."

"Hey, Breanna?" Leo looks up from his phone, before passing it to Alex. "Why were Lily and Hope arrested that same night?"

"What? How the hell can you even know that already?"

"Lily and Hope were arrested? What the fuck for?" Theo and Matteo both question at the same time.

"Says here: for assaulting a police officer. What happened that night, Breanna?" Alex probes.

"Ash beat the shit out of some guy who hit Lily at the club. The girls were trying to get to him when the cops were taking him away in cuffs. One stepped in front of Hope, who slapped him across the face, then Lily dropped the officer to the ground."

The guys are all looking at me with clenched jaws.

"Who the fuck put their hands on Lily?" Alex is seething. He passes the phone back to Leo. "I want a name. Now."

"I don't know his name. Last I heard, he was still in the ICU after the beating Ash gave him."

This makes them all smile. Great, I've managed to surround myself with fucking crazy-ass psychos, just my type of people.

"Okay, now that that's sorted, get strapped up. We're going to get my daughter back." I turn around and pick up a couple of lightweight handguns, before tucking two small knives in my boots. Once I'm satisfied with my choices, I walk out, the four towering men at my heels.

"How do you know where she is?" Matteo asks.

"My dad gave her a bracelet with a GPS tracker hidden in the little gemstone. The location of that bracelet hasn't moved in the last hour."

Matteo looks up and down my body. "What the hell are you looking at?" I ask.

"Just wondering how many trackers Josh has hidden on you?" He shrugs.

"Probably more than I even know about." I laugh.

***

We've just pulled up to a crappy, old, abandoned house, about thirty minutes outside the city.

"Okay, here's the plan. Leo and I will go in through the back. Theo and Matteo, take the front. Bree, wait in the fucking car," Alex orders out, like he expects everyone to fall in line.

I look at him and shake my head. "You can follow whatever plan you want, but I'm going into that house." I jump out of the car, before anyone can try to stop me, and run down the side of the house, stopping at a window. I hear them all curse as they come up behind me.

I peer inside the rundown shack and see an empty room. I push on the glass panel, thanking God that it's unlocked. As soon as it creeps open, I hear Faith's cries and someone else shouting at her to stop. My blood boils.

I go to jump through the window when a pair of arms wraps around my waist. "Wait, I'll go first." Theo leaps over the ledge with more grace and agility than a man his size should have.

"We're going round back. Meet you inside," Alex says as he and Leo run towards the back of the house.

"Okay, come on." Theo holds a hand down to help lift me over the windowsill. Batting his arm away, I jump up and pull myself through. Maybe not as gracefully, but I still did it myself.

"Shut up," I hiss, walking towards the door and opening it just a crack to peek down the hallway. The crying gets louder, and I can hear footsteps pacing up and down at the front of the house. Movement from the other end of the hall catches my attention. Holding my breath, I wait until Alex and Theo come into full view.

They pass me and head straight into the front room without a second thought. I follow, a little quieter with my steps.

"Wh-Who the fuck are you?" a woman screeches. "Get out! This isn't your house."

"Yeah, pretty sure it ain't yours either," Alex replies,

pointing a gun in her direction.

I step into the room, and my eyes land on the bitch. I'm thankful she's not holding Faith. Scanning the small space, I see *her.* My daughter, on the floor, in the far corner. *On the fucking floor.* I run over and scoop her up.

"Wait, you can't have her! She's mine! I want my fucking money, bitch!"

"Shh, it's okay, baby. Mummy has you now. It's going to be okay." I stare at the woman, letting her hear my words too.

"You'll never be her mother. She's my blood. She will always be mine." She laughs.

"Hold her for a second." I hand Faith over to Matteo. I don't want to let her go, but I need to be the one to end this bitch's life. As much as I'd like to take my time and slowly slide a blade across her throat, I want it to be done. For this to be over. And I want to go back to Ash.

I remove one of the smaller firearms from the holster hidden under my jacket. I watch her as I twist a silencer onto the barrel. Pulling out my phone, I call my dad as I stare her straight in the eye.

He picks up on the first ring.

"Breanna, did you get it done? Ash is going crazy here," he asks.

"Daddy, I'm going to need you to send a clean-up crew to the address I'm texting you now." I put on my sugary-sweet voice.

"They're already there waiting. Hurry up and get

back here."

I end the call and smile.

"You know, the thing about being a daddy's girl... is that he'll do anything for me. Even cover up a murder." I take a single step closer. Her face pales as her reality sets in.

"You took my daughter. You should have known I'd come for her." I take another step. "You hurt Ash—nobody hurts the people I love without paying the price." Another step. "You drugged my mother. If I wasn't here ending your life, I assure you my father would be. And trust me, that is one man you don't want to piss the fuck off."

"You're just trying to scare me. Ash wouldn't let you kill the mother of his child," she says with confidence.

"You're right. Ash would never let anything happen to the mother of his child. And that's me. It may not be biological, but I'm her mother in every way that counts. I'm sorry I don't have more time. It would have been fun to see you beg, to see you pass out from the pain. But I have more important things to do. Like being a mother." I pull the trigger.

A single bullet straight to the middle of her head. I walk past Alex and hand my gun to Theo, before taking Faith back from Matteo. She's still crying.

"Shh, it's okay. We're going home, baby," I whisper in her ear as I walk out of the house. I see a van pull into the driveway, the *maintenance and repair* logo on the side telling me it's my dad's clean-up crew. I've seen this van once or twice throughout my life.

CHAPTER 35

*S*he left. I knew when she said she was going to get coffee that something was off. I put it down to her being upset. She did just find her mum unconscious on the floor. I know she's distraught about Faith being taken too. But she left...

We're meant to be in this together, and she just walked out of the hospital, leaving me here. I've called five times, each rejected. What the fuck could have gotten her to leave? Where the hell did she go? Has she finally come to the realisation that this is all too much for her? Being with me isn't easy. I won't blame her for leaving, but she could have at least talked to me about how she's fucking feeling.

I'm barely holding myself together. I need to get out of here. This hospital is doing my head in. I need to find my fucking daughter. I need to find Breanna. As I'm walking out, I send her a text, which she fucking answers with vague messages about how she had to do something and she'll be back.

I run into Chase as I blow past the hospital doors. "Where'd you park? You're giving me a lift."

"Ah, yeah, over here. What's going on? Any word on where she is yet?" he asks.

"No, but I'm not going to sit around waiting either. I need to find her, Chase. I need to get her back." I'm close to losing my shit again.

"Okay, let's go. We will get her back, man. Where are we going?" He starts the car.

Fuck, I don't even know where to begin. "What did you find in all your stalking of Hayley? Any addresses? Places she could be hiding out with Faith?"

"It's a longshot, but I pinged her phone to an old house in The Hills District. But when I scoped it out, there was no sign of anyone having lived there for years. It looks abandoned."

"It's a start. Go there. Did you learn anything else about her? How worried should I be? She has my fucking daughter, man. How fucking unstable is the bitch?" I ask.

"I didn't find anything to suggest she's unstable. If

she is, she hides it well. She moved to Sydney from Tasmania two years ago. She was raised in your typical family: mum, dad, brother, and sister—all still living in Tasmania. There's nothing to suggest why the fuck she would be ransoming off her own child."

"Faith is not her fucking child, Chase. She's mine and Breanna's. That woman may have given birth to her, but I'll make sure she never sees her again." I can't wait to get my fucking hands on the crazy bitch.

The whole drive there, all I can think about is Faith. Does she have everything she needs? Has she been fed? She'd be hungry by now… She would need to be changed by now… Is she cold? Scared? My mind goes over the worst-possible-case scenarios. What if she's hurt? Or that woman has snapped?

By the time we arrive at the house, I jump out of the car. Breanna's SUV is parked on the other side of the road. What the fuck is she doing here? I can hear Chase calling out to me, telling me to wait for him, but I need to get into this house. As I'm walking up the pathway to the front door, the screen flies open. A van pulls into the driveway, and Breanna walks out of the house with Faith in her arms.

"Ash?" she questions as she steps towards me, tears running down her face. What the hell was she thinking, coming here? I pull her in close, wrapping my arms around her. *And my baby girl.* Faith is distraught, her cries breaking my heart.

"My car, I have a baby bag in the car. I think she

needs a bottle," Breanna whispers. I take Faith and hold her to my chest, as four men exit the front door.

"Go and get one." I kiss Breanna on her forehead, although what I want to do right now is shake the shit out of her. What the fuck was she thinking? Anything could have happened to her. And why the fuck didn't she tell me she was coming here?

"Ash, it's not their fault. They were just helping me," she says before running across the road to her car.

"What the fuck is this? Why didn't one of you call me?" I turn to the men in question.

"Why didn't you tell me you've got charges over your head at the moment?" Theo responds.

"That has nothing to do with this. This is my fucking daughter. Someone should have called me."

"You're right," Alex agrees, shocking the rest of us.

I rub circles up and down Faith's tiny back, trying to settle her. She's so fucking upset, and I'm not helping. I need to calm myself down. "Anyone want to tell me what happened in there?" I ask, watching as they all look at each other.

"Not it! Also, I'm never fucking with your girl. Breanna makes most of the made men I know look like pussies." Matteo peeks behind me. Turning my head, I see Breanna shaking a bottle as she makes her way back to me.

"What'd she do?" I ask Alex directly. If anyone's going to tell me, it'll be him.

"She made sure that the crazy bitch you knocked up won't be able to bother you again. Now, you'll have to excuse me, but I have business to attend to." Alex walks off with Leo. They stop and say something to Breanna in passing. She nods her head and looks my way.

I don't like that these fuckers know something about her that I don't. Call me immature, petty, jealous... I don't fucking care. I should have been the one here to help her.

"Yeah, sorry, buddy, but we got shit to do too. Come on, Matteo." Theo walks off in the direction of a blacked-out car that just pulled up.

Breanna finally makes it over to me with a bottle. "Do you want me to feed her?" she questions quietly. As much as I want to say no, that I want to keep Faith in my arms, there's a vulnerability in her eyes I've never seen before. She's unsure about something.

"Sure, let's go sit in the car." I lead her across the street. Opening the passenger-side door, I wait for her to take a seat before I pass her Faith. I close the door and walk around the front of the car. Before I jump in, I turn to Chase, who has been awfully quiet this whole time.

"Thanks, mate. You can head back home."

"Uh, sure. I'll catch you later. I'll be at the club if you need anything."

"Thanks, I don't know what I'd do without you, man."

"Remember those words. They might just save my life one day." He smirks before getting in his own vehicle. I don't have time to figure out the riddle that is Chase. I jump into the driver's side of Breanna's car.

Faith is quiet, drinking her bottle quicker than I've ever seen her. I watch her for a moment before I speak.

"Breanna, what happened in there?"

"I-I had to do it, Ash. I couldn't let her hurt Faith again. I couldn't let her hurt you." She looks at me pleadingly.

"It's okay. What did you have to do?"

"I shot her. I shot Faith's birth mum," she whispers. I wait for the shock of what she's telling me to sink in. It doesn't. I know Breanna would stop at nothing to protect those she loves, to protect her family. And Faith and I are her family now.

"You did good, babe. I'm fucking proud that you're mine. Faith is the luckiest girl in the world to have a mother like you in her life. However, I would have preferred to be the one at your side. I wish you would have told me, instead of keeping me in the dark. But we can talk about that later." I lean over and kiss her forehead before resting my own against it. "I love you, Breanna. Nothing will ever change that."

"I'm sorry. I just didn't want you to get into more trouble… if anything went sideways. I love you, Ash. There's nothing I won't do to protect you."

"Babe, you and Faith are my world. I don't ever want you to put yourself in danger like this again. I can't live a life where you don't exist."

"I promise I won't keep you in the dark again. I love you, Ash."

"Let's get her into her seat and go home," I say, jumping out and heading around to Breanna's side. I take Faith and lock her into the baby seat in the back. I double-check the seat belts securing her in, turn on the little musical toy that dangles from the handle above her, and close the door.

"Think we can run away together, Ash?" Breanna asks me.

"I'd run away anywhere with you, babe. Where do you have in mind?"

"Anywhere other than your penthouse. My dad just texted me. Our parents are currently waiting for us at your place."

"*Our* place, Breanna. We both live there. And as much as I'd love to run away and keep you and Faith to myself, we can't. Your mum and dad would track us down within a day."

"You're probably right." She sighs.

"Don't worry, once they see that you and Faith are *in fact* okay and in one piece, I'll get rid of them all. And I'm changing the code to the fucking lift."

"Deal. I want nothing more than to curl up on the theatre couch with you and Faith, and just stay in our own little bubble."

"Then that's exactly what we will do; the Brash bubble will be in full effect in just a few hours."

"The Brash bubble?" she asks, her eyebrows drawing down in question.

"Breanna and Ash: Brash. Get used to it—it's sticking."

EPILOGUE

*S*ix months later

"ARE you sure you want to go through with this, because I can have the getaway car ready in two minutes," Hope whispers in my ear as she hugs me.

"I'm sure. Have you seen your cousin? He's fine as fuck, Hope. I'll gladly tap that for the rest of my life." I laugh at the pained expression on her face.

"Wrong, just wrong, Bree. Although, after today, I can really say you're my cousin, instead of just pretending you are." She smiles.

"You're right, I couldn't think of anyone else I'd want to be related to."

I look at my reflection in the mirror. My mum comes up behind me with a tissue in her hand. "Breanna, I can't believe we're doing this already. It was just yesterday that your dad and I were bringing you home from the hospital."

"Mum, I'm pretty sure that was twenty-two years ago, not yesterday." I turn around and face her.

"I know, but you're my little girl. You are everything to your dad and me. It's not easy letting go of that." She sniffles again. Oh, God, if she's crying like this, how the hell is my dad coping? He has to walk me down the aisle. I wouldn't put it past him to pick me up and carry me in the other direction.

"Mum, I'm always going to be your little girl. Don't worry, I'll let you come around and pick up after me every day *if you need to*." I smirk.

"Nope, I'm good. My house has never been cleaner than it has been the last six months."

"You have a staff of ten people—pretty sure your house has always been clean."

"But now that you're not there, we don't need a staff of ten people just to pick up after you." She laughs.

"Do I look okay?" I ask, changing the topic.

"You look so beautiful it hurts. I love you so much,

Breanna. I'm so happy for you. I'm happy you found your soul mate in Ash." The tears start to roll down my mum's face again.

"Okay, let's get this show on the road before you make me ruin my makeup." I walk out of the dressing room. Hope, Lily, and Ava are all lined up, waiting for me. My mum kisses my cheek.

"I'll see you out there, baby," she whispers.

"Thanks, Mum."

The music starts, and my three bridesmaids slowly make their way down the aisle. My dad appears in front of me.

"Shit, Bree, are we sure you're ready for this? I can get rid of everyone. I'll hide you away. I'm not ready... Maybe we should reschedule this whole thing for a later date," he suggests.

"Daddy, *this whole thing* is my wedding. We are not rescheduling. Now, tell me I look beautiful and walk me down that aisle." I smile to soften the blow.

"Bree, I fucking love you so much. I never thought I could love anyone as much as your mum. Then you were born, and the minute I looked at you, I knew you'd be the one I'd love the most in the world. You *are* my world, Bree. I'm not ready, but I will put my feelings aside for yours. Let's do this."

My dad lifts his arm, and I link mine through it. I look out at the garden of our family's ranch. My gran sure did outdo herself with this wedding. White chairs, with pink ribbons evenly centred and tied into bows, line the red carpet. The aisle has bouquets of pink and white roses contouring the runner, which has been sprinkled with matching rose petals. There's a small wooden gazebo at the end, where Ash is standing and looking right at me. The white timber tresses are covered in twinkling fairy lights and flowers. It's absolutely stunning.

The song "I Get to Love You" by Ruelle sounds, and that's my cue to start walking. I chose this song because my dad played it when he proposed to my mum. I grew up listening to my parents sing it to each other, while dancing around the house, not caring who saw them.

I scan the crowd, and spot my mum and gran at the front with Ash's parents—his aunts and uncles alongside them. We opted for flexible seating. I didn't want the traditional "his side, her side" bullshit. I look to my bridesmaids, all standing to the left of the gazebo: Hope, Lily and Ava. Ava is holding Faith; my nerves relax when my eyes land on her. Ever since that day at the hospital, I have a hard time letting that baby out of my sight. I get anxious whenever she's not within reaching distance.

I've managed to hide these nerves from everyone but Ash. He put cameras all around the penthouse, so no matter what room she's in, I can look at my phone and see her. I've opted to complete my master's degree online, so I can stay home with Faith. On those days I need to go into McKinley Industries for work, I take her with me.

We never did figure out what her biological mum's plan was. Not really anyway. It seemed she was struggling with some mental health issues following Faith's birth. She thought giving up Faith was going to solve all her problems, but things only got worse. Instead of seeking out help, she turned away from her family and lost her job. She blamed Ash for it all, for each decision *she* made, and when she saw his face plastered next to mine in the social news section, she wanted to make him pay. She wanted both of us to pay.

We don't know if she had a hand in Faith's allergic reaction that day in the park. Chase says that it was more than likely coincidental. He believes she was watching and waiting for an opening, and followed our mothers to the hospital.

Ultimately, none of it matters: the what, why, and how. Because she chose to throw away her opportunity to be a mum. And I embraced it.

My eyes lock with Ash's as I get closer to where he is standing, and all thoughts leave my head. The only thing left on my mind is saying *I do*, and making this man mine in every possible way.

EPILOGUE

I feel like I've been waiting for this day forever. I wanted to whisk her away and marry her six months ago. But I knew both of our families would have shot me if I had. I also didn't want to take away her one chance to have the wedding of her dreams. Because this *will be* her only chance.

I watch her walk down the aisle with Josh. Part of me is surprised he manages to look so calm—and that he hasn't run in the other direction with Bree over his shoulder. He's been grunting and groaning every time someone mentions something about the wedding plans. I can't blame him. If some guy was coming in, trying to lay claim on Faith, I probably wouldn't be coping any better.

Breanna looks like a fucking dream. I've envisioned what she'd look like walking down the aisle in a white dress, but nothing compares to the reality. She's wearing what Ava refers to as a princess dress. It's fitted a little too snuggly around her bodice and flares out in a huge skirt—*it reminds me of something out of one of those Disney fairy tales Ava used to be obsessed with.* However, all I can think about is how I can't fucking wait to get her out of that dress, and see what's hidden underneath.

Breanna reaches my side. I shake hands with Josh, his grip a little too firm. I have to stretch my fingers out when he lets go. But once I'm facing Breanna, holding her hands, everyone and everything else fades into the background. This is the moment my life becomes complete.

The celebrant drones on. I'm not sure what he's saying. When I feel Breanna squeeze my hands, knocking me out of my daze, I take notice. It's my turn to say my vows.

"Breanna, I knew from the moment you were born that you were someone special. I may have only been six, but I knew even then just how great you were. I've loved you from the sidelines for as long as I can remember. In fact, I can't remember a time I didn't love you. My heart beats for you, Breanna. You complete me in every way possible. You are the mother of my child. You are my best friend. You are my life. I promise to love you with everything I have. I promise to hold you above all others—not that that's hard. I promise to always support you in anything you do. I promise to always be yours."

I slide the ring onto her finger. It fits like a glove. She doesn't know it, but Faith actually picked out this wedding band. I had the jeweller line up three bands; the one Faith reached for first is the one I chose.

"Breanna, do you have vows prepared?" the celebrant asks.

She nods before clearing her throat. "Ash Williamson, you are mine, whether you want to be or not. Because I'm never letting you go. You are my person, the one I can always turn to. You love me without judgement, and I promise to always return that love to you. You have given me a family, love, everything. I have loved you for longer than I can admit publicly. I promise that I will always put you above all others. I promise that from today onward, you and I will be one heart, one soul, united for eternity."

Breanna slides a ring onto my finger.

"Do you, Breanna McKinley, take Ash Williamson to be your lawfully wedded husband?" the celebrant asks.

"I do." Breanna's eyes never leave mine.

"Do you, Ash Williamson, take Breanna McKinley to be—"

"I do." I cut the celebrant off, eager to get to the good part.

"Okay, I now pronounce you husband and wife. You may kiss the bride."

My lips are locked with Breanna's before he finishes that sentence. I've been waiting a long time to kiss my wife. *My wife.* Breanna is my wife. I smile into the kiss.

"I love you," I say as I pull back slightly.

"I love you too." She slams her lips back onto mine, pulling my head closer to hers.

THERE IS SO MUCH MORE to come from The Merge World! With all of the children getting their own stories told in standalones.

CLICK HERE TO PRE-ORDER AVA & Noah story to find out all about that necklace he left her - Tethered To Him

FOR A PEAK at my latest release - Holly and T's story (a dark mafia romance) sign up here to download your free preview.... Devilish King

Want to find out how Lily and Alex's story plays out? The whole christmas event is told in An Entangled Christmas

Continue reading for a sneak peak.

Come and check out my website and join my mailing list to stay up to date and gain access to bonus materials.
Website & Newsletter: www.kyliekent.com

Want to be involved in discussions, get early access to cover reveals, excerpts and tons of give-aways?
Join my readers group on Facebook Kylie's Steam Room
Facebook: @kyliekent2020
Instagram Follow: @author_kylie_kent_

ACKNOWLEDGMENTS

First, I'd like to acknowledge you, the reader. Without you, I would not be where I am today. Your constant support and feedback (through your messages and reviews) mean the world to me. They give me the encouragement to keep at this authoring journey. I love everything about conjuring up a story and putting it into words.

I would not be able to do this without the support of my husband. Nate is my happily ever after, my forever person. The one who supports me unconditionally like no one else ever has.

My beta readers are bloody amazing women. Natasha, Amy, and Sam: you girls keep me on my toes, keep me reaching and meeting my deadlines. And make sure I'm not killing off the most important characters! I can't even imagine doing this without you girls.

My editor, Kat: she's the bloody bomb! I always have a slight panic attack when I have to send off a manuscript to her, yet she never gets frustrated or annoyed with my constant need for reassurance. My stories wouldn't be half as good without you, Kat.

ABOUT THE AUTHOR

Kylie made the leap from kindergarten teacher to romance author, living out her dream to deliver sexy, always and forever romances. She loves a happily ever after story with tons of built-in steam.

She currently resides in Perth, Australia and when she is not dreaming up the latest romance, she can be found spending time with her three children and her husband of twenty years, her very own real-life instant-love.

Kylie loves to hear from her readers; you can reach her at: author.kylie.kent@gmail.com

Visit Kylie's website and sign up for her newsletter at: www.kyliekent.com

Manufactured by Amazon.ca
Bolton, ON